SIDNEY CHAMBERS AND
THE DANGERS OF TEMPTATION

Archdeacon Sidney Chambers is beginning to think that the life of a full-time priest (and part-time detective) is not easy. So when a bewitching divorcee in a mink coat interrupts Sidney's family lunch, asking him to help locate her missing son, he hopes it will be an open and shut case. The last thing he expects is to be dragged into the mysterious workings of a sinister cult, or to find himself tangled up in another murder investigation. But, as always, the village of Grantchester is not as peaceful as it seems. From the theft of an heirloom to an ominous case of blackmail, Sidney is once again rushed off his feet!

SIDNEY CHAMBERS
AND
THE DANGERS OF
TEMPTATION

THE GRANTCHESTER MYSTERIES

JAMES RUNCIE

LARGE
PRINT

First published in Great Britain 2016
by
Bloomsbury

First Isis Edition
published 2016
by arrangement with
Bloomsbury Publishing Plc

A catalogue record for this book is available
from the British Library.

ISBN 978–1–78541–296–7 (hb)
ISBN 978–1–78541–302–5 (pb)

Published by
F. A. Thorpe (Publishing)
Anstey, Leicestershire

Set by Words & Graphics Ltd.
Anstey, Leicestershire
Printed and bound in Great Britain by
T. J. International Ltd., Padstow, Cornwall

This book is printed on acid-free paper

For Marilyn

No man is matriculated to the art of life till he has been well tempted.

George Eliot, *Romola*

Contents

The Dangers of Temptation

Although it was Valentine's Day, and also his birthday, Sidney Chambers was not in a happy frame of mind. This was due to persistent toothache, his imminent renunciation of alcohol for Lent and the fact that the recent television series *All Gas and Gaiters* had made fun at the expense of his beloved Church of England, concentrating, quite specifically, on a hapless and drunken archdeacon. This had resulted in much unnecessary teasing from his wife about the similarities between fact and fiction. Could the writers have had anyone specific in mind when they had created such a clueless character? What did Sidney think?

"Not much," had been his reply and, as a result of his grumpiness, Hildegard had asked her husband to spend the morning of his birthday cheering up in his study. In order to do so, he put one of his favourite records on the turntable, Sidney Bechet's "*Si tu vois ma mère*", only to discover that, in the words of the great Christian poet George Herbert, "music helps not the toothache".

His family was coming to lunch: his mother and father (who still treated him as a child even though he was forty-six years old), his brother Matt, his sister Jennifer and her husband Johnny Johnson. Further guests included Inspector Geordie Keating and his wife Cathy, Amanda and Henry Richmond, and Sidney's former curate Leonard Graham. Together with Hildegard, and their four-year-old daughter Anna, this made them a very crowded thirteen at table.

Geordie was amused. "You'll have to be Jesus, Sidney."

"Then I wonder who the Judas is."

Hildegard put down the chicken casserole. "Now then, *mein Lieber*. You promised to be in a better mood."

"I am always cheerful . . ."

"I'm not so sure about that," Geordie interrupted.

"Only, it's this bloody toothache."

Anna poked him in the arm. "Don't swear, Daddy. It's rude."

"I'm sorry, everyone. The truth is, I haven't been myself lately."

"Perhaps you haven't got enough to do?" Amanda asked.

Sidney was just about to answer that a clergyman's life was actually far busier and more serious than anyone ever gave him credit for when the doorbell rang. He stood up and left the room. "What fresh hell is this?" he muttered as he walked out into the long central hall that ran down the length of the ground floor. He opened the door to find a startlingly attractive middle-aged woman dressed in a mink coat.

This was Barbara Wilkinson, a divorcee from Grantchester whom Hildegard had always disliked. "I hope I'm not interrupting anything?" she said. "You do remember I was coming . . ."

"Not to lunch," Sidney blustered. He had completely forgotten about her and compounded the offence by being unintentionally bad-mannered.

"You said midday. I'm afraid I'm a little late."

"No, that's quite all right. It's only that we are about to eat. Would you like to join us?"

"I wouldn't want to intrude."

"It would be no trouble."

"I can tell by the way you are looking at me that's not true, Mr Archdeacon."

There was an awkward pause. Sidney knew that he should try and get rid of the woman but couldn't do so without being even ruder than he had been already.

"It won't take long," she continued. "Ten minutes at most."

Hildegard and Amanda emerged from the dining room to fetch a few more things from the kitchen. A series of awkward salutations then had to be made before Sidney was able to steer his visitor down the hall and into the study. He asked his eyebrow-raising wife to keep the casserole warm and promised he would return shortly.

Barbara Wilkinson took off her coat to reveal a long-sleeved blue and white polka-dot dress, cinched at the waist. Had she deliberately dressed up for this encounter, Sidney wondered, or was this her usual style? It was flash for Ely, let alone Grantchester.

"As you may recall," she began, "I am very troubled about Danny."

Mrs Wilkinson's eighteen-year-old son had joined a commune that had recently been established on a farm outside Grantchester. It was run by Fraser Pascoe, an awareness guru, and was called the "Family of Love".

"Danny has joined of his own free will?" Sidney asked.

"He has."

"And have you found out anything more? Is the community religious at all?" Sidney continued, wondering how on earth he was supposed to help.

"Apparently there was a mystical sect with the same name that flourished round here in the sixteenth century. This is some kind of secular revival. These people say that they have now moved 'beyond religion'. I think they chant, shout out and have visions."

"Sounds as if they go in for mystical experiences. William Blake sang naked in the garden with his wife."

"That's different. He was a poet. My son is supposed to be going into the City. This is not the kind of thing I had in mind at all. And it's not *like him*. He was always such a sensible child. But he's not been the same since his father left home."

"I see."

"As you may remember, I have been on my own for the last two years. Mike thought it would be safe to divorce once our son reached sixteen, but Danny's always been young for his age. I'm so worried. I can't sleep. I think he's been brainwashed." Mrs Wilkinson

4

took Sidney's hand. "There's no one else I can turn to. You have to get him out of that dreadful place."

"Have you spoken to my successor, the vicar of Grantchester? It is his parish. I wouldn't like to tread on his toes."

"He told me that the joy Danny was experiencing in finding himself was something I should celebrate. Honestly. I could kill the man. It has to be you, Mr Archdeacon. Will you go and see my son?" She met his eyes, squeezed his hand and let it lie there rather too long.

Sidney promised to do what he could, stood up and saw his guest to the front door just as Anna had been commandeered to rescue him. "Please call in whenever you like," Barbara Wilkinson concluded. "Lunch, dinner, anything, Mr Archdeacon, I am all yours."

As he closed the door, Sidney could still sense his hand in hers. Scent hung in the air.

He returned to his birthday lunch and was immediately teased. Hildegard remarked that she didn't understand why some women felt the need to dress so provocatively when visiting a clergyman. Her husband tried to justify the interruption by explaining how he knew Barbara. She was, he said, a vulnerable parishioner whose husband had run off with a dental assistant, leaving her alone with a teenage son.

"She looks more than capable of looking after herself," Amanda replied. "Her perfume was so strong I thought your indoor hyacinths had come out early."

"It's Fidji."

"You know the name?"

"I asked her."

"Why on earth would you do that?"

"Curiosity, I suppose."

"Then it's just as well you're not a cat. You'd have been dead by now."

Geordie cut in before anyone else could respond. "If she's what you call your 'pastoral duties' then I can understand why they take a while."

Sidney did not want to darken the mood by telling everyone that he really felt he should go and see Danny Wilkinson because he knew that some cults warned of the impending apocalypse so fervently that they encouraged their members to get the whole thing started by killing each other.

"Anna said grace for you," Hildegard reported. "It was going to be a surprise. She learned it specially. *Sag's nochmal, Kleine* . . ."

A reluctant Anna, disappointed by the earlier absence of her father, repeated her prayer:

> "*Komm, Herr Jesu, sei unser Gast*
> *Und segne, was Du uns bescheret hast. Amen.*"

The company applauded. Sidney was touched and guilty at the same time. How had he missed the moment? Repeating it later was not the same, he knew, but he kissed and thanked his daughter and said that her words were the best present anyone could have given him.

After lunch they retired to the drawing room for coffee and gifts. Sidney's father Alec handed over the traditional copy of Wisden, his mother had knitted him an Aran jumper and Amanda produced twelve monogrammed handkerchiefs.

"SRC — *Sidney Robert Chambers* — or *Senior Roman Catholic* if you're thinking of going over to Rome."

"I think that's unlikely."

"I had the same done for Henry. Details matter, Sidney, people notice these things: shoes, handkerchiefs and cufflinks. It's important to have standards."

"I will do my best. Even though we must all fall short."

"That's enough false modesty," said his father.

"Then it seems I can't win."

"That's the clergyman's lot, Sidney."

"I thought this was supposed to be my birthday?"

He was keen to get a walk in before tea but Mrs Wilkinson's visit, and her son's predicament, provoked a long discussion of the historic idealistic farm communities inspired by Tolstoy in Kharkov, Kursk and Voronezh, after which Leonard Graham left to see his old friend Simon Hackford in Cambridge. Inspector Keating then said that both he and Cathy should be heading home and would be happy to give Leonard a lift, while Amanda and Henry said they had to return to London for a social engagement that evening. Johnny Johnson also needed to get back to his jazz club.

The remaining Chambers family decided on a brisk tour past Cherry Hill motte and bailey and along the River Ouse. It was a damp afternoon and there were few signs of spring. Last year's leaves clung to the hedgerows, while thick sprays of traveller's joy unfolded over the brambles and dead bracken. Out in the stubble-fields a group of chaffinches picked at the grain left by the gleaners. Clumps of snowdrops were scattered under a hawthorn tree but, as Iris Chambers lamented, there was no hint of either primrose or crocus. Spring was going to be late again.

Jennifer Chambers took her brother aside and asked if he really minded being teased about other women.

"I'm used to it now."

"It doesn't make you want to change your ways?"

"I have a clean conscience, Jen."

"You don't think you lead women on?"

"Not at all."

"I don't know why they find clergymen attractive."

"I'm not sure they do."

"It must be the air of distracted unavailability."

"I don't cultivate such behaviour, if that's what you are suggesting."

"But you don't mind the attention when it comes? I'm sure Hildegard does."

"I think she prefers to ignore it. She knows I love her more than anyone else."

"I hope you tell her. Sometimes you need to keep proving these things. It's quite easy to lose faith; not only in religion but also in marriage."

"Are you worried about something, Jen?"

"Not really, only it's sometimes hard to know what men really think."

"Johnny?"

Jennifer swept back a strand of hair that hadn't needed to be tidied and avoided eye contact. "There's this woman at the club. He says there's nothing in it, but he's been coming home later and later. I know it's the jazz world and I'm used to it, but he's been distracted and irritable. He snaps at me more often."

"Is it money worries?"

"It's all kinds of anxiety. I overheard him saying that Blossom was a holiday from his everyday life."

"Blossom? As in Blossom Dearie?"

"I don't know, Sidney. It's always Blossom this and Blossom that. She's a jazz singer. Quite a handful, apparently."

"They often are."

"I only hope she hasn't turned his head."

"I think he's strong enough to resist."

"You were quite keen on a jazzer yourself, I recall."

"Gloria Dee?" Sidney replied. "That was a long while ago; and, don't forget, I wasn't married at the time."

"Then I don't know how you resisted the temptation. Will you have a word with Johnny when you're next in the club?"

Why did people take such risks with their happiness? Sidney wondered. He could not imagine anyone wanting someone more lovely than his sister. She could have doubled for Diana Rigg in *The Avengers*. That was a far better programme than the bloody travesty of *All Gas and Gaiters*.

After the cake and candles and the final farewells at the station, Hildegard suggested a light supper and an early night. As she applied cold cream to her face in bed, she asked about Barbara Wilkinson, Sidney's toothache and then remembered that she had wanted to question her husband about Jen. His sister hadn't been herself. Was anything wrong?

Sidney thought about all the pressures and anxieties of the day. Did he have to tell his wife everything? His birthday had not gone as well as he had hoped. He sighed and put out the light.

"It's been a long day." He said.

Later that week, and still feeling listless, Sidney sat at his desk with gloomy determination, hoping that work might give him a greater sense of purpose and direction. From the window he watched a bullfinch in the garden, strutting around with a sliver of bark in his beak, waiting to be relieved of his duties and clearly cross that he might have to make his own nest. His strut became ever more furious but pointless, like a vain clergyman in mid-procession up the cathedral nave, convinced that he should have been made a bishop.

Sidney put his hand to his cheek where his tooth throbbed. He thought he caught a ghost of Barbara Wilkinson's scent in the air, and found himself remembering the warmth of his hand in hers.

Because it was Lent, he was working on a study of conscience and guilt, trying to negotiate his way through the vexed question of human fallibility and the necessary distinction between the sins we can live with and those we can't. He had read that it might be helpful for a priest, or any other believer, for that matter, to imagine that Jesus was walking alongside you at all times, as if in conversation, on the road to Emmaus perhaps, as guide and conscience.

Sidney was not at all sure he wanted Jesus to be walking alongside him at all times; certainly not when he was with Barbara Wilkinson or having a man-to-man chat with Johnny Johnson in the jazz club. There were times when discretion was needed, moments when surely even Jesus might have to absent himself until things quietened down a bit.

He put down his pen and left to pursue a less meditative type of faith in the form of a visit to the farm where Danny Wilkinson had sequestered himself.

The centre of the commune was a dilapidated farmhouse with a cottage garden, garage, woodshed and barn. An old Land Rover was parked outside and a couple of mongrel dogs ran freely across the front yard. The doors to the barn were almost off their hinges and the outside tap had formed a frozen puddle on the ground below. A cat toyed with a dead yellowhammer. Sidney was on his guard before he had even knocked at the door.

He was greeted by a pale floppy-haired boy dressed in an oversized loose white shirt over jeans. He asked Sidney to sign a book of greeting and wait in the meditation space for their leader. Fraser Pascoe would join Sidney once he had finished his morning trance.

There was nowhere to sit down properly. A series of beanbags and yoga mats surrounded a teak coffee table that displayed an array of self-improving books: Erich Fromm's *The Art of Loving*, Aldous Huxley's

The Doors of Perception, Kahlil Gibran's *The Prophet*, together with Thoreau's *Walden* and Hermann Hesse's *Siddhartha*.

The walls had been painted orange and there was a faint aroma of joss sticks. Sidney noticed a reproduction of William Blake's painting of the twenty-four elders worshipping God in the Book of Revelation, a "Desiderata" poster and a framed wisdom accreditation certificate from an organisation in India.

Pascoe was a man with a strong handshake and a firm jawline, chiselled cheekbones and dreamy blue eyes that could perhaps have been stolen for the purposes of becoming a cult leader. It was rare for Sidney to dislike someone within minutes of meeting, but Pascoe's perfumed cleanliness (Tabac aftershave, minty breath, Italian hair oil) was surely too good to be true.

"Western society is based on converting wants into needs," he explained. "Here, within the Family of Love, we try to do the opposite, reducing our desires to simple daily necessity."

"An admirable idea."

"It was, I think, the aim of the early Christians before they were corrupted by the Church."

"That's true. To some extent."

"That is a very Anglican answer. 'To some extent'."

"And one that you might expect from an Anglican priest."

Pascoe elaborated on the principles of the farm. It was a celibate, self-sufficient, vegetarian community, living entirely off the land, without personal possessions

12

or money. Their aim was to cleanse themselves of capitalist delusion and reach transcendent truth through meditation. "The less you think, the freer you are. We open ourselves to divine dictation; a trance before the revelation of all things."

"And the revelation will come?"

"Before the rapture. When all things will be known."

"And when might that be?" Sidney tried not to sound sceptical.

"That is a secret known only to our adherents, but if you have read the work both of Nostradamus and Hendrik Niclaes and are aware of Mayan astrology then you can make a start. You are, of course, welcome to join us."

"And tell me," Sidney answered, giving the invitation a duck, "how do you achieve the trance-like state necessary for revelation?"

"Silence, meditation; just like your prayers. The aim is to live beyond the body in pure light."

"And how do you find that brightness?"

"We share a loving cup. We discover ourselves through love."

"And is that expressed physically?"

"That is a question that befits a journalist rather than a clergyman. As I have already explained, Mr Archdeacon, we are a celibate group, uncorrupted by human bondage. I hear you would like to talk to Danny?"

"If that is allowed."

"We are a free community. People come and go as they please."

"And you are self-sufficient, I think you said?"

"Everything people need can be found in the community: food, shelter, safety, companionship and, I hope, wisdom."

"Danny's mother is worried about him."

"Barbara Wilkinson is naturally anxious," Pascoe continued. "A man less charitable than myself might even describe her as neurotic."

"Do you know her?"

"I have had conversations and, in the past, I offered her a way of rest. But she is too attached to the cares of the world. Her son needs space and distance. That is why he is safely with us."

"And how did he come to be here?"

"I am sure he can tell you himself. I believe he is in the kitchen. We are having an onion soup with our home-made bread. As I say, you would be welcome to join us."

Given his insistent toothache, Sidney thought that simple food might be a comfort but he did not want to prolong his stay. "That is kind but I think a conversation will be enough . . ."

"To allay a mother's fears. There is nothing frightening about our family, Mr Archdeacon. We live very simply, as you will see. But sometimes people are threatened by simplicity, just as they were by Jesus."

The kitchen still had an old gas range and the peeling paint was partly disguised by hippy posters preaching love and self-improvement: *Your mind is a garden, your thoughts are the seeds; you can grow flowers or you can grow weeds.* One wall had been

14

covered by a recent fresco of a rainbow over the Himalayas; another depicted a field of daisies with peace signs and psychedelic self-portraits at their centre. Danny Wilkinson was slicing onions, dressed in a simple olive-green crew-neck jumper with jeans and plimsolls. He was of medium height, with a goatee beard and hair that fell to his shoulders in a style that most parents would have described as "girls'-length".

Sidney apologised for the intrusion. "I know you are old enough to make up your own mind about the way you live your life."

"I certainly wouldn't follow my mother, man."

"She has had a challenging time, I gather."

"After Dad left? I knew it was bad before anything happened: the rows, the drinking. My parents were swingers. What do you expect? I think they still are. It's too much."

Sidney was momentarily flummoxed by a generational role-reversal in which a trainee hippy appeared to be more moral than his parents. "How did you come to be here?" he asked.

"Life was doing my head in. A friend saw I needed sorting out."

"And who was that?"

"Tom Raven. You met him when you arrived."

"With the large white shirt?"

"That's him. He's the only one who still cares about what he wears."

Sidney did not bother arguing that an untucked shirt worn over jeans hardly required much effort and continued with his questions. "How long do you intend to stay, Danny?"

"I don't believe in time any more."

Pascoe explained. "We encourage all our young people to live in the moment. Now is the only reality. The past has gone; the future will come. Father Time has no place here."

"I sometimes think it's advisable to learn lessons from the past and make preparations for the future," said Sidney.

Danny repeated what was surely a mantra. "Our only reality is now. Love is our truth. Desire is illusion. Simplicity is our only need."

Sidney had had enough of being lectured. "Then I can tell your mother that you are content?"

"You can tell her that I am discovering a happiness that she'll never know."

"I may not put it quite like that. But I will say, if I may, that she has nothing to worry about."

"You can tell her what you like, man. I never want to see her again."

The train back to Ely was delayed by frozen points. The hold-up only increased Sidney's sense of unease. Even though Christmas was long gone, it felt as if he was still stuck in the bleakest of midwinters. He wiped a smear across a steamed-up window to reveal a dull view of the scuffed and bruised earth, wind-damaged fences and empty telegraph wires. The landscape looked abandoned, with only a couple of blanketed horses in the paddocks, a solitary crow and a dead fox that had trapped itself under a railing.

He decided to call in on his friend Felix Carpenter, the Dean of Ely, before evensong. "I don't know why I am so irritable," he confessed. "I think it must be a mixture of cold, toothache and impatience. The visit to the Family of Love has hardly helped. I find those people so difficult. I know it's not very Christian of me."

"Perhaps it is their certainty," the dean replied. "I am not sure faith comes so easily as they seem to believe."

"There's a smugness to them. I don't like it and then I become even more annoyed that they seem to have got to me. Do you think I could be jealous?"

"No, I think you find it simplistic, Sidney. Our faith is born out of the pain and suffering of the Cross. It's about a little more than sharing a bowl of lentils and doing the odd bit of yoga."

Cordelia Carpenter came into her husband's study with tea and digestive biscuits. She asked after Sidney's toothache and recommended the Maltings dental practice and a Mr Wilkinson in particular. Sidney imagined that this must be Barbara's former husband and immediately recognised that he could kill two birds with one stone.

It was impossible, Cordelia Carpenter vouchsafed, to concentrate on anything properly while suffering from such pain.

"Trollope's novels are full of teeth," her husband remembered. "I think he never travelled without a toothbrush and seldom described a woman or a girl without referring to their mouth. Of course in those days there was, I think, greater dental variety. People had teeth in gold, tin, ivory, wood and bone. It made them nervous of smiling. Nothing to do with Victorian propriety; they just didn't want to show their gnashers."

"Didn't they also take them from corpses and reuse them?" his wife said as she removed the teapot to make a fresh supply.

"I think so. Had you been alive then, Sidney, you might have had a teeth-related mystery to solve."

"I am more than happy to live now," their friend replied, eager to return to the subject in hand as soon as Cordelia had left them alone. "The Family of Love are taught that there is no such thing as past or future. They live only in the present."

"And so they are unlikely to appeal to historians or futurologists."

"Their leader is certainly aware of the future. I think there is some preparation for the end of the world; the final rapture."

"Has he been kind enough to set a date on it? Pope Innocent III predicted it would end 666 years after the rise of Islam; Martin Luther thought it would be no later than 1600. Recently I have been told it might be 1968, 1975, or even 1984, but I have my doubts. We don't all live by the same calendar."

"I think you have to be one of his adherents to be illuminated . . ."

"Or indoctrinated. How dangerous do you think they are, Sidney?"

"I'm not sure. It feels rather creepy, that's all."

18

"What about their leader? Is he all he's cracked up to be?"

"Definitely not. I am sure he is a charlatan."

"Has he taken money from the people who stay there?"

"Probably."

"That's what you need to find out. If you can't get them on their philosophy, you have to hit them with their economics. If there's fraud you can bring in Keating."

"I can't see him sharing a loving cup."

"Indeed. But I'd like to see them offer. You will look after yourself, won't you, Sidney? I don't want you taking on too much."

"I'm not sure I'm taking on anything."

"At least go to the dentist, as my beloved Cordelia suggests. I always find it easiest, if you want an untroubled life, to do what your wife says. That's the kind of simplicity that's easy to follow and you don't need to go to the trouble of joining a cult."

Sidney smiled and finished his tea, loving the dean and his wife for their loyalty, generosity of spirit and their unpretentious goodness. Their home was such a welcoming contrast to the commune, with its deep sofas and fresh flowers, its aroma of baking and Brasso, sherry and furniture polish. This was a different, old-fashioned, Church of England timelessness, he thought; the oak and mahogany tables, cabinets, chests and chairs passed down the generations, watched and measured by the reassuring tick and strike of the grandfather clock in the hall.

He was in a far better mood during evensong and returned home almost cheerfully in time for a simple supper of Welsh rarebit and a bit of easy television.

Hildegard had finished her piano teaching for the day and was reading Anna the story of Little Red Riding Hood in the original German. She asked Sidney if he'd like to join them. Perhaps both father and daughter could become bilingual?

Anna laughed. "You can be the big bad WOLF, Daddy . . ."

"I'm not sure I've got the teeth for it," Sidney smiled indulgently before promising that he would try his best.

On Monday 20th February, the Grantchester churchwarden discovered the dead body of Fraser Pascoe in a field between the farm and the church. He had been decapitated.

There was no sign of a murder weapon. The head lay a few feet from the body, as if someone had taken an almighty swing at the victim while he was walking, but the pathologist reported that it would have required several attempts to sever it from the body and that it was more likely to have been tossed or even kicked aside once it was off.

Inspector Keating was on the scene within an hour, the farm was cordoned off and no one was allowed to leave. Road blocks were set up at Coton Road, Broadway and Mill Way, police went door to door asking for witnesses, and Sidney was summoned that evening.

"Why didn't you warn me this might happen?" Geordie asked. "This is the man that woman in the fur coat was telling you about."

"I didn't think it would come to this."

"But you were uneasy. I know you, Sidney Chambers. Do you think Barbara Wilkinson could have done it herself? Taking the law into her own hands?"

"I hardly think she's responsible. She wouldn't have the strength."

"You'd be surprised. If the axe was sharp enough . . ."

"You think it was an axe?"

"What else could it have been? We'll have to interview every member of that bloody cult. Never mind Mrs Wilkinson, I suppose any one of them could have done it."

"Or one of their parents . . ."

"Or a local madman, for that matter. We have no leads. You'll talk to the boy; and his dreadful mother, of course. Did you ever get round to meeting the victim?"

"I didn't like him at all, Geordie, I must confess. Even the dean said he was a 'perfect menace'. Although I wouldn't put *him* down as a murderer."

"All this religion has a lot to answer for."

Sidney tried to explain the difference between good and bad religion; that it wasn't the fault of any individual belief system but misunderstandings by their followers. Even if people fall short of their ideals, it is still better to have them than not.

"I'm not so sure," said Keating. "Wouldn't it be preferable to have no religion at all?"

The next morning Sidney attended a meeting of the Cathedral Chapter in the Lady Chapel. Items on the agenda concerned the maintenance of gravestones in diocesan churchyards, a review of parish tithes for the financial year 1967/1968, forthcoming missionary work in Nigeria, and a discussion of the Church's attitude to homosexuality in the light of the recent Sexual Offences Act.

Despite the importance of the issues, his attention was unsurprisingly diverted to the carved figurines that decorated the chapel. One hundred and forty-seven statues had been mutilated, vandalised and indeed decapitated by the Puritan reformers in the sixteenth century. It was the worst of violent religion, the smashing of images, the stripping of the altars. The stained glass had been destroyed, the walls whitewashed, all colour and imagery removed. A building intended to represent God's green garden had been razed by fire. This was a living embodiment of religious zealotry.

Had someone approached Pascoe with similar fury? Perhaps the motivation for his murder could have been religious after all?

Sidney thought of the saints, martyrs and other victims of decapitation: John the Baptist, St Alban, the first English Christian martyr, St George and Thomas More. He prayed for them all. He even prayed for Fraser Pascoe.

Then he called in to see Mrs Wilkinson. She was wearing some kind of day-gown and although her make-up was incomplete she still looked vulnerably attractive. Ever since his wife and friends had warned him how compromising the woman might be, he had found himself thinking more and more about her. Sidney told himself to concentrate.

"I was afraid something like this would happen," she said. "It's dreadful."

"Have you seen Danny?"

"I went to the farm but there were police everywhere. My son still won't talk to me so I wrote him a little card and included some money to help him along. One of the girls said they would take it to him. I am doing my best."

"I'm sure you are."

"Do the police have any clues as to who might have done such a thing?"

"There's nothing they are prepared to say publicly."

"And will you involve yourself? I know you are friends with the inspector."

"I have come to ask if there is anything I can do."

"I am not sure that is the only reason for your visit. You have come to ask me questions."

"And I have asked one," Sidney replied carefully before repeating himself. "Is there anything I can do?"

"You can get my son out of there."

"I have tried. But now the situation has changed. The police will want to keep them all on site during the investigation. Danny will be a suspect along with the others."

"They all worshipped that man. Why would they kill him?"

"Why would anyone? That's what the police need to find out."

"I suppose you've come to tell me that I might be a suspect?"

"That is a possibility . . ."

"Even though I am 'a weak and feeble woman'?"

"You never spoke to Fraser Pascoe yourself?"

"Not recently. Not at all."

Sidney remembered something the man had said. "Didn't he offer you 'a way of rest'?"

"He made a pass at me, if that's what you mean."

"He claimed they were a celibate community."

"That is nonsense in his case, Mr Archdeacon, and he made it perfectly obvious. I am quite used to men making propositions, as I am sure you can imagine."

"I can."

"In fact, I'm sometimes surprised when they don't. People are never very subtle about it."

"And you refused him?"

"Of course I did. What kind of woman do you think I am?"

"Your son . . ."

"What has he said about me?"

"I think . . ." Sidney hesitated. It was too soon to discuss what he had heard of Barbara's life as a swinger. In any case, it was probably better to give her the benefit of the doubt. "I imagine Danny wants some time away from his parents. It's a process of discovery. I'm sure you know that this is common in adolescence."

24

"But a mother's love never stops. I am still responsible for him."

"I think Danny wants you to let go."

"I can't. He may be in danger."

"Is there anything you know that you're not telling me, Mrs Wilkinson?"

"Call me Barbara, please. I hate this formality."

"Go on . . ."

"Fraser Pascoe may be dead but I don't think the trouble is over. It's my feminine intuition; something I can't quite explain. Haven't you felt something similar, Sidney? It makes me shiver. That place is evil; evil masquerading as love. I am convinced that we haven't seen the last of all this, that there are terrors still to come."

Sidney returned to the Family of Love. The weather was appropriately sombre, with low and heavy skies, slanting rain and a biting wind that seemed to be blowing hard at him.

Inspector Keating asked Danny Wilkinson about Pascoe's background. The cult leader had experimented with alternative medicine, learned Transcendental Meditation in San Francisco, studied under a guru in India, and returned to his home country to teach others what he called "the way of all knowledge". His plan had been to let the mind run freely — "jazz thinking" he called it — in order to find the underlying harmony of all religions and link human consciousness to the beginning of creation. Once a moment of eternal union had been achieved then his adherents could be filled with inner light and find themselves at one with the cosmos.

Geordie pretended to find this appealing but, as soon as they had time alone, he asked Sidney how anyone could ever believe in "such utter crap". They then began to interview the residents.

There was Roger Nelson, a burly young man with a forward stoop as a result of a rugby injury at school; Kevin Jenkins, a boy who'd had rickets as a child and whose father still blamed him for failing his eleven-plus; Sam Swinton, who had the requisite air of sullen silence that suited the most obvious suspect; Tom Raven, the boy in the white shirt who appeared remarkably unconcerned, as if recent events had nothing to do with him; and two women, Bea Selby and Rachel Sladen, who claimed that they had been in bed with what they thought was an out-of-body experience but turned out to be flu.

That left Danny Wilkinson, who swore that, at the time of Pascoe's death, they had been drinking from the loving cup before resting in a state of trance.

"And does that cup have any ingredients that the police might consider illegal?"

"I can't tell you that."

"We'll find out soon enough," Keating snapped.

"Tell me, Danny," Sidney resumed, "do you plan to stay here? It will be very different now."

"I have nowhere else to go, man."

"Your father and mother . . ."

"I said I have nowhere else."

"But you no longer have your leader . . ."

"Your Church follows a dead man," Danny Wilkinson concluded. "Here we are living a life of peace and beauty. That's all there is. All that matters. What we're waiting for."

By the time the questioning had been completed, Keating was unimpressed. "Peace and beauty, my arse. That's got to be one of the least tranquil places on earth. They're all terrified. I don't believe a word any of them say. I presume you're going to keep helping me with all this? It probably means seeing a bit more of the boy's mother, but you won't mind that."

Sidney was part of a working party to discuss the Church of England's attitude to "modern morality", during which everyone spent a great deal of time trying to find the right level of informed tolerance over matters such as sex before marriage, divorce, homosexuality and abortion. After several protracted sessions in dim Westminster basements with lukewarm coffee and stale biscuits, he needed cheering up.

Tubby Hayes was headlining at Johnny's club in Soho. This meant that Sidney could see one of his favourite sax players and question his brother-in-law about the status of his marriage at the same time.

The band was playing "Finky Minky". Sidney ordered a tomato juice and thought through his approach. He would begin by asking about the main matter in hand, not least because Johnny had been present when Barbara Wilkinson had first arrived to discuss her fears about the farm.

"I don't know what it is with those places," Johnny began. "They give me the creeps."

"I think it's an attempt to opt out of boredom and pursue something other than the norm. I suppose jazz started like that. As did the Church."

"You just have to stay true, Sidney: no gimmicks. I hate it when vicars get the guitars out."

"I am not wild about that either, I must say. It's all part of our appeal to 'the youth of today' people keep writing about."

"Those campfire Christians always look like people who are too scared to have sex."

"I wouldn't put it as strongly as that. Perhaps they are just waiting for the right moment."

"That's what Christianity's all about, isn't it: deferred gratification? Waiting for the return of Jesus, hoping for revelation. You'd think they might want to hurry things along a bit."

"Some of them do. This cult I was telling you about. They have a 'loving cup'."

"You think it might be spiked?"

"I'm afraid so."

"And you want me to put out a few feelers? It'll be a local dealer."

"Just the odd discreet word might be helpful."

Johnny pointed to the band as they swung into "Mexican Green" at the start of the second set. "Tubby is no stranger on the scene. Blossom knows people too, but she doesn't get involved."

"The singer?"

"She's become a regular here. Everyone loves her."

"Jen was saying."

"She's worried we're having an affair."

"And are you?" Sidney was surprised by his own boldness.

"So that's why you're here."

"Not entirely . . ."

"Blossom's much older than me and she's not a woman you mess with. I've told Jen there's nothing going on, but she's suspicious."

"Is your artiste married?"

"Not any more. But I'm telling you, Sidney, there's nothing going on. You can meet her if you like. Then you'll see."

"I suppose the late nights can't have helped."

"This is a jazz club, Sidney. What am I supposed to do? Leave after the first set and tuck up early? Come on, let me get you a proper drink."

As the band launched into "Off the Wagon" and Sidney accepted the addition of vodka to his tomato juice, he had to admit that his resistance to temptation was not always as good as it should have been.

Barbara Wilkinson's former husband, Mike, was a strict but efficient Scottish dentist who was keen to instruct his new patient on the importance of "a confident mouth".

"So much goes into it, Mr Archdeacon: food, air, bacteria. It has to be your front line of defence. All manner of things can unsettle, invade and then fester. Your gums have been open to attack for far too long. In fact, your teeth are failing so fast it's like the Battle of Bannockburn in there."

Sidney had not seen a dentist for almost ten years and now remembered why. Mike Wilkinson had a similarly poor attendance record at Sunday services. "I went to church once too bloody often," he volunteered, referring no doubt to his marriage.

Sidney's inability to keep to proper standards of oral hygiene meant that he was now in need of a crown, three fillings and some root-canal treatment, not to mention the fact that it was likely he would soon have to have his wisdom teeth extracted.

"Do you have to knock me out for that?"

"Not completely," Mike Wilkinson explained. "It depends on how complicated it is. Some patients do prefer hospital but we can call in an anaesthetist. We do have everything to hand."

"Gas and air?"

"Yes. Sedation too. We try to make sure people hardly notice they've been here."

"That's not a story I've often heard told."

"I shouldn't worry too much, Mr Archdeacon, although we will have to see you quite a few times. However, one of the side effects of diazepam is amnesia, so you may well forget how many."

Sidney was not at ease. He worried about the misuse of dentistry. Could, for example, a murderous dentist get away with a slow-acting poison inserted into the body of a filling that might not kill until days or weeks afterwards? How easy would that be to detect?

He lay back in the chair and wondered why he was thinking like this. Who else would imagine that their dentist was a potential murderer?

As he was waiting for the anaesthetic to take effect, Sidney mentioned that he had seen Mike's son Danny just before Fraser Pascoe's death.

"A ghastly business. I was in London at a meeting of the British Endodontic Society at the time. We meet to exchange ideas on all aspects of pulp and root-canal treatment. Dr Angelo Sargenti was giving a paper on the use of N2. Barbara tracked me down and told me."

"So you do speak to each other?"

"Not if we can help it. But when it concerns our son, we have to. Hopefully that'll put an end to it all. They can't go on without their leader."

"I think they're going to try. The plan is to live outside the capitalist system."

"Then Danny should move to Moscow."

"I'm not sure that's practical."

"It's no more difficult than living without heat or money in a draughty old barn with a collection of messed-up lunatics."

"I suppose if you put it like that . . ."

The dentist resumed his work. "Let's see if we're ready to continue. A little wider please, Mr Archdeacon."

The drilling began and Mike Wilkinson drew this particular subject of conversation to a close. "You can't force your children to do anything against their will. But you can cut off their source of funds. That's what

I've told Barbara. But she's too weak with Danny. She had a soft spot for Fraser Pascoe too."

"Really?" Sidney mumbled as best he could.

"Oh yes. They were quite close at one stage. Then after a couple of months it all fell apart. That's what happens with Babs. Nothing ever lasts. Rinse and spit please . . ."

That Saturday Sidney took his wife and daughter to lunch with his parents in Highgate. Alec and Iris Chambers had both retired and now that they were well into their seventies they were thinking of selling the family home and moving somewhere smaller and warmer; Devon, Cornwall, or even France. Alec Chambers said that he wanted to "throw some ideas around" but before they did so he would like "a bit of a man-to-man" with his son. Sidney knew it was going to be serious as soon as he was handed a gin and tonic that he hadn't asked for.

"Hildegard has told us what's been going on and we think you need to be very careful indeed."

"There has been a murder."

"I know. However, we are more concerned about the woman who came on your birthday."

"Barbara Wilkinson?"

"Indeed. I hope you haven't been tempted to get involved with her problems?"

"There's nothing improper, if that's what you're worried about."

"I was worrying about the proper, let alone the improper."

"I don't appear to have much choice, Dad. She asked for my help, I went to see her son and his spiritual leader was found murdered."

"But that is a matter for Keating."

"I know. But when parishioners ask for help . . ."

"Barbara Wilkinson is not, as far as I am aware, a parishioner."

"You know what I mean."

"No, I don't. I was wondering if you would have been so eager to help if the boy's father had come to see you rather than the mother?"

"I like to think I would; although there is quite a difference in manner between husband and wife."

"This has got to stop, Sidney. It's not fair on Hildegard."

"Have you asked her?"

"I don't need to. You can't just go charging in all over again. Unless you're trying to impress your *femme fatale.*"

Hildegard popped her head round the study door. "Lunch is ready!"

"Very good," Alec Chambers replied loudly but then added, as a final aside to his son, "she may very well not mind, but it's embarrassing for the rest of us. You have a reputation to keep up."

"And I do."

"We don't want gossip. Once Anna starts her education, you'll have to think about that too. Mothers at the school gates."

"I don't think we need to worry about that. Ely is a decent enough place."

"You don't want to give anyone cause. A priest, like a doctor, must be beyond reproach. Didn't they teach you anything at theological college? If you really must talk to that female again, make sure that it's in your house and not hers. You can't be seen going out of other women's homes. That's all I'm saying. Now let's have some lunch."

Once they were all seated in the dining room, Iris Chambers produced her famous fish pie and Sidney tried to cheer up proceedings by making a jokey reference to Sidney Bechet's "Hold Tight (Want Some Seafood Mama)". This went unnoticed. Undaunted, he then extended his marine sphere of reference by telling the assembled company that he had recently been to Johnny's club to see Tubby Hayes play "Fishin' the Blues".

"I presume you were 'fishing for clues'," his mother replied as she served up the fish pie, kale and a dish of carrots that she was trying in a new way: *à la julienne*.

"I did ask Johnny about things, if that's what you want to know."

"What things?" asked Anna.

"It doesn't matter."

"But," Sidney turned to his mother, switching to French, *"il n'y a rien à faire."*

"You mean *il n'y a pas une affaire?*" his mother asked.

"Non."

"It's not fair," said Anna. "Speak in German."

"I'm sorry, *ma petite*," Sidney continued, "I was distracted by your grandmother's carrots *à la julienne*. I will now speak to you only in German."

"That won't last long," said Hildegard.

Iris Chambers gave her son an extra helping and was assured that there was nothing to worry about. Sidney was certain Johnny Johnson had been behaving himself. "As have I," he added quickly, catching his wife's eye.

"Guilty conscience?" she asked.

Sidney tried to concentrate on the matter in hand. He had always been bemused by family secrets and partiality; how assumptions were made, sometimes based on childhood and teenage years that no longer applied when siblings were fully grown adults; how one member of the family might be trusted more than another and that people never knew everything, either about their parents or their children.

"Are we talking about Sidney or Johnny?" Alec Chambers enquired.

"Never you mind," his wife answered. "Some of this is simply between a mother and a son."

"Does it concern Jen?"

"*Zut. C'est fini.* The moment has passed."

"You promised no more French," Anna complained.

Alec Chambers looked to his granddaughter and winked. "Don't worry, poppet. We have our little secrets too, don't we?"

"And what are they?" his wife asked.

"*Zut. C'est fini,*" he replied, and once Anna realised that he was referring to the box of Cadbury's Lucky Numbers her grandfather had said she could have after lunch, she repeated the phrase again and again until pudding was served.

This was Angel Delight, a new strawberry and cream instant whip that could be made in seconds. "I thought you might be amused by the name," Iris Chambers told her son, "and it's so easy."

Her husband began to sing "Earth Angel (Will You Be Mine)" quietly to himself and then increased the volume once he had the attention of the room. Everyone clapped. Sidney couldn't understand why his mother, who had been so imaginative under rationing and who prided herself in her home cooking, would want to take such an artificial short cut. "I remember the trifles you used to make when I was a child: jellies with raspberries; lemon meringue pie on my birthday."

"Oh, I can't be bothered with all that now. Don't you think it's a wonderful name? Perhaps the angels scoop it all up when they've had enough of playing Bach?"

"There is no such thing as too much Bach," said Hildegard.

When Sidney failed to respond, his mother tried again. "You don't seem to be on top form, my boy. Is it your teeth again?"

"It's a bit more than that."

"You're not still being plagued by that ghastly woman?"

"*Pas devant l'enfant*," Sidney replied.

"Oh, for goodness sake."

"*Zut. C'est fini*," Anna shouted out, only to hear her mother observe:

"If only it was."

Shortly after breakfast on the Thursday, Inspector Keating telephoned to say that Dr Allan McDonald had completed the post-mortem and Pascoe's body had not been drugged. There had been a number of blows, one of which had severed the carotid artery. The resultant bleeding and lack of oxygen to the brain had been the cause of death, but further attempts had then been made to detach the head, which had been kicked away from the body with the force of a footballer's volley.

The blade of the murder weapon could have been up to sixteen inches long, curved like a sickle or grasshook, and there had been some additional hacking with what might have been a serrated carving knife. Whoever did it would have had blood all over them and so it was imperative to continue searching the area for both weapons and clothing.

Sidney tried not to think too hard about the horrors of the scene. "That rules out Barbara Wilkinson, I would have thought."

"Unless she was in cahoots with her husband."

"The dentist? They hardly speak to each other." Even as he said the words, Sidney did not know if this was true.

"Decapitation is going it a bit for a dentist, don't you think? He has so many other methods of murder at his disposal. And why would he want to kill a religious fanatic?"

"Because of what he was doing to his son?" Sidney replied. "He does have an alibi. That doesn't stop him or his wife paying someone to do it for them, I suppose."

"It's too messy for a hitman. This was brutal and personal. We need to find out who could have hated Pascoe so much. We'll have to look a bit harder. In the meantime, there's no harm in you seeing your lovely lady again, Sidney. Perhaps she'll tell you a bit more. Give her a bit of your pastoral care."

"I'm not sure that would be appropriate."

Keating managed a sardonic smile. "It hasn't stopped you in the past."

It had begun to snow, the drifts across the fens covering all the signs of spring. Sidney took Byron, his black Labrador, as well as his bicycle, and caught a late-morning train to Cambridge, determined to get his visit to Barbara Wilkinson over and done with.

Despite the cold outside, her heating was on sufficiently high for her to wear a sleeveless black woollen dress, with her hair in an "updo" style. A soft, dark tendril fell across her eyes. Sidney found himself wanting to move it to one side and touch her cheek. Instead he took her hand as she wept and said that she was frightened of the police. "They came asking the most terrible questions."

"About Fraser Pascoe?"

"Danny too. They asked me how much I knew about 'free love'. It was insulting."

"Fraser Pascoe insisted on celibacy."

"But I don't think that man practised what he preached. I told you that last time."

"He was keen on you."

"That is not too unusual, Mr Archdeacon, as I've said before." Still she held his hand.

"And you didn't respond to his approach?"

"Again, I've told you, no."

"But was there anything about your meetings that might have given rise to speculation?"

"I can't do anything about gossip. That's why your company is so refreshing. I know I am safe. You are beyond reproach." She patted his hand and let it go.

Sidney was reassured and disappointed at the same time. There was something curiously fetching about the woman, despite her bare-faced lie. "I wanted to ask about something that may not be so easy to discuss."

"Oh dear. I hope this is not going to be *complicated*."

"It's money," Sidney said quickly.

"Oh," Barbara recovered. "I thought it might be something else."

"How much did you give Danny?"

"I wouldn't like to say."

"Was he stealing from you, Mrs Wilkinson?"

"You've guessed?"

"How much did he take?"

"I don't honestly know. But there was a forged cheque. Fortunately the bank stopped it. They couldn't believe I would do such a thing."

"Do you mind telling me how much it was for?"

"Five thousand pounds. Payable to Fraser Pascoe."

"That's a vast amount of money."

"Now you see why I had to get my son out of there."

"But you didn't go to the police?"

"I thought if I did that then Danny wouldn't come home. Now the police are involved I'm afraid he never will. What on earth are we going to do, Sidney? You won't desert me, will you?"

Before he left Grantchester, Sidney decided that he needed a moment to recover from the unsettling nature of his conversation with Barbara. She had a tentacular way of pulling him into situations he would rather avoid.

What he needed was something predictably reassuring and so he chose to look in on his former housekeeper. Mrs Maguire was much slowed by arthritis, and she was less confident than usual, but she came to life when the subject turned to her assessment of current events. Barbara Wilkinson had only herself to blame.

"She's a terrible mother. Everyone comments. People who don't have to work for a living can get up to all kinds of mischief. The devil makes work for idle hands, and many are the men who've benefited from her personal touch. I'm surprised she hasn't got her claws into you."

"I have seen her . . ."

"You've got yourself involved, haven't you?"

"Not in any improper way."

"I mean with the crime. My sister Gladys was saying they think the murder weapon was a scythe. That would be appropriate, wouldn't it?"

"What do you mean?"

40

"Father Time, of course. The Grim Reaper, cutting Pascoe down to size."

"Are Father Time and the Grim Reaper one and the same?" Sidney asked. "I'm never that sure."

"Doesn't matter now the man's dead. I wonder if he knew what hit him."

"They think he was attacked from behind."

"He must have known. You can't do that kind of thing with one blow. He would have staggered about and seen his attacker. It's bound to be one of those young men. They'll neither work nor want."

"Do you think they're rich?"

"Only people with money can afford to say they have no need of it."

"That's very wise, Mrs M."

His former housekeeper smiled, grateful for the acknowledgement. "I've always said there's something dirty at the crossroads. It's a fraud. All those boys and girls are rich children with trust funds, I'll bet. Pascoe was raking it in. You need to look for the money, Sidney, isn't that what they say? Perhaps Mrs Richmond's husband could help? He works in the City. He must know people."

"I can't see Henry Richmond troubling himself with this."

"He owes you a favour, doesn't he?"

"I'm not sure he does."

"You approved of him. Told Miss Kendall to go ahead and marry him."

"Only because there wasn't anyone else left."

"That's not true, Sidney. You should be ashamed of yourself for saying such things. I always said she'd have made a good wife for you."

"You never said anything of the sort. Besides, I'm very happy with Hildegard."

"I'll tell you one thing about Mrs Richmond. She'd have given short shrift to that Wilkinson woman. She wouldn't have let you near her."

"Hildegard is a lot more tolerant, I must confess."

"That may be, but I wouldn't take her for granted."

"I don't."

"She's been spurned once and her last husband was murdered. You don't want to start giving her ideas."

"I really don't think Hildegard is capable of murder, Mrs M."

"You shouldn't test her, though, Sidney my boy. People can behave very unpredictably when they're desperate."

Sidney took Byron for a quick constitutional across the Meadows before their journey home. He was annoyed with himself for getting involved in a situation that was now out of control. He should have told Barbara Wilkinson right at the start that he could do nothing for her. But instead he had been initially attracted to her (he could admit that now) as well as vain and flattered into thinking that only he, the great Sidney Chambers, could sort things out. And now he found himself right in the middle of it all. *Never again*, he told himself. What he wanted more than anything was a drink with Inspector Keating. What he would do for a pint of

Guinness in the Eagle, sitting by the fire on this dire day!

At least it had stopped snowing. He let his Labrador roam free during his cogitations and it must have been a good ten minutes before he realised that he had lost sight of him altogether. This was all he needed. To mislay his ruddy dog on top of everything else! *Honestly.*

He called and called but Byron gave no reply. Passers-by offered to help and they finally found him nosing his way through a patch of undergrowth. He had been pawing at a swathe of dirty blue-and-white material, but it wasn't a random item of clothing at all. It was a bloodied cheesecloth shirt wrapped around the blade of what appeared to be the gardener's scythe from Grantchester church.

After that it was bedlam. Keating and his forensic team set to work while Sidney made phone calls to Henry Richmond about the cult's finances. He also telephoned the dean to apologise for his absence at evensong before anyone complained.

"We all understand these are special circumstances, Sidney."

"Sometimes I worry things are never normal."

"Perhaps there's no such thing as normality?" the dean mused. Sidney envied the time his colleague seemed to have available for free-flowing thought.

"I do hope there is. It isn't good for me to spend so much of my contemplation suspecting people of murder."

"I am afraid that being a priest isn't about 'what's good for me', Sidney. It's about what's best for the community we serve."

"I'm not sure I'm even managing that."

"If you are fighting evil, then you are taking steps to help the world become a better place. Try to make your every moment an act of prayer. That is all a priest can do. Take steps. The race is not always to the swift."

Sidney had got away with his ecclesiastical negligence only to be encouraged to work harder at the practical application of his ethics. There really was no respite, not even when it came to sharing a moment of relaxation with the inspector as soon as the pub was open.

"You need to question that dentist again."

"I think that's your job, Geordie. If I ask any more leading questions he's sure to commit an act of excruciating violence. Have you made any progress with the shirt?"

"It's a medium size; and so, if it did belong to the murderer, which seems pretty likely given that it is soaked in blood, that rules out the bulky Roger Nelson, and the diminutive Sam Swinton. It's probably safe to think it wasn't one of the women, which means the murderer must be Tom Raven, your friend's son Danny or his dad the dentist."

"Unless one of the women deliberately wore a man's shirt or it's a stranger after all."

"I'm concentrating on those three men for now. It shouldn't take long for one of them to crack. They're all behaving as if they're in the middle of a nervous breakdown."

"Perhaps they need help."

"And they may get it once we've sorted this out. Then, if they haven't been disowned, we need to get the

44

children back to their families. You said Amanda's husband might look into the finances?"

"Companies House. Other records. I've also asked him to look for the surnames of the people in the cult. Pascoe might have been working with one of the parents. You never know. But if he's got assets, Henry says he will find them: provided they are not in Switzerland."

Geordie offered Sidney and Byron a lift to the station. Before they got into the car, the two men stopped at a makeshift poster advertising a student production of *Orestes*. Geordie asked what the play was about and was informed that the plot concerned a son who murdered his mother, Clytemnestra, and her lover Aegisthus.

"Charming."

"He's then pursued by the Furies and goes mad."

"Any justice?" Geordie asked.

"Funnily enough, there's a trial with a jury of twelve but they can't decide. It's a split vote, but the goddess Athena lets him off."

"Extenuating circumstances . . ."

"His mother was having an affair. He was provoked. A similar thing may have happened here."

Geordie was doubtful as he got in the car and turned on the ignition. "Are you sure? Barbara Wilkinson and Fraser Pascoe hated each other."

Sidney slammed his passenger door shut. "Yes. The kind of hatred that only happens after a relationship. *Hell hath no fury* and all that . . ."

"And so if Danny Wilkinson or his father found out about the affair they could have wanted to kill either of them?"

"Or both."

"It seems a bit extreme."

The two friends drove in silence down King's Parade. As they passed on into Trumpington Street, Keating asked: "Sidney, are you suggesting that Danny Wilkinson might have joined the cult specifically to murder Pascoe in revenge for sleeping with his mother and that he has been faking his cult-like behaviour all along?"

"It's not impossible."

"Tell you what," said Geordie, missing the left turn into Lensfield Road and taking an abrupt right into the Fen Causeway. "Let's go round there now."

"Both of us?"

"Why not?"

"What about my train? I should be getting back. We're going the wrong way. Hildegard . . ."

"Oh don't worry about her. She's used to all this."

"That doesn't make it any easier," Sidney replied forlornly. "I've just come from Grantchester. I don't want to go back there all over again."

Keating turned towards the village and was overtaken by an ambulance going full pelt. "Bloody hell."

It was heading for the farm. By the time the two men arrived a body was being stretchered away.

Barbara Wilkinson was already there. "Someone's tried to kill Danny," she said.

Sidney sometimes wished he had developed a mild form of agoraphobia to keep him at home, since whenever he went out into the world he found himself cast adrift, like a Cambridge Odysseus, wondering when he would ever return to his Penelope.

Danny Wilkinson had either taken an overdose or he had been poisoned. He was not dead but was rushed to hospital to have his stomach pumped. His mother followed the ambulance all the way there. Keating took statements and Sidney offered what consolation he could as Byron slept in the corner. If this was not a straightforward suicide but attempted murder, it could have been performed by any surviving member of the cult.

Keating searched the farm and awaited the toxicology report. There was not much to look for, since the Family of Love, in espousing the cause of poverty, was hippily monastic. There were few clothes, little food and no ready money. The bathroom contained a sliver of soap, a thin ribbed towel with the nap rubbed away and Izal lavatory paper that was so rough it was used only sparingly. But finally, in the cupboard under the stairs, hidden away in the bag of a Hoover that was never used, the police found a supply of ketamine.

"Here we go," said Keating. "There aren't many horses to tranquillise on this particular farm. It must be for the loving cup. Progress at last."

He began by interviewing Tom Raven. The boy claimed that Danny Wilkinson must have taken an overdose. His friend had always wanted to reach for a higher calm and if that meant death then his attempt had, perhaps, been noble.

"Unless he didn't mean to take things so far."

"You have been listening to his stupid mother?"

"I don't need your advice on who I talk to," Keating snapped back. "I make my own observations."

"Then you probably don't need my help."

"I'll be the one who decides that."

Sidney knew that he might be able to lessen the aggression between the two men with a quiet word but decided to remain silent and let his friend press on with further questions about Pascoe's death. Raven claimed that he always wore white shirts long and loose from Hilditch & Key, and he wouldn't be seen dead in the blood-soaked cheesecloth specimen discovered on the Meadows. He had never noticed any other member of the farm wearing it either. Perhaps it was a stranger's and Pascoe's murder had been a random attack? In any case, he had been visiting his father in London at the time of death, so he couldn't have committed the crime even if he had wanted to.

"What about financial gain?" Keating asked.

"I have enough money, thanks."

"I thought that in this place you weren't supposed to have any at all?" Sidney remembered.

"We all need a running-away fund," Tom Raven answered before smirking a little. "I am sure your wives have them."

"Don't be cheeky," said Keating. "What about your so-called friend, Danny Wilkinson?"

"He's still my friend."

"Did you poison him?"

"Why would I do that?"

"You tell us."

"I could have done, I suppose. I could have done anything really. But I didn't. None of us did. We were all together that night, 'in harmony', and then we went to our rooms for jazz thinking."

"Separately?"

"I did."

"What about the girls?"

"What about them?"

"What was their relationship with Danny like?"

"It was groovy enough. But I don't think it was physical, if that's what you mean. Danny was scared of chicks. Something to do with his mum. You'll have to ask him. Her too, if you can stand it."

"You speak as if you know he will survive."

"You think he might not?" Raven asked.

"Sometimes, even after a stomach pump, the damage has already been done. It's either internal bleeding, kidney damage or liver failure: even all three. Do you want that on your conscience?"

"My conscience is clear enough."

"But you are friends," Sidney pointed out. "Don't you care about him?"

"I love him like a brother. But I don't see why I have to talk to you about it."

"Don't take that tone with us, you little shit." Keating exploded at last, getting out of his chair and grabbing Tom Raven by the collar. "I don't see why I have to talk to a spoilt little wazzock like you either but unfortunately that's my job. I have to do it. You think you can give any answer you like? You make me sick."

Tom Raven held his ground and remained utterly still. "Stay cool, man. There's no need to get heavy. You don't want my dad involved."

"Don't think your father can get you out of this."

"My dad can get me out of anything."

"Is that a challenge?" Sidney asked.

He rang Hildegard to explain why he was going to be delayed even further. He did not go into details, and he left out the fact that he had promised to look in on Barbara Wilkinson before getting the last train back to Ely.

He tried her home first and found that she had just returned from the hospital. She said she was just about to get ready for bed but knew that she would not be able to sleep. "Danny's all right," she said. "Thank God. He needs a good night's rest. They all think it's a cry for help but I don't believe that. Someone at the farm was trying to kill him."

"And who do you think might do such a thing?"

"Tom Raven."

"Why do you say that?"

"He got Danny into the cult in the first place."

"But they are friends," Sidney pointed out. "Why would he want to kill your son?"

"Because Danny knew he killed Pascoe."

"And do you have any evidence? Do you even know Tom Raven?"

"He was always an arrogant little boy. I think he's behind the whole thing. It's a money-making racket."

"Then why would he want to kill Pascoe? If they were making money and it was all going well . . ."

"Perhaps his father ordered the murder. I've heard he's a hard man."

"All of this is speculation, Mrs Wilkinson."

"I can't help that. Everything keeps going around and around in my head."

"Then we should rest."

"Would you like to stay the night? There's a bed in the spare room."

"I don't think that's wise."

"I'll give you a lift to the station then."

"That would be kind."

The snow and sleet had turned to rain and it was hard to see the road ahead, but Barbara Wilkinson was a good, confident driver, which made Sidney suspicious about her public insecurities. He looked out through the windscreen, allowing the sound of the wipers to give silence a rhythm against the engine of the car, and wondered what on earth he was doing, travelling through the darkness with a woman from whom he was unable to escape.

"Do you find me disconcerting?" she asked.

"Not at all."

"You can trust me, you know."

"I'm sure I can."

"I suppose you don't want to run any risks."

"I think I just need to get home and clear my mind."

"I hope I haven't contributed to the muddle."

"Not at all," said Sidney before a voice in his head told him that Barbara hadn't *contributed* as much as been the *cause* of the whole damned thing. How on earth had he fallen for the charms of a woman who was clearly trying to manipulate him? It was ridiculous.

"I'll make it up to you one day," she promised.

"That won't be necessary. I'm only doing my job."

"I may insist . . ." Barbara pulled over in front of the station, and gave Sidney a goodnight kiss on the cheek, holding on to him for just a little too long. "You're such a comfort," she said.

It was after midnight when Sidney got home. All he wanted to do was pour himself a whisky, put his feet up and listen to a bit of jazz. He might even have time to read a bit of the Bechet autobiography Hildegard had given him for his birthday. *Treat It Gentle*. Some hope.

He assumed that his wife and daughter were asleep but he found that they were both awake and in their nightgowns. Anna had woken up and was unable to settle, so Hildegard was reading her yet another bedtime story: the tale of "Sweetheart Roland".

"Heavens above — is that a good idea? Isn't that the one that begins with the witch cutting her daughter's head off?" Sidney asked.

"It's just a coincidence and it's a fairy story. Anna loves it."

"I don't want her growing up and thinking these things are normal."

"But in your world," his wife replied, "they are."

On Saturday 4th March Sidney went to see Danny Wilkinson in hospital. It was a bleak day that did nothing to improve his spirits as he took in the winter landscape from the train down to Cambridge: the bare hedges, the skeletal trees with their abandoned birds' nests, the wheat cut short, the last stacks of hay bales, the sheen of green still fragile across the fields.

On arrival the chaplain gave him what he took to be a rather insincere wave, calling out, "Here comes trouble."

"I think you've already got plenty."

"Which is why we don't need any more, Mr Archdeacon. Your reputation precedes you."

"I am helping a former parishioner, that is all."

"And you expect me to believe that?"

"I am only going where the Lord takes me."

Danny had almost recovered. He claimed that he could not remember a thing but that he definitely had not taken an overdose and had not meant to kill himself. What was going on and who could he trust? He didn't want to spend any time with his mother or father but he could hardly go back to the farm if one of the members was out to get him.

"Do you have other friends? Relations?" Sidney asked.

"There's Tom's family. They have a house in London. His dad's rich and never there."

"And you don't think Tom might have poisoned you?"

"He's my best friend."

"And he wouldn't have killed Pascoe either?"

"No. He was in London at the time. I think he was seeing his dad."

"Can you think of anyone who could be behind all this?" Sidney pressed, wishing he could get past this blank state of denial.

"The farm was a refuge. We were all happy there. It can't be any of us."

"I know you've already told me, but we need to be clear. Can you confirm that you didn't take the overdose yourself?"

"I did not."

"You're sure?"

"Yes."

"Will you let your mother see you, Danny? She's very worried about you."

The young man closed his eyes and turned his face away.

Henry Richmond responded surprisingly speedily to Sidney's request for a little financial investigation. He confirmed that the Family of Love operated as a company called Lucis International, and that there were two directors, Fraser Pascoe and Giles Raven, the London accountant who was Tom's father.

"And if Pascoe's dead?"

"All the money would go to the Raven family. They are the nominated beneficiaries."

"And so Tom could be working for his father?"

"He could indeed. In fact, it seems highly likely. But I think that's your territory."

"And he could be in cahoots with Danny Wilkinson," Sidney thought aloud. "Although I wonder if they really are best friends: if not, then what is their game?"

"Perhaps they fell out? They both killed Pascoe to get the money but then Tom tried to poison Danny to get the cash and hoped everyone would think that it was a guilt-ridden suicide attempt?"

Sidney was surprised by Henry's ability to think through the implications after he had been given so little information about the crime. Perhaps Barbara Wilkinson was right after all?

He took a bus into Soho and found Johnny Johnson at the bar of his club. He seemed unusually mellow, even for him, and after he had revealed that Blossom Dearie was playing once more, Sidney wondered, uncharitably perhaps, if Johnny had been lying all along and the couple had spent the afternoon together.

"You do seem to have a soft spot for her."

"You're one to talk. How is the lady Barbara?"

"She is at the heart of a murder investigation."

"Well, Blossom Dearie is my main act. I have to look after the talent and she's quite a handful, believe me. Don't be nosy, Sidney."

"I'm not."

"Why are you here then?"

"I wondered if you had ever come across a young man called Tom Raven?"

"And how on earth would I know him?"

"Because his father used to be your dad's accountant. Giles Raven."

"Oh," said Johnny, "He sails close to the wind, I'll tell you that. They call him 'The Magician'."

"I think I can guess why."

"He makes money disappear. I wouldn't mess with him."

"Do you think he could make people disappear too?" Sidney asked.

"More than likely."

"And could you introduce me to him?"

"I *could*, Sidney. But I'm not sure I want to."

"You're trying to protect him?"

"No, Sidney, I'm trying to protect *you*, you clown. That man's so rich he doesn't have to worry about the law. If he's anything to do with your investigation you won't be able to pin anything on him; and if he finds out you're meddling then there'll be trouble."

"I'm used to that."

"Not his kind of trouble, I can assure you. Let's have a drink and listen to some music."

Blossom Dearie had a light pixie voice with husky undertones of barbed romanticism and she was determined to put down anyone who might make the mistake of patronising her. She opened with "Let's Go Where the Grass is Greener", continued with "You Turn Me On Baby", sashayed into "Peel Me a Grape" and ended her first set with the satirical cabaret song "I'm Hip", which had the audience laughing at their own pretentious modernity.

Once the first set was over, Sidney told Johnny he really should be going home. "Do you stay until the end every night?" he asked.

"That's my job."

"Hard on Jen."

"She's pretty cool about it all."

"Are you sure?"

Johnny hesitated and then told Sidney that he should go backstage and check Blossom had everything she needed. His brother-in-law could meet her if he wanted. Sidney shook his hand and grinned. "Rather you than me. She seems a volatile lady."

"That's nothing unusual round here."

They were just about to make their final farewell when Johnny suddenly opened up. "Jen's afraid the love's run out. It hasn't. I just don't want to have to force things or pretend. Distractions keep me happy."

"As long as it's not more than a 'distraction'. There are limits to my tolerance — and Jen's."

"And I'm not going to test them, Sidney. Please. Don't worry. I love your sister. She loves me. Marriage is what it is. We can't all be like you and Hildegard. We're different. It's not about passion all the time. Sometimes you just have to let things drift."

" 'Treat it gentle', as Sidney Bechet advises."

"Yes, although the great saxophonist had his women troubles and spent plenty of time in the nick. I wouldn't follow his example too closely if I were you."

Back at Cambridge police station Keating was annoyed. He just couldn't get anything out of Tom Raven, a boy whose effortless southern English confidence had got under the detective's Northumbrian working-class skin. "We've always suspected that cult's a scam, but it's proving impossible to nail the bastards."

"It seems a very odd way of making money, doesn't it?" Sidney observed. "You pretend you don't believe in worldly goods and then cash in."

"The Church has been doing it for years."

Sidney gave his friend enough of a look to force an instant apology.

"Sorry, that was ungenerous of me. I didn't mean it."

"I think you did. Working in a cathedral like Ely, one can't deny that the Church has wealth. Fraser Pascoe did have a point. It might be better if we conducted ourselves more monastically."

"But the monks were just as bad, Sidney. Isn't that why their monasteries were all dissolved? People had had enough of them, and went round hacking away at all that wealth and corruption, cutting the heads off the statues in the Lady Chapel and then decapitating human beings as well. They were filled with the passion of the Lord, I seem to remember."

Sidney tried to concentrate on the motive behind the murder. "The Raven family do seem pretty suspect."

"Giles Raven, 'The Magician', has already got his lawyers on to us. His son has a very strong alibi. Father and son were both in London at the time of Pascoe's death. Loads of people saw them. They were at the greyhounds."

"That's unfortunate."

"I don't know, Sidney. When I started out in this job, a senior officer told me that crime was nearly always

58

about sex or money. You just had to follow one or the other. In this case it's probably both."

"Do you think the Wilkinson family are wealthy?"

"Not any more. Divorce soon sorts that out. And if you start handing out cash to a dodgy cult then you're asking for trouble."

"Which brings us back to Danny Wilkinson."

Sidney had a little walk around the room to help order his thoughts. "You don't think that in some strange way he's been trying to save his parents' marriage? If his mother did have an affair with Pascoe, he then kills her lover, pins the blame on Tom Raven and attempts suicide in the hope that his parents will be so shocked by his unhappiness that they reunite?"

Geordie thought things through. "And Danny could have stolen the sedatives from his father. When's your next appointment? You will have to make it sharpish, Sidney. Unless you want another session with the boy's mother?"

"I'd rather leave Barbara Wilkinson to you, if you don't mind."

"You're lucky I don't fancy her."

"Geordie, I don't fancy her *either*. In fact, come to think of it, I *can't stand her*."

"Oh dear," his friend replied. "It's as bad as that, is it?"

Sidney's prayers to St Apollonia, the patron saint of dentists, to relieve his toothache had gone unanswered. He therefore made further arrangements to see Mike Wilkinson, both to sort out the vexed matter of his teeth and to ask a few more questions about Mike's wife, his son, and his recent whereabouts. It was not going to be easy, not least because his mouth would be open and anaesthetised, there would be padded wool along his gums and both the sound and no doubt discomfort of continual drilling. There would not be long to ask questions, but as he had deliberately booked the last appointment of the day, he hoped there would be no emergency patients and that the receptionist might have left, giving Sidney the time and privacy for an unofficial interrogation.

Mike Wilkinson saw through the ruse. And although his attitude was curt (a quality often wrongly attributed to his Scottishness) the information post-surgery was revealing. He was sure his son had taken an overdose in a bid to attract his mother's sympathy and contrition. It turned out that, despite Barbara Wilkinson's protestations, Danny had been all too aware of her infidelity.

"Did you tell him?" Sidney asked.

"I didn't need to. He witnessed how his mother behaved."

"Children often find their parents embarrassing."

Mike Wilkinson gave Sidney a weary look, as if he was too tired to spell the whole thing out. "It wasn't just that."

"What was it then?"

"He walked in on Babs and Pascoe. Came home early from school. Wasn't feeling well. They were *in flagrante;* too busy to notice him. He ran away and came straight to me. I already knew what Barbara was up to and tried to calm Danny down, but it wasn't much use. He said he was never going home again, which was complicated, as he was supposed to be at school and we had hopes that he was clever enough to go up to Oxford. That's all gone now."

"So he stayed with you?"

"Not for long. He was sixteen and his friend Tom had already left to make money in London. I confronted Barbara, told her that Danny wasn't coming back and that everyone knew about her carrying on. I didn't say that Danny had walked in on them because I didn't want her making everything worse with a scene. I didn't tell her where he was, either. She went mad and denied it all but I think that's when she ended the relationship. I heard that Pascoe went to India and we all thought that was that, but then he returned and set up his cult."

"Which Danny eventually joined . . ."

"It was either Tom Raven's idea or his father's. He probably offered a cut of the money. I think both boys knew the whole thing was a scam."

"But it involved living with his mother's former lover."

"That was also his way of getting back at her."

"I think there may have been more to it than that," said Sidney.

"I'm not sure if I understand the psychology of it all or even if I want to," the dentist replied.

"Is there anything more?"

"I don't think so. There comes a time when you just have to let your boy find his way in life. He turned away from us both, his mum and me, just as we had rejected each other. Barbara was impossible to live with, as I am sure you can imagine. Then she got it into her head that I was having an affair with my assistant — something that was plainly untrue — and I just couldn't stand it any more. I let her believe it and I left them both. Selfish, I know. But you don't want to hear about all this. I should get on. Don't leave it so long next time. There's enough pain in the world without your teeth adding to the sum of human misery."

"I'm sorry to have asked so many questions, Mr Wilkinson. Actually I can feel the sedative wearing off. Do you keep a supply of it at home?"

"Yes, but it's strictly controlled, as I am sure you know."

"And none of it has gone missing recently?"

"Not as far as I am aware. If you are suggesting that I've either given some to my son or he has stolen from me then you are mistaken. It's more likely to be his mother's sleeping tablets."

"That would involve going back home and getting them."

"It wouldn't be hard to do that without her noticing."

"And if any had disappeared then your wife should have told us."

"She may have decided that you didn't need to know. Babs likes her little games. She can be quite cunning. I think that's where Danny gets it from."

"You mean that both mother and son are capable of deception?"

62

"I don't know, Mr Archdeacon. There are times when I don't know who anyone is any more. So many people spend their lives trying to become someone they were never intended to be. I try to concentrate on my job and earning enough money for a roof over my head, a car that works and a decent holiday twice a year. It's simpler that way and it leads to less trouble."

"Have you seen your son in hospital?"

"Of course. I do care about him. It's been a difficult time."

"It has. I'm sorry."

The dentist stretched out a hand in farewell. "I'm hopeful that Danny will be all right in the end. He just needs to find out who he is and get on with his life."

Sidney shook the man's hand and tried to find reassuring words but felt, in his heart of hearts, that it was almost certainly too late. The rest of Danny's life was likely to be entirely different from anything either of his parents had ever hoped for.

Sidney checked with the doctors that their patient was now recovered sufficiently to go home and then alerted Keating. He went to see Danny Wilkinson in his hospital room and told him that the police were convinced he had killed Pascoe in an act of revenge and had then taken an overdose that was intended to look like a murder attempt. Danny, still pale, and propped up on his pillows, seemed shocked. Sidney got to the point straight away: "Is there anything I can do to explain your story or stop you going to jail?"

Danny wondered whether to maintain his denial. "I don't think you have any actual witnesses to the murder."

"There is plenty of circumstantial evidence. And it was your shirt."

"I don't see how you can know that."

"There are your fingerprints on the scythe."

"Don't you think that, if I had done it, on a cold winter day I would have worn gloves?"

"Not if you wanted to get caught."

"Why would I do that?"

"Perhaps you wanted to send a message to your mother?"

"My mother?" Danny's voice was filled with contempt.

Sidney had had enough. "Danny we all know you did it. The evidence is there. You have no alibi."

"I was in my room at the time he left us."

"No one saw you. The only thing I don't understand is why you needed to go through the whole business of joining the cult. Pascoe walked freely around Grantchester. He was an easy target."

"And so anyone could have killed him."

"Not anyone. You."

Danny sighed. It was as if he was wearied by his denials at last.

"Tell me, Danny. It will only get worse if you don't."

"I don't know. I suppose I don't care any more."

"It must have been an extraordinarily hard decision to take. You must be exhausted. Don't bear this burden alone."

"I had to learn to hate," Danny began. "I had to despise Pascoe even more than I did already. I had to prepare for so long in order to kill him. I had already had fantasies about punching him in the face or kicking his head in but I wanted to do something so violent that I needed fury and desperation. So I had to see him up close. Let the anger build. If it was to be a crime of passion I was going to show him what that really looked like."

"But you had to disguise all those feelings when you were with him."

"I let them build up inside. I had never felt so alive than when I thought of that man dead."

"And no one else knew?"

"Tom helped. I talked to Tom."

"He knew about your plan?"

"His dad too."

"But surely they warned you that you would be caught?"

"I said I didn't care. They said I needed to be clever about it. Tom's dad knew people. They were going to come up with the perfect murder for me but I couldn't wait. I remembered the old gardener at the church cutting back the long grass and the hedges and I noticed the shed was never locked. I remembered something from school, *As for man, his days are as grass, and grass needs to be cut down, doesn't it? Thrust in thy sickle, and reap, for the time is come for thee to reap; for the harvest of the earth is ripe.*"

"So you stole the scythe and hid it until the time was right?"

"I told Pascoe I wanted to talk about the nature of love; what it really meant. He fell for it. That's a joke. As if he knew about love, real love. He said we should go for a walk. I suggested the river past Byron's Pool. It was a cold day and there was no one about. I waited until we reached the pool. I had brought a rug and a bit of the loving cup in a flask. We sat down and talked about love and how you had to really trust someone to love them completely. I asked more and more questions because I wanted to see how hypocritical the man was. He went on and on and I almost laughed when he talked about the dangers of betrayal. I could only think about my father and what my mother had done to him. I said I needed a pee and walked off to get the scythe. Pascoe got into one of his crazy yoga positions, closed his eyes and started to meditate. I knew that I would have to attack him from behind and that it would have to be a surprise and this was the opportunity. I took off my coat and jumper so I just had my shirt on. I wanted to have my arms free. The first swing was right into the neck. It was hard to get the blade out. I even thought it might be stuck. I had imagined one blow, like an executioner. Then I realised it would need more and more and I was glad. It would take longer. He would feel more pain. I could take time to enjoy that, knowing that there was no one there to stop me."

"Did Pascoe know what was happening?" Sidney asked. "Did he see the 'necessary hatred' on your face?"

"I wasn't expecting so much blood. The man — I won't say his name, I've always hated it — managed to gargle some kind of plea to stop but I just kept on. I had a little chant going. *Thrust in thy sickle and reap.* I was almost singing it. In the end it must have taken fourteen or fifteen blows and his eyes kept on blinking at me even after the head was off. That was quite funny. I thought he was still going to say something. The man looked surprised. He didn't seem to be dead. Yet there it was, a severed head. Still bleeding, still living. I couldn't believe that he could go on like that. It must have been pulsing for ten or fifteen seconds longer and I wondered whether he was still able to think; if he realised that he was dying and knew why and felt horrified. Did he think those things? Perhaps it was just horror. I looked down and it was almost as if I wanted to make the whole thing last longer. I could have started all over again, or cut his body to pieces, but then I hated myself and it was cold and I knew I had to get away and I didn't want to look at that stupid face any more and so I kicked his head as far as I could and ran back to where I'd left my stuff."

"And that was where you hid your shirt and scythe?"

"I shoved them into the undergrowth and put my jumper and coat back on. I looked back to check that I had really done all that, that it wasn't a dream. I wanted to laugh. I had done it, after waiting so long, and no one had been able to stop me. Part of me wanted to take a photograph and post it to my mother. That'll show her, I thought. But I knew that would incriminate me. So I just looked back and saw the body. I couldn't see the head any more. Then I got closer and stood over the body and started swearing at it. Then I found his head and kicked it around until I was bored.

"I went back to my room and lay on the bed and looked at the ceiling. I kept saying the mantra, *As for man, his days are as grass.* Pascoe taught us to keep a phrase in our heads when we meditate and it felt good to have used one to kill him. I turned his teaching back on him. *Thrust in thy sickle. What's the mantra in your head now, you bastard?*"

"And did you tell Tom what you had done?"

"He guessed as soon as the police arrived."

"And afterwards, I think you took an overdose and pretended that it was a murder attempt. You must have taken sedatives from your father's practice. Or perhaps they were your mother's sleeping tablets? I remember when she first came to me she said that she could not sleep."

"None of this was hard."

"Your mother was frightened you might do something like this and brought me in to try and stop it. Unfortunately she didn't spell out her concerns as boldly as she thought. Perhaps she was worried she would sound mad."

"She is mad."

"That may be the case, but she knows you far better than you might like to admit. She had a mother's intuition, and she was right."

"Will I have to see her again?"

"Very likely, I am afraid, and probably in court."

As Sidney left the hospital and crossed Grantchester Meadows, he thought about the power of hatred and the nature of revenge. He wasn't at all sure that violent action had done anything to make Danny Wilkinson feel better, either about his mother or himself. Would there be any redemption at all from this, and what could Sidney have done to prevent it happening? Should he have guessed, on that first visit, that the boy's membership of the Family of Love was just a front?

He had to see Barbara Wilkinson one last time. She had come to him in distress only a few weeks ago and the least he could do now was to tell her that Danny had confessed to the murder of Fraser Pascoe.

"What's he gone and done that for?" she asked. "They must have threatened him. He's protecting Tom Raven. His dad must be behind this. You can't honestly think my son is a killer?"

"He has confessed."

"Under duress."

"He told me. There was no pressure."

"He must be afraid. Let me see him."

"I do not think that will help, Mrs Wilkinson. Perhaps you should have been more honest about your relationship with Fraser Pascoe from the start."

"I would hardly call it a relationship."

"Your son thought it was."

"He didn't know anything about it."

"I'm afraid he did."

"Well, whatever it was it can't have anything to do with what happened. I know my son. Why is he confessing to something he couldn't possibly have done? The fact is that those people tried to kill him. Have they now brainwashed him into thinking he killed Pascoe as well?"

"You should have been clearer with me from the beginning, Mrs Wilkinson."

"You can't point the finger at me. I told you all you needed to know. I tried to stop all this."

"But it wasn't enough."

"What more could I do? I was trying to save my son. What mother could have done more? You can't blame it all on the past."

"For Danny there was no past. He lived with the memory of your actions all the time. I think he still does."

"You think this is some kind of revenge?"

"I'm afraid so."

"For Pascoe?"

"Yes."

"But that had nothing to do with him."

"He is your son."

"You are making a mistake. I'm the only person who tried to help Danny. Now you're implying that it's all my fault?"

"I think the issue of blame can be complicated and it is not always helpful."

"Has Danny really confessed?"

"He has."

"Why?"

70

"Because he killed Pascoe."

"But what about the attempt to murder him?"

"It was an overdose, designed to deflect attention. Danny took your sleeping tablets. They've gone missing, haven't they?"

Barbara Wilkinson did not answer the question directly. "I only came to you because I was frightened all this would happen."

"Had Danny been violent in the past?"

"He has a temper. But he's clever. He made me believe he was serious about the cult."

"It's strange Pascoe didn't guess what was going on. You didn't think of warning him?"

"Fraser thought that everyone loved him. He believed he could turn hate to love. He could never imagine meeting anyone who wasn't pleased to see him."

"Why didn't you tell me exactly what you feared when you first came to see me?"

"I thought you wouldn't believe me."

"Did Danny take your sleeping pills?"

"I suppose so."

"You never told us."

"I didn't want to say anything that might incriminate him. He is still my son. And I won't accept what anyone says. Do you think the police will blame me too?"

"I don't know. Perverting the course of justice is not the best way of going about things."

"You won't put it as strongly as that, surely?"

"That's not my decision. I can only tell the truth about what has happened."

"Without pity or mercy, it seems."

"That has to come after the whole truth . . ."

"And nothing but the truth."

"Remorse follows, then pity, then forgiveness. I think that's the general order of things, Mrs Wilkinson."

"You never called me Barbara."

"You have to start with the truth. Everything flows from that."

Sidney realised he was being harder on her than he had originally meant to be. Perhaps he was making up for all his softness at the start.

By the time he reached the Eagle in order to talk things over with Geordie he had still not made a decision on how much he should say. He should really tell his friend that Mrs Wilkinson had withheld information about the extent of her relationship with Fraser Pascoe, the forged cheque and the sleeping pills. She had also attempted to mislead the police by accusing Tom Raven. Was this enough for a charge of perverting the course of justice? Or should he adopt a more forgiving tone after all that trauma and remember Christ's words to the woman taken in adultery: "Go and sin no more."

In the end, he told Geordie everything. "I thought hell had no fury like a woman scorned," his friend began as he handed Sidney an inadequate tomato juice. "It turns out that children are even worse. It's like a Greek tragedy out there."

"Well, the Greeks did write the first crime stories. They had murders all over the place."

"And they were supposed to be the greatest civilisation known to man. Just shows how little human nature changes."

Sidney picked up his drink. "Barbara Wilkinson and Fraser Pascoe. If they'd known about the results of their affair they'd never have started it."

"I don't know, Sidney. People are reckless. Sometimes these things are unstoppable."

Geordie had that dangerous look in his eye that meant he was not going to hold back on what he was about to say, whatever the consequences. "You got off lightly when you think about it, old boy. Just imagine if it had been you and Babs instead."

"That was never a possibility."

"You are not going to admit that you were attracted to her when all this began?"

"Never." Sidney stood up to order another round. "I love my wife. Restraint has always been my watchword."

"As long as you keep saying that."

"I mean it."

"Do you think you're bored, Sidney?"

"No. Too much to think about."

"Perhaps we still hanker for the drama of war-time?"

"I don't miss the loss of my friends."

"It's funny, though. It seems religion is never quite enough for you."

"We have to keep searching. Sometimes people need distractions and moments of respite. They just have to choose the right ones."

"Drink is safer than flirtation."

"Sometimes one follows the other."

"In both cases you have to know when to stop."

Sidney hesitated. "Have you ever given up alcohol, Geordie?"

"I certainly have."

"When?"

"I can give up for several hours at a time. Now stop getting so anxious about life, faith and women. Buy yourself a pint or a bottle of dog."

"Perhaps I will."

"You've earned it, man. No one's looking."

"I feel a bit bad about it."

"If that's the only temptation you're submitting to then you're doing well. Have a chaser while you're at it."

"No, I think that's too much."

"Howay, man, I'll pay."

Geordie barged his way past Sidney to the bar and bought beer and whisky for both of them. After they had settled back down in their seats and got out the customary game of backgammon, he mentioned that he thought he had seen Hildegard talking to Barbara Wilkinson in town. "But that can't be right. Your wife wouldn't bother passing the time of day with a lass like that. Just as well you kept your distance."

"I've told you, Geordie, there was never any danger of impropriety. I do have some standards. And I love Hildegard."

"You had a bit of luck in finding a wife like that. But I suppose you deserve it. You took a risk on a foreigner with a murky past and it paid off."

"Hers wasn't the past that was murky."

"As far as you know."

"I do know. And, by the way, while we're on the subject, I'd like to take some of the credit for my marriage."

"No one's going to believe you, Sidney. Hildegard saved you. You may think it's the other way round and even let people come to that conclusion . . ."

"I'm just very grateful to be so blessed."

"I'm glad you realise. If I behaved like you do Cathy would give me hell."

"What do you mean 'like you do'?"

"Being all sympathetic to the ladies."

"That's my job."

"No, it's not. It's what you like. That's different. You can't fool me."

"Hildegard knows all this. I tell her everything that's been going on."

"Like hell. Does she do the same?"

"Not always. I think she likes to retain a bit of mystery."

"Most women do. Canny, aren't they?"

"Would we have it any other way?"

"We would not," Geordie replied, before downing his pint and contemplating his next move on the board.

"I am glad we agree then."

"You know what they say about marriage? A man can either be right or happy. At least neither of us would be foolish enough to carry on, like Barbara Wilkinson, with someone else in our own home and be discovered by one of our children."

"No, we certainly wouldn't," said Sidney, as seriously as he could before catching his friend's eye. "We'd book a hotel room."

Both men laughed. It was the first time they had done so in ages.

Grantchester Meadows

The University of Cambridge was celebrating May Week and, as with many superior organisations that never feel the need to explain themselves, the celebrations lasted longer than a week and took place in June.

The students had completed their exams, the punts were out on the river, picnic rugs fluttered down on to daisy-decorated grass, Pimm's was poured, strawberries were served and the barefoot dancing began.

Sidney had just finished a meeting in King's Parade for a diocesan ministry commission that had been asked to set up a new payment scheme for clergy. The plan was to abolish the current system of private patronage, introduce compulsory retirement at the age of seventy and establish a level of remuneration that neither excited financial ambition nor resulted in economic embarrassment.

It had been a long, dull affair and Sidney was discombobulated by the contrasting elitism of May Week with its collision of youthful exuberance, alcohol and high expenditure. He was due to head on into Grantchester to visit his former curate, Malcolm Mitchell, but decided to cheer himself up by popping in to see Geordie at the St Andrew's Street police station. This certainly livened up his day, as his friend immediately reported that one student had narrowly escaped being trampled to death by a herd of cows while another had had a family heirloom stolen.

The crime scene was a party on Grantchester Meadows, organised by a Magdalene College drinking club in memory of their founder, Sir Joshua Wylie. Twelve executors had dressed up in tails to serve vodka and grapefruit juice out of watering cans at the end of the May "Bumps" on the river. Within hours the ground had resembled a medieval battlefield, with drunken students sprawled across the Meadows in varying stages of consciousness and undress. At one point in the proceedings Richard Lane had ended up in the middle of a herd of cows that had banded together to fight a rearguard action against the excess. By the time the ambulance arrived, the student was half-dead, having caught his ankle and fallen into a cattle grid while trying to escape.

"He made it that far?" Sidney asked.

"Accounts are hazy. Students may be able to study the origins of the Agricultural Revolution but most of them are incapable of walking across a field. In the meantime, another of their number, one Olivia Randall, 'lost' her mother's necklace."

"Valuable?"

"It's worth about a thousand pounds, she says."

"And no one has so far suggested that the stampede of cows was a deliberate distraction to facilitate the disappearance of the jewellery?"

"No one, Sidney. Not even you. Yet."

"Olivia Randall, you say?"

"Helena's sister. She's eleven years younger; an afterthought, apparently. Although you would have thought her parents would have had misgivings after they saw how their first child turned out."

"Is Olivia anything like our friend, the great investigative journalist?"

"On the contrary, she seems a bit of a hippy."

"And could she simply have mislaid her necklace?"

"Yes she could; not that she's going to admit to it. The whole situation has got out of hand. The parents of the injured boy want to sue the farmer, whom we both know is trouble from past encounters, and the Randall sisters are terrified their mother will find out about the necklace and are making all manner of fuss."

"When the thing might not have been stolen at all."

"They want us to get it back. They seem to think it's far more important than a half-dead student with a broken leg, smashed ribs and a fractured collarbone."

"But in both of these cases it may be the victim's fault; a mixture of drunken cow-provocation and careless necklace-wearing?"

"Yes: which is why it's so annoying we've been called in to sort things out."

"Do you have to?"

"There could be a case of negligence against the farmer. That'll go down well. He will retaliate with claiming wilful damage by the students. And if the necklace has gone . . . well, theft is theft."

"I presume it was insured?"

"Belongs to Mummy. She lent it to her daughter for May Week. Made quite a fuss about her not losing it, probably because I am not so sure the insurance covers them if a loopy daughter with a skinful of Pimm's dances half-naked across the Meadows."

"Half-naked?"

"You know what I mean. Anyway, apparently we have to get the necklace back before Mummy finds out it's missing."

"This is, presumably, Helena's instruction."

"I am afraid so."

"Do you need my help at all?"

"I certainly do; both with the cow incident and the question of negligence. You have a history with the Redmonds."

Sidney knew the farmer all too well. Harding Redmond's wife Agatha was a formidable Labrador breeder who had provided Sidney with both Dickens and Byron. His daughter Abigail was a great beauty who had attended the same antenatal class as Hildegard.

However, Harding Redmond's brother and sister were both in prison for poisoning a young Indian boy at a cricket match, and the farmer's terrible temper had not endeared him to the police in the subsequent investigation.

"I wouldn't mind if you paid the old bastard a visit," Geordie continued. "He's funny with the police, as you know."

"He has form. As do you . . ."

"I'll ignore that. He won't take kindly to anyone suggesting that his animals might be to blame. Then there is the small matter of the Randall family. You are probably on better terms with Helena than I am these days, especially since you're taking her wedding. I am sure that she and her sister will let you know more than they'll tell me. And you've got Malcolm, the fiancé, on your side too."

"I'll do what I can."

"We'll interview all the students who were at the party, but some of your more discreet enquiries wouldn't go amiss."

"Not that they're very discreet these days."

"It might be easier now people are used to them. They accept you. You've interviewed many of them before."

"Which means they will be more prepared."

"I'm sure you can lull them into a false sense of security."

The Cambridge quads were full of large marquees and bands unloading their equipment. This particular year the May Ball committees had secured the services of The Who, The Moody Blues and the New Vaudeville Band, who were soundchecking a jaunty number called "Winchester Cathedral". Sidney wondered why on earth it was called that, and he was just thinking about the need to concentrate on his regular duties, and find a new vicar for All Saints in Newmarket, when he saw Harding Redmond on the edge of Spring Lane Meadow. The farmer was getting out of his Land Rover to look in on his herd after the drama of the near-stampede. There were about seventy cows in all, a mixture of breeders, heifers, yearlings and four or five calves, dark red in colour with white touches on the tail-switch and udder.

Redmond was an imposingly broad-framed outdoor-hued man in his mid-fifties who preferred animals to people. In his youth he had opened the bowling for the village cricket team but age had lessened his physical presence, boiling it down to a simmering aggression.

On being asked to recall the events of the previous week he said he hated the students thinking they owned the place, interfering with innocent cows and then blaming him. He'd already had the police round, explained what had happened, and didn't fancy going over it all again. The students had been mucking about by the river in an area known as Little Fen. The herd was in Trench Meadow and the victim had got between a cow and her calf. The animals thought they were under threat and so rushed towards one of the partygoers. The boy could only make his escape uphill and that slowed him down. He fell and the cows surrounded him. It had been a job to get them all off.

"When did you arrive on the scene?"

"After the ambulance. My daughter sorted it all out. Saved the boy's life."

"I'm sure he'll be grateful."

"We won't be expecting thanks."

"And that must have been Abigail? How's she keeping?"

"Baby John isn't so much a baby any more." The memory brought the farmer's guard down. Sidney had been instrumental in persuading a grieving woman to return the child she had snatched from hospital in the Christmas of 1963. "We'll always be grateful to you, Mr Chambers, for getting him back."

"I didn't do very much."

"We all know you did. But you're getting yourself involved in this now? I hope you're not going to cause trouble."

"It's not so much about the cows. There was a crime committed at the same time."

"Apart from the one against my animals?"

"I'm afraid so. But please tell me: what did Abigail do?"

"She reunited the calf with the mother. It was a third-calver and she knew our Abi straight away. As soon she'd got them back together it was all over. They're not normally so aggressive, not like the continental breeds — the Limousin or Charolais. Polled cattle are born with no horns. They're a cross between the Norfolk cow that was bred for beef, and a Suffolk, which is used for dairy. So they're dual-purpose . . ."

"Two for the price of one."

"Not that they're cheap. But they're docile and friendly in the main. If that boy had got under some horns he'd have a punctured lung, so he's lucky they were our polls. They're the best cows you can get, in my opinion. The meat's like fine wine, the beef of old England. The Queen keeps a herd at Sandringham. Not that she has to put up with students messing about."

"I'm sure they won't be doing that again."

"A new generation comes every autumn. They never know better. They don't understand that the land needs to be worked. It's not a private park where they can swan past peasants doffing their caps. Those days are gone."

"Indeed they are, Harding. But the Meadows are common to us all."

"King's College own the land. They should control it better."

"I'm not sure how you can police the whole countryside."

"None of those students know what it's like to work for a living."

"They'll find out soon enough."

"As long as they don't start thinking I'm responsible. The police said I should have put up warning signs and fenced it off better. One of them told me I ought to have known that particular cow was a liability. But what about dangerous students, that's what I want to know? If they think they can sue then they've got another think coming. I'll give as good as I get, I can tell you that, Mr Chambers."

"If there is any problem with the university I am sure I can help."

"That would be good of you, I must say."

Sidney remembered that Harding Redmond never knew how to end a conversation. He called Byron back.

"Mind the herd with your dog, Mr Chambers. The cows will get funny if he comes too close."

"Don't worry. I'll make sure he gives them a wide berth."

"You should come round and visit our Abi some time. She'd love to see you. So would the wife. Is your Lab holding up all right? Dickens, isn't he?"

"That was the last one. This is Byron."

"Looks like he knows his own mind."

"Byron has a relaxed attitude to discipline but is easily bribed by food. If he senses the possibility of nourishment he is immediately obedient."

"You'll let us know if you want another? Agatha's got some puppies on the go. You may have moved up to Ely but there's always a welcome for you down here."

This was about as good a farewell as Sidney was going to get. Harding Redmond climbed back into his Land Rover. It was a new series IIA, he said, and he had paid nearly £2,000 pounds for it.

"That's about twenty-five cows or a grant for five or six students. Funny thing money, don't you think?"

"It is indeed," said Sidney, realising that the amount was twice the price of Olivia Randall's necklace and almost £700 more than his annual salary.

Sidney loved the Meadows around midsummer: the comfrey, lady's-smock, water figwort and arrowhead along the river; the commas, brimstones and meadow brown butterflies in the hedgerows with swifts and house martins overhead. The blossom on the hawthorn was starting to turn but the elderflower and honeysuckle were out, young jackdaws skirred in the sky and swallows hawked midges over the water. He wished he could stop and laze away the rest of the afternoon, but those student days were long gone.

At least he could watch a few overs of village cricket on Audley's Field. He could perhaps enjoy the end of the game in Malcolm's company and share a pint or two in the Blue Ball afterwards.

Grantchester was playing Hemingford Grey, a rival village that was coasting towards a five-wicket victory requiring only twenty-eight runs to win. Because he had a strong throw, Malcolm was fielding at long leg, close to the boundary, and Sidney walked round so that he could talk to him between overs. Reclining in a deckchair nearby was a retired Welsh undertaker, who reminisced about fielding in the long grass in the 1920s and jumping out of it to catch a batsman who thought he'd hit a six.

"I was like a whale rising out of the sea. And I took the ball that was Jonah."

"Presumably," Sidney could not help but ask, "you didn't swallow it?"

After just missing a difficult high chance, Malcolm said that he needed to concentrate, but the game was finished in the next twenty minutes and the two former colleagues were soon ensconced in post-match conviviality, during which various cricketing metaphors were extended towards the curate's forthcoming nuptials; how he'd at last bowled a maiden over, that Helena Randall was quite a catch and that he'd need his third man once the covers came off.

Malcolm was, it has to be said, uncomfortable with the joshing and confessed to Sidney that he was worried about his ability to fulfil Helena's expectations. He was sure that she was more experienced than he was and he also wanted to ask about her relationship with Inspector Keating. Had there been any funny business? They were always so odd when they were together and the inspector had been hostile towards him from the start.

"I shouldn't worry about Geordie. He's always trying to bat above his average. It was a flirtation, nothing more. I think Helena just used her feminine wiles to extract information for the newspaper."

"It's the feminine wiles I'm worried about. I'm not entirely sure what I'm in for. What's marriage like? Is there anything I should know?"

"This is not something that's easy to talk about, Malcolm, especially here. All I can say is that if your love is tender and considerate and sometimes forgiving then you won't go far wrong. It's a matter of mutual compassion. Do you think you understand Helena?"

"She's a complex creature."

"She's about to be your wife. You should know her pretty well by now."

"But do you *understand* Hildegard, Sidney? How much should a man know the woman he is going to marry and how much should be left to discover? Sometimes I think it's like half-opening a present, guessing what it's going to be and finding that it's something entirely different."

"Then I look forward to being unwrapped."

Helena had arrived in the pub, approached Malcolm from behind and put her arms around his neck. She was wearing a white smock with Jackie O sunglasses perched on her head. Neither of the men had seen her but there was a raucous jeer from the cricketers to her left.

After buying the couple drinks and talking about the arrangements for the wedding rehearsal, Sidney dared to switch the subject and ask about her sister.

"You've heard already?"

"Geordie told me."

"We have to stop my mother finding out about the necklace . . ."

"She's that formidable?"

"Will you talk to Olivia, Sidney?"

"If you think it will help."

"Fortunately her boyfriend is in Corpus. That gives you an excuse."

"Now I am no longer the Vicar of Grantchester I do not have so much access to the college."

"I am sure you can find a reason."

"What do you have so far?"

"Olivia's twenty-one and she's what you might call a free spirit. She's always threatening to drop out and go and live in some godforsaken ashram, so I think Mummy and Daddy just kept bribing her to finish her degree. They paid for a party, to which they weren't even invited, and Mummy lent her the necklace for the May Balls."

"She's going to more than one?"

"She could go to them all. She's very in demand, my sister, as you'll see. She combines beauty with availability. If her degree was in flirting, she'd get a first."

"But it's not."

"No, it's in English. I think that's almost as easy. You end up studying books that most educated people are supposed to read anyway. But that's by the by. Mummy told Olivia that she was only supposed to wear the necklace to the May Balls but my sister couldn't resist showing it off at some ludicrous drinks party where they all got completely smashed. Now she can't remember a thing. Sometimes she says the drinks must have been spiked. At others she blames one of her many boyfriends. The one thing she isn't prepared to do, it seems, is to accept any responsibility herself."

"She's not upset?"

"She's attempting a casual bravado. At least the whole disaster has happened after finals. She's got no excuse if she's messed them up."

"I suppose I should applaud your sense of priority."

"Don't be pompous, Sidney. I'm annoyed with her more than anything else. Olivia could have been killed. Instead, she's lost one of Mummy's most valuable pieces of jewellery. I could kill her myself, I'm so annoyed."

"You're keeping it out of the papers?"

"The jewellery but not the cows. My colleagues are on to all that. You can imagine the fun they're having. Anyone would think that they had invented the art of alliteration. *Meadows May Week Mayhem. Cow Carnage. Terror Trampling.*"

"Have they interviewed your sister yet?"

"I've told them they can't. A friend of hers has piped up instead. She was near enough to the drama at the time and used to go out with the victim. That should be enough. They love a girlfriend angle and her picture will help the story. I'm sure Emily can look appropriately distraught. One of the boys has already told me she's 'an absolute corker'. That was helpful, I must say."

"She's a friend?"

"Of Olivia's, but she won't mention her. We want the cow story and Emily and Richard to take all the attention. Daddy's certain to read about it and we just need to make sure that he doesn't feel duty-bound to tell my mother. If she finds out, she'll either phone Newnham to ask what the hell's going on, which will be easy enough because she's an old girl, or she'll take the next train up, check that Olivia's all right, and then ask where the bloody necklace is."

"What's it like?"

"It's a single large sapphire, but very rare: cornflower blue from Ceylon. It was fashioned into a pear shape and then set within what they call a 'sparkling halo' of small mine-cut diamonds."

"A 'sparkling halo'?"

"Don't go all ecclesiastical, Sidney. It's Victorian. It's been in the family for almost a hundred years."

"Why didn't you have it? You're the eldest."

"Mummy said I didn't have the right colouring. Olivia's the one with the bright-blue eyes. Besides, it was only a loan."

"I don't suppose . . ."

"She could have pretended to lose it in order to hang on to it? I don't think you know my mother."

"And you didn't mind the favouritism?"

"They gave me a coral teardrop for my twenty-first. It was supposed to set off my hair. I hated it because, as you may remember from when we first met, I am prone to spots. It looked like a skin complaint. I couldn't exchange it fast enough."

Malcolm interrupted to get out a gallant "you have perfect skin, my darling" but Helena was having none of it. "Happiness certainly improves it; but this whole business with my sister is still going to bring me out in a rash."

Sidney resumed his inquisition. "And do you know what Olivia was doing before she discovered that she had lost the necklace?"

"I am afraid so."

"Would you like to tell me?"

"I think she was having a bit of fun."

Malcolm elucidated. "Doing what students do in May Week."

"With a boyfriend?"

"Alexander," said Helena. "The one that wasn't trampled."

"You mean that the victim of the stampede was also her boyfriend?"

"I think she had a bit of history with him too. You know what it's like these days. One man is never enough for some people. Good vibrations and all that!"

"And so could the necklace have been pulled off in a moment of passion? It may have fallen where they lay."

"I've already asked. They say they went back to the spot to look for it. It was far enough from the cows not to have been trampled by them. They were down by the river. In a dingly dell. Olivia called it their very own hobbit-hole. I've always hated Tolkien. But, anyway, they went back and necklace was there none."

"And you don't suppose her boyfriend could have pocketed it in the ensuing chaos?"

"I suppose he could have done. You'll have to ask him. I've told Olivia that you'll sort it out if Geordie can't."

"I'm not sure about that."

"I've given you a very good write-up. And you know Mummy is a good friend of Henry Richmond?"

"I thought you were trying to keep your mother out of this?"

"I am but if she *does* get to hear of it, and you were unable to help us, then you wouldn't want Amanda finding out that you are mortal after all, would you?"

"Amanda is well aware of my failings, as am I."

"Don't let us down, Sidney. We're relying on you."

"But if it wasn't the boyfriend then it could have been anyone. And the Meadows are vast."

"Who knows them better than you? You could take Byron. Didn't he find some kind of axe last time he was here?"

"He did."

"There you are then."

"Lightning seldom strikes twice in the same place, Helena."

"It does where you're concerned, Sidney. You're our very own conductor, attracting heat wherever you stand."

"I'm not sure I like that idea."

"Yes you do. You positively crackle with electricity."

"I rather think you and Malcolm are the ones with the electricity," said Sidney.

"Not if her mother's got anything to do with it," his former curate replied.

It seemed appropriate to their conversation that the next time Sidney found himself in Grantchester he was caught in a storm and forced to take shelter by the willow trees in Long Meadow. It arrived more quickly than anticipated, the Cambridge-blue sky overrun by dark clouds and then merging to form a whitish grey, before the rain fell and sounded like an orchestra tuning up; the smither turning into a gulching hail in under a minute, a burst of Beethoven before a slow diminuendo into a shatter that lasted far longer than Sidney thought it would; almost an hour.

Sheltering close by was a tall young man with long hair, dressed in a lacy shirt and velvet and brocade flares that had been bought from the fashionable London store Granny Takes a Trip. He was carrying a small microphone attached to a Grundig tape recorder. After he had hit the stop button he nodded; indicating that he was ready for conversation.

"I wasn't expecting the rain," he said. "But I like the sound. I've been here for days."

"Making recordings?"

"I want to use nature musically; to see what silence is really like."

"I imagine there's no such thing."

"Even when everything stops there's still the sound of the water, the drone of hoverflies, a lark or a distant dog barking. I'm Roger."

He held out a hand. Sidney took it and introduced himself, explaining that he used to be the Vicar of Grantchester.

"You haven't stopped, though? You're still a clergyman. You haven't been defrocked or anything like that?"

"Not so far. I came back to see one of my parishioners. The farmer with the cows."

"The ones that attacked the students?"

"Were you here at the time?"

"I was the other side of the river," said Roger. "One of the girls came to talk to me. She wanted to know if I was spying on them."

"How did she get across?"

"She stopped a punt. I was a bit scared of her at first. But she was all right when I told her I was in a band. That's why I was doing the recording. It got much better after that. I even started to like her. She said she preferred jazz. I quite admired that. It's not the kind of thing many people admit to. I told her she should have been born fifty years ago."

"What was the girl wearing?" Sidney asked.

"That's kind of weird too. She was dressed as if it was the 1920s."

"Any jewellery?"

"A silver band, I think. And something in her hair."

"Nothing blue?"

94

"No, she wore green. She looked like she belonged in the trees. I told her that. Some people have an aura to them. Hers was clover green. She laughed when I said so. She had a nice smile. I've been thinking about laughter quite a lot; how we each have our own. You can be recognised or given away by enjoying yourself. It's strange, don't you think?"

"Do you say this because the students were laughing?"

"I suppose so. They were mucking about with the cows. I'm not surprised the animals got fed up."

"Did you see what happened?" Sidney asked.

"It was quite far away. The green girl had gone by then. She said she'd had enough of them. I didn't think I'd ever see her again, but I think she came back later, on the other side of the river. Perhaps she'd forgotten something. I don't know."

"You didn't help when you saw the cows?"

"I was over here and there was the water between us. Besides, there were loads of them. And it looked dangerous enough without me adding to the situation. The cows wanted to kill the student that got into trouble. It was a job to get him out. I don't think any of them were medical students. They were probably too pissed anyway. But then this woman with a dog came along. She knew what she was doing. I think she must be something to do with the farm . . ."

"So you definitely saw the attack? The student couldn't have been injured by anything other than the cows?"

"You mean he might have been attacked first, left lying on the ground and then the cows did the rest? I don't think so. You've got a strange mind for a vicar."

"It's not my only job, I'm afraid."

"I didn't realise times were that hard. But it must be difficult when your faith's going out of fashion."

"It's not that," Sidney replied quickly. "I can explain. But, in the meantime, you didn't by any chance see another couple, by the river's edge?"

"I didn't look too closely but there was plenty of what my friend Emo calls ummagumma going on."

"I'm sorry?"

"Sex. I think that's why the girl came over. She must have thought I was some kind of pervert watching them. I'm not, by the way."

"I'm sure you're not."

"So I didn't see much. And I didn't record any of the kerfuffle. It was people shouting and I didn't want that. As I said, I like natural sound, stuff we don't always notice that just carries on no matter what's happening."

"The flow of the world."

"That kind of thing."

The rain had eased off, but an after-drop fell on Roger's forehead and he wiped it away. "It's hard to see the river unseen beneath the trees, don't you think?" he asked. "But when you do, it's like laughter. Perhaps it's laughing at us?"

After this somewhat disorientating encounter, Sidney tried to call in on Alexander Farley in his rooms at Corpus. A neighbour on the staircase said that he had gone to London with Olivia Randall and wouldn't be back for a couple of days. This was odd in May Week, with the summer holidays so close, and it turned out to be misinformation. In fact the couple had gone to Ely, having been dispatched by an impatient Helena and were waiting for Sidney on his return. A bemused Hildegard had told them to have a look round the cathedral, visit Cromwell's house and come back for lemonade and biscuits once she had finished her piano teaching.

Olivia was a tall young woman, bigger-boned than her sister, and appeared to have a slight stoop from trying to make herself look smaller. She was wearing a sleeveless mini tent dress in fused stripes of shocking-pink and orange; while Alexander had a floppy-collared floral shirt and white cotton flares.

Olivia told Sidney that she thought the farmer must have taken the necklace during the clear-up. "He was so annoyed about the cows perhaps he assumed it was his reward."

"I'm not sure Harding Redmond's the kind of man who would do that sort of thing."

"Why not?" Alexander asked. "He could have given it to his daughter."

"I suppose that's possible, but I imagine both of them had more important concerns. I'm sure they would have seen to the victim and then worried about their cows. They wouldn't have had time to consider the necklace unless it was right in front of them. Did it take long for the ambulance to come?"

"About twenty minutes," Olivia replied. "It was horrible. We thought Richard was going to die. The cows were determined to kill him. They kept pushing each other as if they all wanted a try at stamping on him and they were butting him with their enormous heads. Alex ran to the phone box, but one of the villagers stopped him and said that she had already called for help."

"It was like a rugby scrum," said Alexander, "and Richard was the ball. The cows kept turning him over and over. The farmer's daughter saved him. She swore about how irresponsible we were and how lucky we were that more of us weren't killed and that we had no right to be on the Meadows."

"She's wrong about that," said Sidney.

"I never know why some of the people who live here hate students so much."

Olivia was looking for something in her net bag. "It's so unfair. It was only a party."

"Not for the farmer or his daughter," Sidney pointed out. "How long did everyone stay?"

"Once Richard was taken to the ambulance everyone left. It was definitely over after that. We couldn't really go on."

"And who went to the hospital to see Richard?"

Olivia started on a roll-up. "I think Emily might have gone."

"Emily?"

"She's in love with him."

"I see. And is Richard in love with her?"

98

There was a silence as the roll-up was completed and shared between the two students. "No," said Alexander. "He's in love with Olivia."

"I see."

"Most people are."

"That's not true," Olivia replied while sounding as if she hoped it was.

Sidney tried to stick to the matter in hand. "When did you notice your necklace was missing?"

"She didn't," Alexander answered. "I did."

"And when was that?"

"When we went back to get our stuff. We were going to pick up our things that we'd left by the river and then go on to the hospital, but we realised the necklace had disappeared and we had to find it. We looked around, retraced our steps. It could have fallen off, but if it had, we would have found it. Someone must have taken it when we were dozing."

Sidney wanted to see what Olivia had to say. "Are you sure you had the necklace on when you fell asleep?"

Alexander spoke for her. "Oh, definitely. I remember."

"You do?"

"It was between her breasts."

"So when you woke it was gone?"

Olivia tried to explain that she couldn't recall what had happened at the crucial moment. "Everyone was screaming because of the cows. I put on my blouse, I can remember doing that, but I must have left my bra behind. I'm not really sure. It was all a bit mad, to be honest."

"So you think your necklace was gone when you woke up?"

"It had to be."

"Before all the drama with the cows?"

"Yes."

"And so you think it was stolen as you both slept? Was there any redness on your neck?"

"From it being yanked off? I don't think so."

"So," Sidney continued, "if it was taken when you were asleep then it must have been someone who knew how the clasp worked."

"That means it was probably a woman."

"And could that have been your friend Emily?"

"She was the other side of the river. And she had already gone off once she realised that we wanted to be alone."

"And do you know where she went?"

"Further downriver. There was a man there, making recordings. She wanted to see what he was doing. She thought he looked a bit spooky."

"And is Emily a close friend?"

"Yes. But I don't think she'd take my necklace if that is what you are suggesting."

"Then who would?"

"I don't know. That's why we think it must have been the farmer or his daughter."

Sidney had had enough of this. "I think I know Harding Redmond well enough to be sure that he wouldn't approach a sleeping student and take a necklace from her naked breasts."

"His daughter might," said Alexander.

"I understand she was nowhere near the Meadows and only arrived in time to help with the rescue."

"But no one knows what happened afterwards."

"As I have already said, I imagine Abigail had enough to do setting the cows right."

Olivia had another suggestion. "Perhaps the man doing the recordings stole it?"

"I thought you said he was the other side of the river?"

"He could have swum across."

"Why would he do that?" Sidney asked.

"Because he saw the necklace lying on the ground?"

"Even though you were sure it was taken from your neck?"

"I can't be positive."

"In any case, it was too far away for him to see anything lying in the undergrowth across the river."

"Unless he had binoculars."

"I think you're clutching at straws," said Sidney.

He was becoming increasingly irritable. Could these people not remember anything? How had they ever been able to pass an exam?

"I don't know how criminals do these things," Olivia replied.

Sidney said that he would talk to Harding and Abigail Redmond once more. It was also important he spoke to Emily Hastings.

"She's at Newnham. It's a girls' college."

"I know that," said Sidney. "The principal is a friend of mine."

"Emily's quite an eccentric," said Alexander. "She makes her own clothes; dresses as a 1920s flapper. I think her father might even be a vicar."

Things were looking up. "Then I'm sure she'll tell me the truth," said Sidney. "If she can remember it."

Before visiting Newnham, Sidney decided to go to Addenbrooke's Hospital in order to find out how Richard Lane was recovering from the stampede. Perhaps he might be able to provide a clearer account of what had happened on the Meadows.

On arrival, the hospital chaplain told him the boy's parents had just left and that it had been a job to pacify them. "I'm afraid they want compensation."

"I suppose you can't really blame them. How is the patient?"

"He'll live. It was a stupid thing to do; not that he's taking any responsibility. Students hardly ever do. Lane comes from a family that can't ever accept that anything might be their fault. There always has to be someone to blame. It's something of a Cambridge disease, I find."

"Perhaps it's one we should try to cure."

"They're only just allowing visitors. The boy's been drifting in and out of consciousness. I'm not sure if he can cope with two clergymen. He'll think he's still delirious."

"It'll be a novelty for him," Sidney replied. "Perhaps he can find a way to blame us for something."

"Unhappiness at school. Sunday boredom. Unrealistic expectations . . ."

"Omnipotence and the problem of evil; a loving God who allows accidents to afflict the innocent . . ."

"We'll be ready."

Richard Lane was propped up in bed. The covers were damp because he was on so much morphine that he kept blacking out between picking up a beaker of water and trying to drink it. A nurse patted down the sheets and told Sidney he could have five minutes.

Once the explanations had been made, Richard told them what he could remember.

"Once I realised what was happening it was too late. The cows were charging at me and I had no time to get away. I felt this thump against the side of my back when the first one hit me. I stumbled and thought I could stagger on but then I was hit again from the opposite side and fell over. They began to head-butt me. They were right on top, blocking the light from the sky. I cried out for help but I knew it was hopeless. There were so many animals. I tried to protect my head and rolled up into a ball but they kept butting me and trying to kneel down on me, wanting to get me to uncurl. In the end, I thought that if I gave up the struggle and pretended I was already dead they would stop. But I didn't have time to do that because there was then this enormous weight on my back and shoulder. One of them must have knelt right on top of me. It was trying to crush me to death. I must have passed out. That's all I remember, apart from thinking that it was the most humiliating way to die."

"It's a wonder you survived."

"The nurses said there was so much blood that it had all clogged up and they had to cut my clothes away. It was a cream linen suit. I've got a broken leg, collarbone and cracked ribs. I don't know how the cows missed my head. They say it'll take months to get better. I was planning on going to India."

Sidney asked if anyone else had been near the cows at the time.

"Everyone was lying down on the grass, playing some kind of weird game of listening to grasshoppers. We even started imitating them at one point, I seem to remember. But we were really just drinking away and having a good laugh. I was looking for my friend Emily. Olivia and Alexander had just wandered off to find a secluded spot."

"I don't know if you've heard about Olivia's necklace?" Sidney asked.

"No one's told me anything. But then I've been so out of it."

"Has no one been to see you?"

"They haven't allowed anyone in except my parents."

"I am sure your friends will come."

"It's the end of term. You know what it's like."

"What about Emily Hastings? Alexander Farley? Olivia Randall?"

"I suppose so. But it's been a bit complicated . . ."

"Do you mean, Olivia?"

"Well, yes. She's lovely. But she's a bit of a lunatic."

"Do you think so?"

"She makes things up."

"You've not been sweet on her yourself?"

"She thinks everyone's in love with her or, if they're not, they should be. It's a pain. I'm keener on Emily, to be honest, but she's out of my league and I'm hardly in a fit state to do anything about it now. Missed the boat on that one."

"I don't know," said Sidney. "Life is long."

"Nearly wasn't, though, was it? Bloody cows. And why me? Do you think they singled me out? I wasn't doing anything wrong. I was just trying to cross a field."

"I don't think anyone tried to set them against you. That would be a hard thing to do, I imagine. I assume it was simply a case of bad luck."

"You're not wrong."

"I am sorry," Sidney continued, "but could I just ask one thing before I go? The main party was in Little Fen. The cows were in Trench Meadow which is on the way back towards Cambridge. Were you actually leaving the party when this happened?"

"I thought I heard Emily calling, some more friends arriving, but I was mistaken. I was hot and confused and the drink was stronger than we all thought. God knows what was in it."

"I understand. I must let you rest."

"What were you saying about a necklace?" the boy asked.

"It doesn't matter," Sidney replied. "It can wait."

As he left the hospital he wondered if Richard could have been responsible for the theft after all. Could the cows have set upon him *after* he had stolen the necklace and while he was making his escape; taking some kind of short cut that had gone disastrously wrong?

Because Sidney was due to dine at High Table that evening he decided to pay the Master of Corpus a quick visit. It was a while since they had spoken and he thought he could use the opportunity to find out if Richard Lane's parents were well off, if their decision to sue Harding Redmond was unalterable and whether their son might be in need of money.

The master was concerned about the boy's health and stated how predictable it was that there always seemed to be some kind of post-exam disaster when the students were winding down at the end of their university career. It was similar to coming down off a mountain: the descent was always more perilous than the ascent.

Sidney discovered that, like Alexander Farley, Richard Lane had been reading law (his father was a QC) and he didn't appear to have any financial worries. He had been a diligent pupil, spoken at the Union, written the odd article for *Varsity* and had caused little trouble during his time at Cambridge.

"I'm sorry he's sustained such an attack," the master said, "but they tell me he's likely to make a full recovery. He'll be able to continue his training in the autumn. I gather there was a related incident?"

"I am not sure about 'related'."

"Inspector Keating let slip that it wasn't just the business of the cows that interested him. A priceless jewel, I hear?"

"I don't think it's priceless."

"The girl's mother told me that it was a family heirloom which could never be replaced."

Sidney tried not to be surprised. "Mrs Randall knows about the theft?"

"Hermione is a friend of mine. I thought it was only right to tell her. We were in an amateur production of *A Midsummer Night's Dream* in Vienna before the war. It's where she met her husband. We were ex-pats together. Geoffrey's a great Shakespearean; named his daughters after famous heroines. Helena and Olivia. I've got a daughter called Rosalind, although everyone calls her Lindy. It's good to keep Shakespeare in the bloodline, don't you think?"

As ever, Sidney was keen to stick to the point. "The girls were hoping that they would find the necklace before their mother discovered it was missing. Then she would never have needed to know."

"Well it's too late for subterfuge. Hermione is not one to waste any time. I think she'll be here the day after tomorrow.

"That won't go down well with her daughters."

"It's not the daughters we need to worry about. Their mother is a very formidable woman."

Sidney was unsure how far his responsibilities extended. If Keating was already on to the theft and Hermione Randall was about to turn up, he didn't see what more he could do to help proceedings. However, he did take up Harding Redmond's offer to talk to his daughter Abigail. He had always admired the girl's free-spirited, untutored perceptiveness and what had eventually become a firm moral stance.

He began by congratulating her on saving the situation and preventing a death.

"It was a close shave, Mr Chambers, I'll tell you that. I've never seen anything like it."

"Did you ever fear the animals might turn on you?"

"Not really. I know those cows. We've all grown up together, you might say."

Sidney suppressed a smile at the young woman's carefree comparison of herself to a group of heifers. "I was just wondering: if someone knew them well, might they be able to predict or even direct their behaviour?"

"What do you mean?"

"If two students were playing around, for example, causing mischief, might it be possible for one of them to set the cows on the other?"

"It would be a risky thing to do. They could just as easily turn on you."

"Unless," Sidney suggested, "the person managed to organise the attack from behind."

"But why would anyone want to do that?"

"To create a distraction."

"In order to commit some other crime, you mean? It doesn't seem possible, Mr Chambers. Unless someone was behind the victim, with fodder, and the cows thought they were going to be fed. That might work, but not in the summer, when there's plenty of grazing. Those cows were all full up and enjoying the sunshine until the students started messing about."

Redmond joined them by the stables and, overhearing this, realised what Sidney was up to. "The other day, when you first came round, you mentioned another crime, one that happened while all this was going on. Are you going to tell us what it is?"

Sidney came clean about the theft of the necklace, described what it looked like and asked if Abigail either remembered Olivia wearing it or if she had seen it anywhere on the Meadows in the aftermath of the accident.

"I can't say I looked too closely. I was more concerned with saving the boy. Then we had to set the cows right, get them all back together as a herd, check none of them were injured."

"I just wondered if a necklace had come off in the mêlée," Sidney continued, "or even if the boy was carrying it in his pockets."

"Are you suggesting that he might have stolen it before the cows got to him?"

"I'm trying not to rule anything out."

"Got his comeuppance if he did," said Abigail. "But if it was on his person then wouldn't they have found it in the hospital?"

"Unless it fell out in the rumpus."

"But I would have seen it when we rescued him."

"And you didn't?"

"No."

"Which means it must have been taken from the couple either while they were sleeping or after they had left their things and come to help."

"I definitely didn't see any necklace," said Abigail. "The boy could have swallowed it, I suppose."

"Surely not," said Sidney. "That would be far too dangerous."

"And I don't think that would be the first thing on his mind, would it, Mr Chambers?"

"There's no lengths some folk won't go to," her father added. "Stealing jewellery and suing hard-working farmers. Haven't they got better ways to earn a living?"

"The necklace has sentimental significance," Sidney replied.

"The kind only the rich can afford. Is that all those people can think about: their jewellery? A boy was nearly killed, his parents are likely to sue, I may go out of business and all they want to talk about is a bloody necklace."

Emily Hastings was indeed a clergy daughter. Her father was the Vicar of St Mary Redcliffe in Bristol, a well-known figure who used his church as a political debating chamber to campaign for CND and annoy the government. His daughter was a languid, somewhat eccentric figure with a round pale face, shell-rimmed glasses, and long dark hair that was parted in the centre and decorated with a peacock-blue flapper headband. She smoked Balkan Sobranies as they drank Noilly Prat and listened to jazz. Sidney was so dazzled by her company that he ended up discussing the difference between Bechet's clarinet and saxophone playing for a good fifteen minutes before they got round to recent events on the Meadows. Even then Emily wanted to talk about other things, tactfully removing her copy of Wilhelm Reich's psychoanalytical book *The Function of the Orgasm* from the floor and putting it back on the shelves.

"I don't know why you've come to visit me, Mr Archdeacon. Your company is very pleasant, but if it's about the incident with the cows I am afraid I left before the drama."

"So you didn't witness the incident?"

"In the distance, but I was already on my way home. I heard a commotion as I was leaving Long Meadow but it was too late to turn back and I wanted to get to Newnham. There wasn't much about the party that excited me, to be honest. Too many boorish public-school boys who've no manners. I'm quite a dull girl really."

"I reckon you protest too much."

"I don't know. I had to ask to be taken to a May Ball. Can you imagine the humiliation?"

"Some people might find that a good thing. You had the ability to choose rather than to be chosen."

"I think a man can sense desperation in a woman."

"I'm not so sure." Sidney was surprised by this shift in tone. "Perhaps you have to disguise it as confidence."

"Exactly." Emily gave her right arm an airy waft. "I am sure you can tell this whole thing is an act; a mask; a charade in which I pretend to be someone I'm not."

"I think we can all be a little bit guilty of that. Who did you ask?"

"Richard, as a matter of fact. Well, he won't be coming with me now, will he?"

"Had he said yes?"

"I think I'd served a purpose. It was one way of getting back at Olivia."

"She had left him for Alexander?"

"Without bothering to tell him. I think she let him find out."

"At the party?"

"No, a few days before."

"I'm amazed he showed up."

"It was his party."

"Then I'm surprised she came."

"I wasn't. Olivia has a relaxed attitude to physical proximity. I don't think she really minds who she sleeps with. She once told me that it was just another form of exercise. Whereas I . . ."

"Think it might have to involve love?"

"Affection, at least. We're not animals; although the veneer of sophistication can be removed by alcohol all too swiftly. Would you like a top-up?"

Sidney thought of his father's watchful eye and how inappropriate it was to be spending so much time in a young student's rooms. "I'd better not."

"You don't mind if I have one?"

"Not at all."

"There's something delightfully decadent about getting sloshed on a Tuesday afternoon, don't you think? Where were we?"

"The party."

"Oh, yes. I didn't join in the so-called fun because I was dressed for cocktails rather than anything else."

"I imagine you looked very stylish."

"I was wearing a dark-green sequin dress with a fringe hem. I thought I'd try to blend in with the landscape. The back was too precious to sit down on so close to the river; the ground wasn't dry enough so I went home when things started getting fruity."

"Can you remember what Olivia was wearing?"

"A powder-blue floaty dress, strappy sandals."

"Her necklace?"

"Oh yes, that."

"You saw it?"

"Everyone did. She wore that colour of dress to set it off. It matched her eyes, she said, not that any of the men looked into them for too long. The necklace gave them the perfect opportunity to stare at her breasts."

"Was it the kind of necklace you would have worn?"

"It's not really my thing. Too Victorian."

"So if, for example, Olivia had offered to lend it to you . . ."

"I see where you are leading, Mr Archdeacon. I am reading experimental psychology, you know. It's not the kind of thing I would have wanted to steal. Believe me, I have my own style and my own studies to keep up. I don't seek out trouble. That seems to be your job."

Once Sidney had confessed to Amanda what he had been up to in one of their "catch-up" telephone calls, he was warned that Hermione Randall was a well-known socialite and "a very forceful woman".

113

"More than you, Amanda?"

"Definitely. You don't need to worry about me any more. I've lost half my confidence. I think it must be age. That and marriage. People look straight past me these days."

"Nonsense."

"It's true. I don't count. I'm old. I'm invisible. I could get away with all manner of crimes."

"Don't start on that."

"I won't. But it's true."

"So you think someone older could have stolen the necklace? Not a student at all, but an intrepid passer-by?"

"I don't know, Sidney; but certainly someone who wasn't young, giddy and drunk. Perhaps you should ask Henry. He might have been in Cambridge at the time."

"Don't be absurd."

"I'm not. He's been behaving very oddly lately. He works late and keeps disappearing."

"He likes his privacy."

"I only hope he hasn't been seeing his ex-wife. I can never quite trust her to keep away."

Henry had divorced Connie Richmond eight years previously but it hadn't stopped her sending threatening letters to Amanda in an attempt to disrupt the romance.

"Do you know we've been married nearly three years and I still can't quite tell what my husband's thinking. Do you have that with Hildegard?"

"All the time."

"It's irritating, isn't it?"

"I think it's supposed to keep us interested."

"Oh, is that what it is? What if we give up and look for entertainment elsewhere?"

"That isn't advisable, Amanda, and well you know it."

"It's what you're doing, though, isn't it? It may not be the amorous activity of a bounder or a rake but you're still away from home, running around the countryside looking for a necklace in a field full of cows and nubile young women. A needle in a haystack is a bit too prosaic for you, isn't it, Sidney? A needle? Oh no, that's not valuable enough. A haystack? Too banal. You need a whole field, mad cows, drunk students, young lovers, glamorous women, an angry farmer . . ."

"Stop it, Amanda."

"I'm right, though, aren't I? You're enjoying all this."

"I'm intrigued. That's different."

"Well, I can't wait to hear what you make of Hermione Randall. I think you may be about to meet your match."

Sidney decided that he had better talk through the case with Geordie over a couple of pints in the Eagle. Were the two crimes connected or were they not? And why was there still no sign of the necklace?

"I don't know what they've all been playing at," said Keating as they sat outside in the yard. "The whole thing's just a cock and bull story, without the cock."

"Or, indeed, the bull," said Sidney. "I did have a mad idea that the culprit could have been Richard Lane, who having been spurned by a former girlfriend took the jewel as an act of revenge. But I think that's too far-fetched."

"And we would have found the necklace in his clothing, unless Abigail Redmond picked it up in the aftermath."

"She even suggested he swallowed it."

"Then they would have found it in the hospital. Blimey, is that how her mind works?"

"I don't think she would pick up a necklace from the ground and not tell me about it."

"The family's criminal record says it all."

"But not her, Geordie. Abigail's always been a good girl. I've never found her to be envious or irresponsible."

"You've always had a soft spot for that woman."

"I've seen her grow up. I think it has to be one of the students."

"What about Emily Hastings? From what you tell me, she seems the most likely suspect."

"I've been thinking about that. It may be a question of timing. If she arrived later than we think, approaching from the town and across Long Meadow, she might have been behind Richard Lane just before the cows attacked."

"You mean they could have been going for her?"

"Possibly."

"But they didn't reach her because they got to the boy instead?"

"And she managed to escape along the riverbank, possibly getting across in a boat or a punt."

"But then she would have been breathless when she met the weird musician."

"He's not that odd."

"Did you ask him if she was breathless?"

"No, not yet. I hadn't even met her when I first spoke to him."

"Then perhaps you should see him again?"

"I will, Geordie. But even then she would have had to recross the river to steal the necklace when Olivia and Alexander had gone to help. And how would she know it was there? She hadn't even reached the party."

"Unless she'd seen Olivia beforehand."

"We need to ask her about that too. We could also search her rooms if you like. I'm sure I could swing it with the principal of Newnham."

"Let's not get ahead of ourselves."

"Then there is the happy or not-so-happy couple . . ." Geordie checked his notebook. "Olivia Randall and Alexander Farley. I suppose the girl could have kept the necklace all along, but I don't think she has the cunning to do that. The new boyfriend is a different matter, though. He could easily have taken it."

"But why would he? And how could he have kept it from her?"

"I don't know. Maybe he wanted it as some kind of proof that he had known her."

"But he must have thought Olivia was enough of a catch."

"His boat had come in, his icing was on the cake and all his Christmases had come at once. What's he like?" Geordie asked. "How new a boyfriend is he? How much does he love her? And would he have the means to sell the sapphire? It's certainly easy enough for him to have taken it as she slept. He'd already removed half her clothes; a necklace wouldn't have been too much of a challenge. It could even have fallen off in their little tryst. I think you need to get to see him on his own, Sidney, unless you want my help. I don't seem to have done very much so far and we're not making a lot of progress with the other students. Who are you talking to next?"

"I fear that decision is out of my hands. Helena's mother is about to arrive. Have you ever met her?"

"Fortunately, not."

"Perhaps you'd better keep it that way."

"I've nothing to hide."

"If Helena's told her anything about you, there'll be trouble. A married man like you, flirting away with a woman young enough to be his daughter . . ."

"She's not that young."

"She was when you started."

"Started what? My relationship with Helena, not that it ever *was* a relationship, has always been above board. There might have been a mild flirtation, mind, but I have always behaved in an appropriate manner and anyone who thinks that there has been anything untoward can . . ."

"Teasing again, Geordie . . ."

"You bastard, Sidney. What about you and Barbara Wilkinson? Don't get me started on that."

"A mere bagatelle. Shall I get the drinks or not?"

"It's definitely your round. And time to talk about something else; cricket, perhaps."

"Cricket? You must be desperate."

"I am desperate, Sidney — for another pint, if nothing else. We'll have to be on best behaviour when that woman arrives, especially if she's anything like her eldest daughter."

Hermione Randall — "that woman" — was a briskly efficient, tightly groomed society lady who wore a pink and cream Chanel two-piece suit with a Maison Michel hat and spoke with a snappy bravado that put action above thought. As they took Earl Grey and scones at the Orchard Tea Rooms the following day, Mrs Randall told Sidney that she was already "more than irritated" as she was almost certainly going to have to delay her forthcoming motoring tour of the Loire Valley. This was a considerable disappointment as it jeopardised the highlight of the entire trip, a chance to meet Robert Carrier, chef and author of *Great Dishes of the World*. "We're due to have dinner with him in the Château de Chenonceau. I've already bought the dress. Courrèges. I chose one in midnight-blue silk and satin that would specifically suit my necklace. And now that fool of a child has contrived to lose it."

"To be fair to Olivia," Sidney replied, "it may have been stolen."

"That would not have been the case if she had looked after it properly."

"It is something of a family heirloom, I gather?"

"My grandfather brought the jewel back from Ceylon after working for the governor, Arthur Hamilton-Gordon. They went on to run the Pacific Islands Company, which dealt in mining, and so he had it set in diamonds from South Africa. The platinum for the chain is apparently from Colombia. He liked to say that it came from all over the globe. When he first put the necklace round my grandmother's neck he said she was the centre of his world."

"Very romantic."

"My mother wore it when she was one of the last debutantes to be presented to Queen Victoria. Then it was passed on to me, in 1930, when Haile Selassie was declared Emperor of Ethiopia. I was going to give it to Helena but she has such unsuitable skin and I couldn't bear to hand it over. Even then I only loaned it to Olivia. I don't know why I did; to part with something that is so inextricably linked not just with the story of our family but with history itself was madness. I cannot understand how my daughter has been so careless with such a treasure. To leave the thing lying in a field!"

"Olivia is convinced that it was taken from round her neck."

"While she was too drunk to wake up. You don't need to spare me the details. We have to get it back, that's all. I've had a word with your man Keating and any jeweller worth his salt will know that the necklace has been stolen. It will be almost impossible to resell. I've also put up a reward of one hundred pounds."

"You're making the theft public? I remember that Helena wanted the whole thing to be kept low-key."

"That is hardly the case now I know all about it. She's a *journalist*, Mr Archdeacon. We might as well put her to some use. It's about time that girl did something for her family rather than herself."

When he next saw Roger Waters, the thoughtful sound-recordist, working further upriver by Byron's Pool, Sidney asked if Emily Hastings had been wet or breathless when she had spoken to him that day on the Meadows. He also wanted to know how soon the incident with the cows occurred after they had met. Could the stampede have already begun by the time she had reached him?

"No, it wasn't like that. We had a good chat. Then we spotted what was going on."

"And did you see the lovers run towards the cows?"

"There was so much happening."

"But were you aware of a canoodling couple?"

"I've already told you. But I don't like to look at that kind of thing. I get plenty of that at home."

"You have a girlfriend?"

"Yes, I do. Not that it has much to do with all this."

"She doesn't mind you going off, making recordings and talking to strangers?"

"She's used to that. I'm in a band. It happens all the time."

"And when Emily left, did she stay the same side of the river?"

"As far as I could see, yes she did."

"On the Cambridge side, not the Grantchester side?"

"That's right. She went back towards Coe Fen."

"She couldn't have crossed the river and stolen the necklace from the spot where Olivia and Alexander had been doing their . . ."

"Ummagumma? No. I don't think so. In any case, she didn't seem like that type of girl."

"And you never crossed the river yourself?"

"Why would I do that? Do you think I took the necklace? Blimey, you've got a nerve. I didn't know it was there, did I? I can't see anything from here. I hardly move. That's the point. Sound washes past me. I stay still. I let the sounds come to me."

"I'm sorry, I was only wondering."

The man was almost amused. "In any case, what are you doing involving yourself in all this? You're a vicar."

"I know the girl's mother. And her sister."

"Are you keen on either of them yourself? Is that what it is?"

"That's quite a direct question."

"You started asking them."

"I am married."

"Still, to be married and yet to be at the beck and call of three other women; that must take some doing."

"Believe me, Roger, I won't be involving myself again. I'm sorry to have asked such questions. It's all got out of hand. I've just about had enough."

"I'm more interested in music than ummagumma. You should come to one of our concerts; the band might take off."

"Is there any hope of that?"

"We're playing all the universities and we're going to Holland. And we've got a record deal. I think there's a chance we might be on *Late Night Line-Up*. So it's possible. Just let me know if you want to come."

Sidney smiled. He couldn't imagine it at all. "I'd like that," he said. "And my wife might too. She's the musician in our family."

"I might even write something about that girl," Roger continued. "There's something about her. The sunlight on her eyes."

"Well, you know where to find me."

"I don't actually."

"Ely Cathedral."

"But are you ever there?" Roger asked.

Sidney thought that he should visit Abigail Redmond once more, not because he considered her a suspect, but because he wanted to know if she could remember anything further about the immediate aftermath of the accident. He also mentioned the hundred-pound reward.

"That's not going to make much difference, is it?" she said.

"Whyever not?"

"If a poor person stole the necklace they can get more for it when they sell it, and a rich person doesn't need the money."

"I think it's a reward for information. So if you know anything . . ."

"Don't insult me, Mr Chambers. I don't need to be bribed to tell the truth."

"I just wanted to check one thing. You can't, by any chance, remember if Olivia Randall was wearing a necklace or not at the time of the accident?"

"She could have been. I might have noticed. I might not. I did have other things on my mind."

"But she was definitely there when you were trying to get the cows off?"

"Oh yes. She was there all right, screaming away with her shirt half-undone. So there was no necklace, come to think of it. Her boyfriend wasn't with her, though."

"Yes, I remember. He went to get help."

"That's what he claims."

"Why do you say that?"

"He didn't return by road. He came from the river. You won't get much help from there."

"Are you sure?"

"I remember seeing him do some kind of arc. I thought he was trying to avoid the cows but now I realise that he was making it look like he was coming from somewhere else."

"And it was definitely Alexander Farley?"

"I don't know his name. He had one of those floppy floral shirts with a big collar and he made a great song and dance about how help was on its way."

"Do you know something, Abigail?" Sidney replied. "You might just have earned yourself a hundred pounds."

In order to make sure this was possible he went back to Corpus to talk once more to its guest of honour, Mrs Hermione Randall; a woman, Sidney surmised, who was in desperate need of a title before her name. He only hoped she would be appropriately ladylike when she heard his proposition. He was now pretty confident that he could ensure the discreet return of the necklace in exchange for the reward.

"You have secured the necessary information?" she asked.

"I think so."

"And are you prepared to reveal the name of the culprit?"

"Not until I have hold of the necklace. It is a delicate matter."

"I hope that doesn't mean you have stolen it yourself, Mr Archdeacon."

Sidney decided to be amused rather than insulted. "Not at all. I am afraid that you will have to take it on trust that I am acting in the best interests of everyone."

"If you maintain your secrecy, I am not sure the police will agree with you."

"I am hoping they will never know."

"You mean to keep this from Helena's friendly inspector?"

"He is my friend too."

"I hear that Helena has him wrapped round her little finger."

Sidney could have made it clear that their relationship had been slightly more complex than that — a flirtation that had lasted for over a decade — but he did not want to make matters worse. "I don't think anyone would wish to get on the wrong side of either of your daughters."

"Oh, Olivia is a pushover. Helena has a bit more grit. That's from my side of the family."

"I don't think anyone would take any of you lightly. You are a formidable unit."

"That is kind. I see you mean to flatter me into submission."

"If I could possibly have a cheque for the reward? Then we can move swiftly towards resolution."

Mrs Randall reached for her handbag. "Whom shall I make it out to?"

You don't catch me out like that, Sidney thought. "If you would leave me to fill in the name of the payee."

"You are worried that if I know the perpetrator I shall report them?"

"This is not the perpetrator but a witness."

"And will we ever know who that is?"

"I hope not. But I am sure the money will be put to good use. Think of it as a charitable donation."

Hermione Randall wrote out the cheque. "I give enough to charity as it is. This feels more like blackmail."

"I can assure you it is not. Once the money is cleared . . ."

"Cleared? You mean we are going to have to wait another three days?"

"I am afraid so."

"You think I might cancel the cheque? That is not very trusting."

"I know that a *lady* would never do such a thing. But a bank might."

"I do have sufficient funds."

126

"I am sure you do."

"All I want is the necklace. Three days!"

"You could look upon it as an opportunity to spend more time with your daughters. We could even discuss Helena's wedding."

"I am in no mood for planning celebrations."

"Then I can only hope that will change. What was lost is about to be found."

Mrs Randall signed the cheque and tore it from her book. "Is that the parable of the lost sheep? It would be more appropriate if it was a cow."

"It's the parable of the prodigal son; or in this case, perhaps, the prodigal daughter. Thank you, Mrs Randall."

"I suppose you may call me Hermione."

"I am not sure I am ready for that," Sidney replied.

He made his way across to the fourteenth-century buildings of Old Court, pretending to leave the college by St Bene't's Gate, but turned left up a staircase that led to Alexander Farley's rooms. Fortunately the student was in, alone and almost unsurprised by Sidney's visit.

"I assume you want to ask us some more questions," he said. "I am seeing Olivia later. We are having lunch with her mother."

"That must be something of a challenge for you. I don't imagine you were expecting to spend so much time with her."

"She is quite a difficult woman, I admit."

"I mean," Sidney cut to the chase, "that it must be hard for you to keep silent."

"What are you implying?"

"I am talking about the necklace."

"You think I stole it? Why would I do that? If Olivia found out she'd be furious. It would be the end of everything."

"But I don't think you expect this relationship to last long, do you?" Sidney persisted. "Once she is back in London and you are doing your vocational training, it's going to be hard to continue."

"I don't know about that."

"I think you do, Alexander."

"But why would I steal?"

"To prove you could. I think it's a kind of trophy, a souvenir of something you know will never last. Olivia is very beautiful, probably the most stunning girl you have ever known. I wonder if you think you will never find someone as attractive again. It's the end of Cambridge. You are in a field, the celebrations are all around you, it couldn't be more perfect, and then it all goes horribly wrong; the violent accident; the ex-boyfriend; you see how upset Olivia is, her mood changes, and you pick up the one thing of beauty that remains: the necklace. It's an impulsive decision. You somehow believe you have a right to it, your very own Cambridge blue."

"That's ridiculous."

"I actually think you meant to give it back. You could have said that you held it for safekeeping, you could even have pretended to have found it. But during the search you became aware that Abigail Redmond, the farmer's daughter, could be blamed. Emily Hastings could also have stolen it. Even poor old Richard Lane could have taken it before the accident, while you were asleep. So you decided that you might as well hang on to it. And you did so for so long that it soon became too late to do anything other than keep it. You were stuck with it, unable to give it back without looking stupid, guilty or causing an enormous fuss."

"An interesting theory . . ."

"Now the situation won't go away. The longer it goes on the worse it gets. I know the necklace must be here, in your rooms, or you have hidden it somewhere. I'm giving you the opportunity to return it. This is your only hope, Alexander. Otherwise I will call in the police. And then your troubles really will begin. You will have a criminal record, there will be no chance of practising law, and your career will be over before it has begun. These are your choices. You can either confess what you have done and give the necklace back to Olivia, taking a risk on her forgiveness, or, alternatively, you can hand it to me."

"Olivia would have to pretend to her mother that she had mislaid it all along. I don't know how we could explain it without looking like idiots."

"Then I think you should give the necklace to me," said Sidney. "I will make sure it is returned without anyone knowing how it disappeared."

"And why would you do that?"

"Because I believe in second chances, especially for the young. You're a lucky young man and I hope that one day you will be aware of how privileged you are and will show mercy and generosity to others — especially if you ever become a judge. Perhaps that's naive of me, but I think this was a desperate impulsive act, an opportunist moment of temptation, and you didn't think through the consequences. As a result, you have been paralysed into silence. The more you kept your secret the harder it became to confess and so you have ended up doing nothing, hoping that the tension would dissipate or, at worst, that someone else would be blamed. But no one can be prosecuted as long as you have the necklace. And so the case will remain open, and you will live in fear unless you do something about it now. I am perhaps the answer to your prayer. I can make the whole thing go away. Only then need you decide how honest to be with Olivia."

"And do you think I should tell her?"

"In time, perhaps you should. But if the relationship comes to an end, then perhaps you will only have taught her to be more careful; in what she does with her necklace and with her future choice of boyfriend."

"She's not an easy girl."

"And you are not a simple man, Alexander. Give me the necklace."

"I have your word?"

"I hope this unfortunate event will have taught you not to keep souvenirs of your conquests. Now please either give me the necklace or assure me that you will find a way of returning it anonymously."

A few hours later, a package arrived at the Porters' Lodge addressed to Mrs Hermione Randall, care of

The Master, and Abigail Redmond was £100 better off. The mystery was not exactly solved but there was insufficient evidence for the police to proceed.

Geordie was relieved to be rid of the case but wasn't prepared to let it go without comment. As he bought the first pint of the evening in the RAF bar of the Eagle, he noticed that his friend was smiling.

"You've been up to something, Sidney, I know it."

"It's nothing that need concern you. I have talked to people, that is all."

"I could have you for wasting police time."

"What about clergy time?"

"Your attitude is very different to ours. You've got all day, or rather the whole of eternity."

"Not in the material world where all flesh is grass."

"And cows trample over it. Honestly, Sidney, I sometimes wonder if you really are on the side of the angels. I know you have been protecting the privileged."

"That's not true."

"Students . . ."

"And others too. I have been looking after the young who make mistakes and haven't yet found out who they are or what they'd like to bring to the world. Think of all the errors we both made in our youth."

"I'd rather not . . ."

"Well, when I do I always remember those who gave me the benefit of the doubt. I think I was more shamed by them than those who set out to punish me straight away. Gracious behaviour can inspire others to do the same. People starting out in life need a little slack from time to time, whether it's Abigail Redmond or the students or, indeed, anyone else. The quality of mercy is not strained."

"Say what you like. The whole lot of you have been wasting police time."

"On the contrary, Geordie, if I told you the full story I think you'd find that I've prevented a lengthy court case and have *saved* police time."

"Would you like to go into details, or am I just to trust in your promises of salvation?"

"I think you can guess the answer to that by now."

"I won't press you then. I know that you prefer the mystery of silence. But let me simply point out that although you may be able to preserve my time and rescue my soul, the one thing you're not going to be able to save is money. It's your round."

"I will be happy to oblige."

"In this case the wages of sin is not death but another pint."

"I think I can bear that purgatory, Geordie."

"Purgatory? With me? You don't know you're born, man."

"''Tis virtue, and not birth that makes us noble: great actions speak great minds, and such should govern.' I'm on my way."

Sidney put his order in at the bar. He was just about to pay when Helena Randall arrived. "I'll get these," she said.

"Where's Malcolm?"

"At home. I thought I'd surprise you. It's a Thursday night. It'll be like old times: just the three of us."

"Has your mother gone home?"

132

"She has indeed."

"What about your sister?"

"She's with Alexander. I think he's about to be dispatched."

"And why would that be?"

"You know perfectly well, Sidney Chambers. I can read between the lines and so can Olivia. But don't worry; your sleuthing is safe with us. I should thank you."

"Yes, you probably should."

"Then I will." Helena leaned over and gave him a peck on the cheek. "I knew you'd turn up trumps."

"Officially, of course, I have done nothing."

"Yes, and it is probably best if it stays that way."

"Don't worry. I won't tell."

"Not even Geordie?"

"Mum's the word."

"No," said Helena, "it most definitely is not. Thank God she's left. Now where is that man? Time for a final flirt!"

She winked at Sidney, picked up a pint glass and blew the inspector a slow-motion kiss.

The Trouble with Amanda

It was a summer's day on the fens in the middle of the haymaking season, with the swifts too high to be heard, cabbage white butterflies hovering over cow parsley, grasshoppers chattering, moths hatching from their cocoons and green woodpeckers flurrying across the sky in search of rain. Behind the thirteenth-century wall of Canonry House, Anna was making a little den for her dolls, Byron was sleeping in the shade of an apple tree and Sidney was just finishing his correspondence.

Hildegard had laid a table for a picnic in the garden with elderflower cordial, quiche, salad and a lemon syllabub. Amanda and Henry were coming to lunch and the family was looking forward to a lazy sunny afternoon in the historic comfort of a cathedral cloister.

Just before the guests arrived, Hildegard had one more chore to complete. This was to persuade her husband to part with an old bottle-green jumper for one of the forthcoming church fêtes. His mother had knitted it for him some ten years previously.

She stood in the study doorway and held the innocent garment out for inspection. She was unsurprised when Sidney appeared reluctant to let his jumper go. "It has great sentimental value," he said.

"But the moths have got to it."

"Then no one will buy it, my darling. The good people of Ely have taste and discretion. They will be after a better class of sweater. Besides, no one will want such a thing on a warm summer's day."

"I don't know. There's always some kind of chill in the air."

"We are fortunate that there's a breeze. Think how stifling it would be if we were in the south of France."

"You have so many clothes to keep you warm, Sidney. I can't believe you are making such a fuss about giving away one stupid jumper."

"I'm not making a fuss."

"You've got that hurt-little-boy look on your face that always makes me cross. This is for *charity*, Sidney, and it's not much of a sacrifice." Hildegard shook out and folded the jumper. "You never wear it anyway."

Her husband was not convinced. "I find it a comfort to know it's there."

"You have others. Your mother seems to knit you something every year. I shouldn't have asked. I could have just taken it away. I am sure you wouldn't have noticed."

"All right," Sidney conceded. "I suppose I can live without it."

"There's no need to be in such a mood."

"I'm not."

Hildegard snatched up the jumper and left the room without another word. Even though her husband was infuriating, she was not going to pick a fight and she, at least, had better things to do than stand around discussing her husband's knitwear. There was a Schubert impromptu to practise for a start.

This seemingly trivial scene, however, disguised a more unsettling touchiness about the subject of generosity in the light of recent events. The previous week, Sidney's friend, Dr Nicholas Stacey, had telephoned in a fury to ask for help in persuading church leaders, politicians and people of influence to do far more for the suffering in Biafra. The television news showed malnourished children, victims of genocide by starvation, the result of a secessionist plan in Nigeria in which both sides blamed each other in a war that showed no sign of ending. The last time Sidney had seen such images had been after the liberation of Belsen. It was impossible to turn away without feeling appalled, guilty and determined to do something, however small, to alleviate the suffering.

When the Richmonds arrived for the garden picnic they were equally anxious about food, waste and unnecessary expenditure. Amanda said that she had recently attended a fundraising dinner for potential philanthropists at the National Gallery and hadn't had the heart to enjoy it. "I hardly eat anything these days. I keep thinking about those poor children instead. What are we going to do, Sidney?"

"Raise as much money as we can."

"I've made a donation but I still feel so helpless. People don't realise how privileged we are in this country."

"Some things are hard to justify," Sidney replied. "Even the wealth of the Church makes me feel a bit queasy."

"At least it pays your salary," said Henry. "One can worry about these things too much."

"And it's still a pittance," Amanda chipped in. "You've no need to be embarrassed about *that*."

"I have to confess that I do also have some anxiety about the cathedral itself," Sidney continued. "All that pomp and circumstance. It doesn't sit very easily when you consider the simplicity of the early disciples breaking bread in the upper room."

"What about the parable of the talents and the Good Samaritan?" Henry asked. "He had to have money to pay for the charity. And isn't all that architecture supposed to reflect the glory of God? You need a bit of majesty don't you? I thought that was the point; a glimpse of heaven on earth."

"I'm going to try and organise a concert," said Hildegard. "We might have some African music like the Missa Luba. And we're going to ask Dusty Springfield."

"Those poor little children," said Amanda. "I wish I could go over there and take them home. Adopt one of them, even."

"I'm not sure about that," her husband replied.

"Wouldn't it be the right thing, though? Something practical."

"It sounds very *impractical* to me."

Hildegard served up the quiche with new potatoes and a green bean salad as Sidney discreetly opened a bottle of white wine and tried not to be embarrassed by the conspicuous consumption. At the same time Byron padded round the guests with a baleful look in his eyes that attempted to persuade everyone present that he had never been fed in the whole of his life and that it was surely his turn for some food.

"Whenever I see photographs of such helpless little creatures I weep," Amanda continued.

"There are some things that are inexplicable," said Sidney. "How can those children be to blame? They cannot. We have to do whatever we can and fall on the mercy of God's grace."

"But why have I got that grace and not the children in Biafra, Sidney? Why me and not them? I don't deserve my good fortune. All I do is shop. Now I can't even do that without feeling guilty."

"Anything you *can* do to alleviate the situation is better than nothing."

"I will and I have. But it frightens me."

"Why?"

Amanda looked down at a plate of food that she had not finished. "Because it shows me how shallow my life has been."

A few days later, Sidney bumped into Henry's first wife, Connie Richmond, walking on the fens to the north of Ely. She was a patient in a hospital for the mentally fragile outside Chettisham. As a charitable foundation, it believed in giving patients as much freedom as possible within a secure environment. Henry was still paying for her care.

It had been a long time since Sidney had seen her, a couple of years he thought, and at first he tried, rather uncharitably, to avoid her by changing the direction of his walk. Unfortunately he had failed to communicate this plan to his Labrador, who made straight for her.

"I see that Byron is keener to speak to me than you are, Mr Archdeacon," she said.

"I wasn't aware that you knew my dog's name."

"I know a lot more than you think I do."

"I don't believe I have ever underestimated the wealth of your knowledge, Mrs Richmond."

The woman had been a formidable opponent in the past and Sidney still suspected her of the murder of her friend, Virginia Newburn, who had drowned almost four years previously. He still couldn't understand how the psychiatric institution where she lived allowed her the freedom to roam around the fens, seemingly at will. She must have been drawn by the heat of summer, a clear day and the need to appreciate the breezy air.

"Do you think my husband is happy with his new wife?" she asked. "Or, more relevant to your enquiries . . ."

"I'm not involved in any inquiry . . ."

"Do you think his new wife is happy with him?"

"I have always assumed that to be the case."

"You have, have you?"

"Every marriage has its ups and downs."

"That is especially true if one part of the so-called couple has already enjoyed a past with someone else. You know all about that, don't you, Mr Archdeacon?"

Sidney just stopped himself questioning the word "enjoyed" and replied simply. "I don't think it's helpful for anyone in a marriage to dwell too much on what has gone before." He did not want to say anything provocative that might prolong the conversation.

"But what if that history clouds the present?"

"I try not to let it do so myself."

"Or if the past keeps yielding up its secrets in bits and bobs?"

"Sometimes you need a clean break."

"'Bits and bobs' is such a funny phrase, is it not, Mr Archdeacon? Straight from the sewing basket. You remember I am a seamstress?"

"I admired the wedding dress you made to resemble Miss Kendall's."

"You noticed."

"It was quite a bold thing to do, Mrs Richmond, to approach Ely Cathedral on the day of the nuptials wearing the same outfit as the bride. I don't know how you discovered what Miss Kendall's dress was going to be like."

"There's a lot about me you'll never know, Mr Archdeacon. Perhaps my husband sees me more often than anyone suspects?"

"He may well do so. But I don't think Henry's the kind of man to retain an intimate knowledge of dressmaking."

"You are right. But he can be 'intimate' in other ways."

"That is a scandalous suggestion."

"I am talking about my husband."

140

"Your *former* husband."

"Joined together in holy matrimony in the sight of God. 'Let no man put asunder.' You should know that, Mr Archdeacon. People say that love has such complexity, but it should be simple, shouldn't it? You keep your promises. That's all there is to it, surely?"

"I am not going to argue with the principle."

"But then," Connie Richmond continued, "people make the mistake of thinking they can change everything and get away with something else and it leads to all manner of complications. They start to have secrets and do strange things and then no one knows where they are any more. If you want to find out what's been going on then you have to start unpicking things and if you try and sew the original back together after all that, well, someone like me can always tell a garment's never as good as it was the first time."

"Mrs Richmond, I'm not sure what you're trying to tell me. I should really be getting on; and so if you do have something specific to say . . ."

"Look at your dog," Connie replied as Byron was pawing at the mud on the edge of a reservoir. "Who knows what he's going to find? He'll always be interested in what's underneath the surface; what's been buried. Just as you should be. No matter how deep he goes, there's always more to uncover."

"I have already had difficulties with my Labrador's discoveries. He's a very inquisitive animal."

"It's like history, isn't it, Mr Archdeacon? I call it emotional archaeology. Just when you think you've buried something, someone can come along and dig it up again. And who knows what could be lying down there covered in the silt of good fenland. There might be a bone and, if there is, then one would have to ask: whose bone was it, and are there any more? Might there be enough to make a body?"

"I'm sorry, Mrs Richmond, I really must be getting on." Sidney no longer cared how rude he was; he just had to make his escape. He could not be a Christian all the time. He called Byron and, fortunately, his Labrador obeyed. Even he had had enough.

The meadows were a buttercup yellow that merged into the orange of bird's-foot-trefoil and the pinks of ragged robin. A brimstone butterfly fluttered across the white clover and wood pigeons called from the elms.

A week later Sidney was back in Grantchester to take the funeral of the sister of his former housekeeper Mrs Maguire. It was another hot, still day, the only natural sounds being the *pseep pseep* of hidden blackbird fledglings in the hedgerows, the murmur of bees and the irritation of flies. Like almost everyone else, the vicar was on holiday and although Malcolm Mitchell was perfectly capable of conducting the service, he reported that Mrs Maguire had insisted that her dead sister Gladys had specifically asked for Sidney.

"A prophet is without honour in his own land. You're considered far more special now you've left."

"I don't know about that."

"You're one of her success stories, Sidney."

"If I have had any worldly achievement then I am very happy to give Mrs Maguire the credit. Perhaps I'll even get to try one of her walnut specials again."

"That is more than likely. She is doing a big 'bake for the wake' as she calls it, but there's a twist. She wants people to pay for what they eat."

"After they've kindly come to her sister's funeral?"

"She is sure Gladys would have approved. It's in aid of Biafra. I think even Mrs Maguire is aware of the irony of raising funds for famine relief in this way but she doesn't have much money and she told me that the disaster was on her conscience. She had to do something, make use of her talents, and she said that this was the only thing that she knows how to do well. I told her that it was an admirable idea. She was very gratified to have my blessing."

"You have such a way with her, Malcolm. I would appreciate a tip or two."

"I don't think you need my help. We all bring different skills to the table. I will say that she does seem a bit lost without her sister. She said she wished her husband was still with her."

"I don't think there's much chance of that, I'm afraid. He went missing a long time ago."

"Nevertheless, Sidney, I think one of your pastoral visits will do her good."

"I'll gladly take the funeral if it's all right with you and it's what Mrs Maguire wants."

"And I'll be happy to assist."

"That would be good of you, Malcolm. It will be like old times. I might even ask Hildegard to contribute."

"I don't think that will be necessary. You don't want to inflame Mrs Maguire's competitive spirit. I think the venture is planned as a solo effort."

And indeed it was, with Victoria sponges, poppy seed, lemon drizzle, chocolate, carrot, fruit and the famous walnut special all laid out on trestle tables in the village hall for the eighty mourners. The bake yielded a grand profit of £7 5s 3d which was efficiently collected in special donation boxes that Malcolm made ready for dispatch.

Sidney told Mrs Maguire that she had admirably fulfilled the commandments in the Book of Isaiah, honouring the dead, respecting the living and treating the unknown stranger as her own flesh and blood. He was proud of her and said that he was sure that her sister would have been too.

"It's what she would have wanted, Mr Chambers. She saw those news reports just as she was in her final decline. She cried about it. We both did. And Ronnie and I never did have children. It's all I can do for those poor little mites."

"And you've done them proud, Mrs M."

"I feel heart sorry. It's been a sad time."

"It has indeed."

"I think I need a bit of a lie-down after all that worry."

"You mustn't overdo it."

Mrs Maguire gave her former boss a shove in the arm. "You're a fine one to talk, Mr Chambers. I bet you've got something up that sleeve of yours."

"You're wrong there, Mrs Maguire. For once in my life my pastoral duties are my only concern."

"Then I hope you enjoy them. You never stay out of trouble for long."

"I don't seek it out."

"I know what you say. 'Sometimes trouble comes to me.' You attract it, that's your problem, Mr Chambers, and you don't know how to resist it. You need a repellent like they have for insects. Something that keeps danger away."

"If I had that then I might be out of a job."

"Not at all. You could just enjoy the services and be paid like any other clergyman."

"Ah yes, the quiet life."

"Except you don't really want one of those, do you?"

Sidney knew that this was true and felt a little guilty stopping off and spending money on a pint with Geordie after the funeral, but he felt that he could do with a bit of cheering up. It was a Thursday. He missed his friend and felt in need of a chat about recent events.

The inspector was in a genial mood and looking forward to his summer holiday in Dorset. Sidney suggested that one year perhaps they should join forces and spend some time together. Hildegard had even suggested that they all go to Germany, but Geordie wasn't too sure about that idea. He liked his routine. Besides, he told his friend, he had too many children and now that the eldest had started producing her own, his home was overrun. Three of his grandchildren were currently staying while their parents both worked.

"Although Cathy and I don't mind," he said. "They are God's reward for having children."

"You seem a bit young to be a grandfather."

"No. I'm the one that's normal. You started late, remember? I can enjoy them and throw them up in the air while I've still got the energy. You'll be an old man when the time comes. People have kids later and later these days; Helena and Malcolm need to get on with it. You've had yours but it's probably too late for Amanda, don't you think?"

"She has raised the subject of adoption."

"Any child would be lucky to have her as a mother . . ."

"She is upset about Biafra. She even mentioned . . ."

"Blimey. That would be brave. I wonder what her parents would say to a black baby?"

"Amanda's beyond caring what other people think."

"I don't know how you'd go about adopting one of them, though. You'd have to go there and find an orphanage while there's a war on."

"Her husband isn't keen. I would even say that he was quietly hostile. I imagine he hopes it will all blow over. He probably feels he's had enough drama after his first wife and would prefer a quiet life. I saw her only the other day."

"Connie Richmond? They let her out?"

"I don't think she goes far. It's only for walks on the meadows near Chettisham. She hardly strays further than a mile or two."

"Still, she should have someone with her from the home, Sidney."

146

"Perhaps they're short-staffed?"

"Quite easy to get lost on the fens."

"As you know, I don't think she is as helpless as everyone supposes. She's more calculating."

"You still think she killed that friend of hers, Virginia Newburn, don't you?"

"Accidents happen; but I am a bit worried, Geordie, if truth be known. Virginia Newburn's may not be the only death she knows about. Connie Richmond hints at something more."

"There have been no reports of anything untoward recently. Perhaps she enjoys making threats?"

"Put it this way, I don't think Amanda will ever feel quite secure as long as that woman's alive."

"I can't see her being much trouble as long as everyone stays well away."

"It may not be that simple. Something's wrong, Geordie. I don't quite know what's the matter with Amanda either."

"You're always worried about *her*."

"It's not just her marriage or the Biafra situation. I think she's having some kind of crisis. She seems a bit lost. She feels her life is petty, pointless and banal."

"She's not the only one."

"Now then, Geordie . . ."

"Don't you 'now then' me, man. What's Amanda's beef? She's got a decent enough husband, a nice house in London, and all the clothes she could possibly want. She lacks for nothing. If she's that concerned about whatever she's worried about, she can always give money to charity. Or go shopping again. The main problem with Amanda is that she's got no problems."

"There's something she's not telling me."

"Perhaps it's that she knows she should have married you all along. She's made an almighty mistake."

"It's not that, Geordie."

"It bloody well is."

"No. It's something else; another layer of truth."

"And are you going to uncover it or wait until you're told what it is?"

"I don't know, Geordie. I think I'd like to find out before anything dramatic happens."

"Well that would make a nice change for once," his friend replied. "Stopping something before it starts. It'd be a bit of a first for us."

"You'd think we'd be getting better at this kind of thing, wouldn't you?" asked Sidney, finding no answer at the bottom of his empty pint glass.

It was Day Two of the last test match of the summer: England versus Australia at the Oval. The weather was set fair, England were batting with D'Oliveira and Edrich at the crease, and Alec Chambers was in an expansive mood, chuffed to have been introduced to Wilfred Rhodes shortly after he had arrived.

"You know, Sidney, his first game for England was W. G. Grace's last? Meeting him is like shaking hands with history."

Rhodes was the first Englishman to have scored 1,000 runs and taken 100 wickets in test matches. "He did it sixteen times," Sidney's father continued. "No one's bettered that, you know."

"I thought he was blind?"

"He can still follow a game. Someone told me that his hearing is so good he can tell when the new ball's been taken because it makes a different sound on the bat. We mustn't judge by appearances. You, of all people, should know that."

Sidney was not quite in the mood to be lectured at by his father so cheerily, but they soon settled down to enjoy the game. The sun was out and D'Oliveira was in an imperious mood, batting in a sleeveless sweater. It was the perfect time for idle conversation. In the breaks for drinks, lunch and tea, father and son could discuss anything from family news to the ebb and flow of the game.

Sidney saw a young couple eating ice creams with their son. It was his first cricket match and he filled in a scorecard after every ball. "Training him up," said Alec Chambers admiringly. "Do you ever wish you'd had a son, Sidney?"

"No, I'm happy with Anna."

"She's a bright little button. Jen's got the boys. I've given up hope with your brother. He tells me he isn't ready for commitment. That's one excuse for being a layabout."

"He's a musician."

"You know what I mean . . ."

"I hope I haven't been a disappointment to you, Dad."

"Not at all. I was only wondering. It was the sight of that young man with the scorecard. He reminds me of you."

"I don't remember being that diligent."

"No, but you were a very serious little boy. You had such concentration."

"I think I've lost all that now. Hildegard is always complaining about how distracted I am."

"We both think she's been the making of you, Sidney. You've done well there, my boy. You took a risk and it paid off."

"I hope I'm enough for her."

"You can't always make up for the past."

"She would have liked more children. But we met too late for that."

"I always think it sad that those who want children so badly often have such difficulties, while other people can't stop having them or even try to get rid of them. And this Biafra business is dreadful. I've sent some money but there seems no end to it. Such a waste. So many children. It's heartbreaking."

"Hildegard's organising a concert. Amanda's made a hefty donation."

"Good for her. It's a pity *she* doesn't have any kids. Bit of a mess there, I must say."

"What do you mean?"

"Henry Richmond, of course."

"I didn't know you knew him?"

"I don't, really."

"Then why are you mentioning him now?"

150

"I don't know, Sidney. Perhaps it's because I once had to look after his wife."

"Connie?"

The two men stopped to applaud a D'Oliveira cover drive to the boundary, silently acknowledging that this was a breach of confidence. Then Alec Chambers resumed.

"I knew Henry's father. It was a rum do. I don't think I've ever told you. Bill Richmond telephoned on a Sunday evening of all things, telling me that the case required my utmost discretion. The woman was in pieces. It was a sad state of affairs, I must say."

"Can you tell me what it was?"

"A mental breakdown . . ."

"Do you know what caused it?"

"It was a long time ago: 1957 or 1958, I think. I'd better not go into details. Patient confidentiality, you understand."

"I was just wondering, Dad. Might Connie Richmond have had an illegal abortion? One that went wrong and you had to sort it out?"

"Sidney, that is alarmingly astute of you but you must know not to ask a doctor such questions."

"It's true, though, isn't it?"

"The law is different now, thank God. At least the politicians have done something about it."

"So you did?"

"Sidney . . ."

"It's just the two of us, Dad . . ."

"And several thousand spectators."

"They're watching the cricket."

"All I will say is that I helped patch her up and things have improved a great deal since then. It doesn't make the business any less grim but there's less chance of a death now that proper doctors can get on with it when it's necessary and the mother's life is in danger."

"Were they married at the time?"

"I'm pretty sure they were not. The girl was lucky to survive the trauma of it all. She was only seventeen. Irish, I remember, from County Clare. Such a pretty little thing. Very frail."

"She doesn't seem so fragile now."

"You know her?"

"She lives just outside Ely."

"Well, well . . ."

"I think Henry still sees her. She's in some kind of institution. He must assume that he is responsible."

"He was. I'm sorry if she's no better."

"She has other issues. There was a bit of shoplifting and feelings of panic and abandonment. I know Henry married her eventually but unfortunately that didn't work out or make anything better."

"He probably proposed out of guilt. That's never a good start to a marriage."

"Do you think he's a good man?" Sidney asked.

"I don't know, Sidney. I deal with health rather than morality. How people behave is more your department. I'm only left to deal with the consequences."

There was a change in the Australian bowling and Alec Chambers was clearly growing tired of the conversation. "It's easier in cricket, isn't it? You're judged by how you play when you're out in the middle.

You play each ball on its merits. There's nothing you can do if you fail. In football and rugby you've got the rest of the game to try and redeem yourself. In cricket, if you make a mistake and you're out then it's all over."

"It can be a very unforgiving game."

The crowd applauded a lovely leg glance. "I tell you one thing. I don't know whether Basil D'Oliveira's a good man or not but he's a great cricketer. He bats without a hair or a nerve out of place. It'll be impossible not to select him for South Africa."

"Do you think so?"

Sidney knew that this was a political hot potato. A naturalised Englishman, D'Oliveira had originally come from South Africa, where he was classed as a "Cape Coloured" and would not be welcomed back by a regime that practised apartheid.

His father did not think this was a problem. "On this showing? That's how you judge a man, Sidney, form. You look at what he's like out in the middle, playing under pressure. Can he respond to changing conditions? Has he got the stomach for the fight? The odd thing about D'Oliveira is that he's not so good when it's easy. He's a pressure player. Remember the way he stood up to Sobers and Hall in his first test against the West Indies; the eighty-seven not out he got at Old Trafford, the eighty-one against Pakistan last year . . ."

Alec Chambers stopped to admire a fine sweep to the boundary. "He times the ball so sweetly; it's not always about strength but judgement."

"Wasn't he dropped when he was on thirty-one?" Sidney asked.

"Doesn't matter. You ride your luck. The cricketing gods gave him a second chance. I suppose Henry Richmond's had one of those too. Dolly wasn't picked for the third and fourth tests and is only playing because Knight's injured. It's how you take your chances, and how you respond to adversity that matters. Now look at him. That's a beautiful late cut. He's got a hundred. Well played, sir."

When Sidney returned, after one too many beers with his father and a long hot train journey from London, his hope of a quiet evening in front of the television watching Spike Milligan's *World of Beachcomber* was soon dashed.

Hildegard had news. A few hours earlier, Connie Richmond had been found dead. She had drowned.

"Like Virginia Newburn?"

"They discovered her in a reservoir just as it was getting dark."

"Could it have been an accident?"

"No. Geordie says she was bound and gagged. They think Henry must have done it."

"How can anyone come to such a conclusion; and so soon? Has Henry confessed?"

"He's denying the whole thing; but one of his handkerchiefs was found at the scene."

"But that could have belonged to anyone."

"Not really. It was monogrammed; the same as the ones Amanda gave you. HJR. Henry John Richmond."

"I don't think the man's capable of murder and surely he wouldn't have been so careless as to leave a handkerchief lying around?"

"It wasn't lying around, Sidney. It was stuffed into Connie Richmond's mouth."

At first, Henry had denied that he had been anywhere near Chettisham at the time of his former wife's death; a claim that was disproved all too swiftly by Dr Evans, the head of the psychiatric institution. He told police that their suspect had, in fact, paid a visit on the morning of the disappearance in order to take Connie out for a walk. The couple had some kind of altercation as they were leaving the building and the patient had been so upset that Henry had produced a handkerchief to assuage her tears. Dr Evans had intervened and specifically asked if Connie was sure she wanted to go out to the meadows. She had taken a good ten minutes to calm down. Then her mood switched and she was bright again.

"She could be like that," Dr Evans said, "particularly after Henry Richmond referred to her as his 'wife'. They left hand in hand."

It had been touching to see the equilibrium restored, although the doctor was sure the peace would not last long. Connie Richmond was too volatile and the situation had been sufficiently dramatic to stay in the memory. He was in no doubt that Henry Richmond had seen Connie on the day of her death and now, as a result of his initial denial, he was the chief suspect.

"What is it with you and your friends?" Geordie asked.

"It doesn't look good."

"Your man couldn't have made a better job of appearing guilty if he had planned the whole thing."

"He must have been framed. Why would he be stupid enough to leave his handkerchief at the scene of the crime? I am convinced Henry is innocent."

"Well, he's done a very good job of making us think he is not. He's already told a whopping great lie."

"That must have been panic. Does Amanda know?"

"I'm surprised she hasn't telephoned you already. Perhaps she's in shock?"

"She's more likely to be finding a lawyer. Were there any witnesses?"

"None so far. The farmer's son found her as he was bicycling home. Not something he'll be able to forget in a hurry, poor lad. Dr Evans said that Connie Richmond often liked to walk on the meadows but never went near the reservoir because she couldn't swim. He told us she had always been careful near water."

"Except when Virginia Newburn was killed."

"That's true. But then it was winter. This happened on a clear summer's day. That makes it all the more strange. We'll have to wait for the pathologist to tell us whether she drowned or if she was dead already and her corpse was dumped in the reservoir. I don't know if the body was weighted down or not. If Connie Richmond was killed somewhere else, whether it was by Henry Richmond earlier in the day or by someone else, then we need to find out where that was and why she was moved. We'll also need to establish the time of death."

"Was the body well hidden?"

"Not exactly. There's a bit of woodland nearby and even an old clay pit that would have been better."

"So 'death by water' may be a deliberate statement?"

"Possibly."

"I can't believe that nobody saw anything."

"We're going round all the farms. There's a private road and a couple of drovers' tracks. The weird thing is that the body was found at the far end of the reservoir from the road. That's a long way to carry a corpse. It's nothing that Henry Richmond couldn't have managed but it's quite a difficult way of going about things. They're not getting much out of him, incidentally. He's very evasive."

"I am afraid that's his natural state."

"Well, he's going to have to change his personality if he wants to save himself."

"I don't think he's a killer, Geordie."

"Do you know, Sidney, I am not sure he is either. But a man can do strange things when he is desperate. I certainly think he wanted to get shot of her."

"Connie Richmond was a threat, I'll give you that; but I don't think she would be provocative enough to inspire murder."

"You saw her recently."

"I hope that doesn't make me a suspect, Geordie."

"Don't be daft. But what was she like? You thought something like this might happen, didn't you? You told me you were worried. Do you think she could have threatened Henry and he retaliated? What could she have against him?"

"A final secret, Geordie."

"And what is that?"

"A lost child."

"One that Amanda doesn't know about, you mean?"

"I'm afraid so."

"Is this child alive?"

"No."

"Did Connie Richmond tell you this?"

"Not exactly."

"Then I must ask you, Sidney, how did you find out?"

"I'm not at liberty to say."

"You'll have to be if this is a material fact."

"I'm not sure that it is."

"You won't let me be the judge?"

"You know what I am saying."

"An abortion?"

Sidney nodded.

"When was this?"

"About ten years ago."

"You know we can still prosecute? There was a Harley Street doctor around that time who carried out a therapeutic abortion on a woman in order to avert her threat of suicide. He charged her seventy-five pounds, she ended up dying of renal failure and he got five years for manslaughter."

"I don't know the circumstances but I think Connie may have threatened to expose the truth and tell Amanda all about it."

"And Henry Richmond would have wanted to prevent her from doing such a thing?"

"I'm afraid that is possible."

"On the other hand she might have threatened other people with further revelations. Connie Richmond was not a stable woman."

"You'll ask Dr Evans who else she saw?"

"We will, Sidney, but you know how often in these cases it's the closest relative that matters? Henry Richmond was paying for her care. You don't get much closer than that. You might like to find out if he's as comfortably off as he says he is. Perhaps he's been using money from wife number two to pay for wife number one? If that's the case and Amanda finds out, it'll be curtains for him."

"Then I hope you'll be the one to tell her, Geordie."

"Oh no, Sidney, I think you'll find that'll be your job."

Amanda telephoned that evening. She said that she was not sure of anything her husband told her any more. She felt too sick to eat or drink and she couldn't sleep. Sometimes she thought she was going mad.

Sidney tried to persuade her not to give up hope. It was perfectly possible someone else had killed Connie Richmond and framed Henry.

"But can you think of anyone who would want to do that?"

"I can't. There is no suspect other than your husband."

"I could have killed that woman myself."

159

"Please don't say that to anyone else, Amanda."

"She's been nothing but a menace. Henry has been keeping it all from me, I know. It would have been so much better if he had told me everything from the start. Then I might never have married him."

"It's too late for that kind of thinking."

"It isn't if I can't help it. Do you know anything more? I bet you do. You know I couldn't bear it if I found out that you were keeping things from me too?"

"We'll have to talk about that, Amanda. A telephone call is not ideal. We should meet . . ."

"That means you do know something. What is it?"

"I can't be sure of anything at the moment. When I am, I will tell you."

"But what are your *suspicions?* You're good at those."

"I can honestly say that I suspect that Henry did not murder Connie Richmond."

"Then who did?"

"I don't know."

"Do you think the woman could have killed herself?"

"She was bound and gagged. They found Henry's handkerchief in her mouth."

"I wish I'd never given them to him. I hope you're not so careless with yours."

"That's nothing to do with events as they stand. Our concentration must be on Henry and the death of Connie Richmond."

"What will they do if he's found guilty?"

"He won't be. I will make sure of that."

"I don't know how you can be so certain, Sidney. A man can be rash. Henry could be lying. He's lied to me so much in the past. And that woman was very strange. Who knows what they got up to? Perhaps they planned it together and Henry has framed himself to get out of being married to me. Perhaps she isn't really dead? Are the police sure the body is that of Connie Richmond?"

"They are, Amanda. Don't get in a state about all of this."

"What else do you expect me to do?"

"Be as sensible as you can."

"I've already done that. I've found Henry the best lawyer in London. I know when I think about it properly that he is unlikely to have killed that woman. He's too weak. But he doesn't help his cause by being so evasive and then by lying. Perhaps the only murder he's committed is the one to his own marriage."

Half an hour later, Alec Chambers phoned in a fury. He had just listened to the news on the radio. Had Sidney heard? The MCC had selected their tour party to South Africa and had left out Basil D'Oliveira.

Sidney did not welcome the distraction and was not in the mood to discuss the matter, but at least all he had to do was listen patiently as his father ranted about the injustice. "There may be good cricketing reasons. Colin Milburn's not going either. But this is a craven decision, Sidney. It's not wanting to cause any political trouble; sucking up to the South Africans when we should be telling them that we can pick whoever we like. How can we call it progress if all we do is change from judging a man by the colour of his tie to the colour of his skin? We cannot base our morality on convenience or the fear of offence. We have to select our team on the basis of form alone. Dolly's 158 at the Oval was masterly, was it not? We were *there*, Sidney. Did the selectors not see the same game as us? A man cannot be judged by appearance or upbringing but by what he has done. As I said, *form*. That's the only thing that matters."

Now Hildegard called her husband to the kitchen table. Anna was refusing to finish her fish fingers and she wasn't going to be given any pudding until she had done so.

"Think of the children in Biafra," Sidney cajoled.

"I'm not in Biafra," his daughter replied.

"Then eat what you can, my darling."

"Don't spoil her," Hildegard warned.

Anna was adamant. "I don't like this."

Sidney leaned forward. "All right. I'll have them. Yum, yum, yum. Then I can have all your pudding too."

"Don't, Daddy. That's not fair."

"Oh it *is* fair; fish fingers, yum, yum yum. Chocolate pudding and ice cream, yum yum yum. Let me count to three . . . one . . . two . . . th . . . th . . . th . . . th . . .?"

Sidney pretended to have an unstoppable stutter and began to dance round the room, unable to say the word "three".

Anna tried to look cross but then laughed, obeyed and finished up her plate.

"That's my girl."

"Do you realise how irritating this is?" Hildegard asked.

Her husband knew that the next day would present an even greater challenge. He would have to go and see Henry in custody. He should also help Amanda in any way he could. That would be the charitable thing to do. There was no friendship without loyalty.

Having moved through the stages of refutation, discovery, humiliation and further denial, Henry Richmond cut a tired figure at the station. He had taken off his jacket, there were sweat stains under his armpits and his thinning hair needed a good comb. All his worldly concerns had simplified into when he could possibly leave police custody.

"Have you told them everything?" Sidney asked.

"It depends what you mean by 'everything'. I have explained all that is relevant."

"That may not be for you to decide, Henry."

"I don't know what they want."

"I think that is fairly straightforward, as I am sure you know. They need to find a way of explaining Connie's death."

"I can't do that. I wasn't there at the time."

"But you were possibly the last person to see her alive."

"Other than her killer, Sidney."

"You think she was murdered? Who would want to do a thing like that?"

"I don't know. I can't be sure. I have been thinking of all the things Connie said to me on that last day."

163

"What did you argue about?"

"You know we had a fight?"

"I know more than you think I do, Henry. Was it about whether you and Amanda were going to have children?"

"We're not."

"That is not the answer to my question. Let me ask another. This is more direct, I'm afraid. Was it about Connie's abortion?"

"Your father must have told you. That would be a breach of confidentiality."

"The least of your concerns, Henry . . ."

"It was a long time ago."

"Not in Connie's memory."

"I think it was her seeing the Biafran children on television; their suffering. She imagined her own; the loss and the waste. That was what she said. We could have had a child, and we didn't."

"Did you pressure her into having an abortion?"

"I know the Church doesn't approve of such things."

"We don't," Sidney replied, simply. Now was not the time for moral ambiguity. "But we do try to understand human behaviour and how people make mistakes. Sometimes there are mitigating circumstances, the health of the mother being important."

"And that, I hope, includes her mental health."

"It does. It also depends on when the procedure is carried out."

"When life begins? I would imagine you considered that being the moment of conception."

"The views of the Church and the laws of the land do not always work in tandem; but when both are disobeyed there are consequences in this life and the next."

"You believe that?"

"We must all account for our actions. It is often just a matter of when."

Henry reached for a glass of water. He said that it was impossible to rationalise or justify impetuous decisions. "I don't know if either of us knew what we were doing at the time. Connie was so young, she was only just seventeen, and we both panicked. I was scared and I couldn't promise anything by way of marriage and respectability."

"You could. But you didn't want to."

"I suppose so. She wasn't 'the right sort of girl', I know. That was very cowardly of me. I should have gone ahead and loved her. Connie was frightened she would lose her job. She had to keep on working for the money and her family back in County Clare. Then, after the abortion, she had a nervous breakdown. She was never really right again. I wanted her to go home, back to Ireland, but she said she could never do that. I tried to pay for her to get better, offered to cover her wages if Mr Lowe kept her job open, but in the end Connie said the only thing that would heal her was marriage. So I tried that, and she was better for a while. Then she said she wanted children to make up for what we had done, a new life for old, but it didn't work out for us, her insides were damaged, and then things got

165

so bad I was sure we were making it worse for each other."

"So you divorced."

"I've told you the story before, the last time I was in trouble."

"And then you sent her to Chettisham?"

"She's been there for over ten years. I didn't think she ever wanted to leave. I even thought she was happy, but as soon as she found out about Amanda things changed. She could not accept that there was another Mrs Richmond. She kept saying Amanda was an imposter, as if she was a rival claimant to the monarchy or something. I could calm her down often enough but then she started to become obsessed about the child. She kept threatening to write to Amanda. I knew I couldn't allow that. One more secret would have endangered my whole marriage. I begged Connie not to write but she wasn't having any of it."

"And that was why you argued?"

"I didn't kill her, Sidney."

"I don't think you did. But you have to tell the absolute truth."

"Connie said that if she couldn't write she would punish me in other ways. I asked her what she meant and she just smiled."

"Are you suggesting that she has committed suicide and deliberately made it look like murder?"

"I am."

"She tied herself up?"

"She knew how to do that. She was always good with knots. Her fingers were so dexterous. There was no note, but the handkerchief is a deliberate touch. It was Connie's final act of revenge. I'm sure of it now."

"Your certainty doesn't make much of a difference, I'm afraid. It's convincing Geordie Keating that matters."

"Have you spoken to Amanda?" Henry asked, now more concerned about his wife than the police investigation. "Is she very angry with me?"

"I fear so."

"Will you stick up for me?"

"I am happy, as always, Henry, to support your marriage. That is what I pledged at your service of blessing and I wouldn't be much of a priest if I didn't keep my promises. But you must tell her what you have told me."

"I'm frightened of losing her."

"Then you must say that too."

"Is honesty the secret?"

"Not always, I fear, especially when our feelings change or are misleading."

"I'm not sure Amanda's ever loved me."

"That's not true."

"She thinks I'm still in love with Connie."

"And are you?" Sidney asked.

"No. I can't be. But the guilt was so strong."

"'Was'. Has her death come as a relief?"

"I don't mind admitting that it has. But that doesn't make me a killer."

"You must be careful what you say."

"That's what I've been doing and it's got me into all this trouble. I was trying to protect people from the truth. I didn't want to hurt Amanda and now everything's far worse than I could ever have imagined. But I couldn't just abandon Connie. That would have been a horrible thing to do."

"You divorced her."

"And I still feel guilty about that."

"Do you think you ever recovered?" Sidney asked.

"Me?"

"Yes. I am asking about you, Henry."

"Perhaps not. I knew I would always feel bound to her. And I knew Connie loved me. That has been the trouble with Amanda, I feel. I've always thought that she preferred you to me."

"You're wrong. She loves you."

"How can you be sure? Has she told you?"

This was not a subject Sidney wanted to discuss in detail. "Amanda and I are friends, Henry. We have known each other a long time. That is all. And we are both married to other people whom we love."

"You've been lucky with Hildegard."

"And you have found Amanda."

"It doesn't feel like that. It seems I have lost her."

"Her fury is a sign of love, you know . . ." said Sidney.

"Fury? Is that what she feels?"

"I'm afraid so. We have a lot of work to do, Henry, and it's probably more than either of us realise."

After Sidney had told Geordie about Henry Richmond's theory, the two men drove out to the crime scene on the fens. It was an intensely still August day with so few people out in the open landscape that the countryside felt as if it had been abandoned. The hay bales were stacked in the edges of the fields and the water on the surface of the reservoir hardly moved. There was that sickly-sweet late-summer fenland smell that combined meadowsweet, nettles, honey and cowpat.

Sidney thought he could hear the *crex crex* of a corncrake but couldn't be sure. It might have been warning him of unspecified danger. A buzzard hovered over them, high and in the distance, waiting for prey.

The pathologist had confirmed that Connie Richmond's death was caused by drowning. "There's a blow to the skull and she's been bound and gagged," Geordie reported, "but there are anomalies about both. The first is that the blow on the side of her head would not have been enough to knock her out."

"Perhaps it was caused by Henry Richmond earlier in the day. He has admitted to a scuffle."

"And that's about all he's prepared to confess. Next time, Sidney, perhaps you could advise him not to start his story with a lie."

"I assume, Geordie, that you have frightened him sufficiently to make sure that there never is a 'next time'."

"The other thing is that her wrists were bound in front of her in a position from which she could easily have wriggled free."

"Is there any evidence that she was held under water?" Sidney asked.

"There's no pressure on the chest; no markings round the neck; and no movement around the knots. In fact there's no sign of a struggle at all."

"So to prove Henry's theory she would have had to have sat by the side of the reservoir, tied her feet together, put the handkerchief in her mouth, then knotted her arms in front of her and slipped into the water as she lost consciousness. It seems an incredibly elaborate plan."

"All to frame her husband," said Geordie. "She probably thought it was worth it. There's no sign of any overdose either so no giveaway sedation for us to discover."

"And she deliberately provoked a fight in order to steal his handkerchief."

"That may just have been a bit of fortune."

"No, I think it gave her the courage to think she could get away with it, as well as the opportunity. Do you believe all this?"

"I am beginning to think that way, Sidney."

"And so do you think there's a chance Henry will get off?"

"He will if he's innocent. The pathologist is pretty sure that the death happened in the late afternoon. In other words, a good few hours after Henry had left. He was back at a concert in London with Amanda at the time."

"And she will vouch for him?"

"Reluctantly. I don't think she's in much of a mood to defend him, but she won't lie."

"That's one thing about Amanda. She's not one to hide her feelings."

Connie's room at the psychiatric hospital was not as spartan as Sidney and Geordie had been expecting. There was a single bed, a lamp and bedside table together with a worn sofa. What took the attention was the desk. It looked like a seamstress's work table with its Singer sewing machine, baskets of thread and material, scissors, tape measure, needles and pins. It was clear that no one had worried about the patient harming herself.

In the drawers were notebooks and sketchpads, drawings of wedding dresses and newspaper cuttings that included Connie's wedding announcement (but not Henry Richmond's subsequent union with Amanda). The wardrobe contained outfits from the 1950s and a bookcase featured a host of pulp fiction and romantic adventure.

Dr Evans assured them that Henry had never been present in his former wife's room, but he couldn't remember her carrying a handbag when she had left for her walk. She was, however, wearing a light jacket over her summer dress in case it got chilly, and the pockets could well have contained pre-cut lengths of string. Her "murder" was quite a far-fetched thing to have staged but, he admitted, desperation carried its own logic.

After a visit from the most expensive lawyer in London, Henry Richmond was bailed for £150, pending further enquiries. It was deemed likely that he would escape

171

without charge. Dealing with his second wife was, however, a more complicated matter.

"She thinks there will always be more to discover," he explained to Sidney over a large whisky at the Lansdowne Club. "She says she can't ever trust me and will never be completely sure I didn't kill my wife; or at least drive her to her own death."

"Amanda is your wife. Did you tell her?"

"About what?"

"The lost child."

"I am not sure she believed me."

"I think she always suspected there was something wrong."

"I knew this would happen if I told her anything more about the past. It's why I didn't."

"Timing matters, Henry."

"She's gone away for a few days to think about what she's going to do. She won't tell me where. I have no idea where she is. I am in total limbo."

"Perhaps we all need to consider the consequences of our actions."

"Amanda's left you a note. She says you will know where she has gone and will tell her the right thing to do."

"I'm not sure about that."

"Will you go and see her, Sidney, wherever she is?"

"It's not that straightforward. I'll have to ask Hildegard. I can't go to see Amanda unless she thinks it's a good idea."

"You're a kind man."

"No, I am very flawed," Sidney replied. "I can assure you of that. I just try to make people aware of my failings before it's too late."

Back home, he read his friend's note.

You will know where I have gone. Please don't worry. A.

For a moment Sidney thought Amanda might have done something extreme, such as fly to Biafra in search of a child, but then he remembered her telling him about her happiest memory as a child on holiday on the island of Skye. It had been a day with strong winds and dark skies, the barking of dogs, the bleating of sheep, the collapse of telephone wires — with no boat daring to go out to sea, and everyone stuck inside.

He could hear her voice saying, "No one thought we would ever go out again, but then the dark clouds moved across the Cuillins and the sun came through the clouds and light darted over the mountains. The wind was stilled and we were free and I felt such happiness that the darkness had passed. I often think that if I ever go back there then the same thing will happen, that the clouds will vanish and the wind will be still but fresh, and the dogs will stop barking, and the light on the mountains will be sharp and clear, even if it's only for a short time. Do you understand, Sidney?"

"Will you go and see her?" Hildegard asked.

"If she is in Skye then it's a very long way. I don't know if the old Morris Minor can cope."

"I think you should go."

"I'm not sure it's appropriate. She has a husband."

"She'll listen to you. It would be an act of charity."

"Amanda's not one for pity."

"Perhaps because she has not truly known it."

"Would you mind if I went?" Sidney asked.

"I don't think it would be a good thing if I stopped you."

"That's not the same as approval."

"I know you love me."

"I do, Hildegard, believe me, more than anything."

"Even if you are not always so good at showing it. But I will not become the nervous woman I do not want to be. We trust each other."

"We do."

"Then you must go if you want to."

"Do you want me to go?"

"That is different, *mein Lieber*. The trouble with Amanda is that you are the only person she believes; and now you will prove it all over again."

"I don't have to go."

"You do."

"I won't if you tell me not to."

"I would never do that. You must do what you think best. Do not worry. Anna and I will still be here when you return. So go. Behave well."

After he had driven for three hours up the A1, stopped for petrol, a cup of tea and a baked potato at Scotch Corner, Sidney began to have reservations about the trip. It was going to take for ever. What on earth was he doing leaving his wife, his child, his friends, his parishioners, his job and his life?

He stayed at a hotel just south of Glencoe that was filled with eager beer-drinking climbers who planned to head on to Ben Nevis, and had an early night with a Michael Frayn novel he was too tired to start. The next morning he drove on to Fort William and the Kyle of Lochalsh and took the ferry across to the island just as the mist was beginning to clear over the Cuillins. He stopped in Broadford to acquire rations — milk, eggs, bread, cheese, ham, mince, potatoes and the all-important Talisker whisky — before heading on to a village which was, in his namesake Sydney Smith's words, "so far out of the way that it was actually twelve miles from a lemon".

He had ascertained that Amanda was in Elgol on the south-west of the island but did not know the exact cottage where she was staying. On enquiries, first down at the harbour and then at the little post office, he discovered that she had rented a place on the headland from a woman who used to work the telephone switchboard in a solicitor's office. It was famous for its sunsets, she said, and had a view straight out to Rum, Eigg and Soay that was both the end of Scotland and the beginning of a new world far out in the Atlantic.

Even though he was almost there, after what must have been a thirteen- or fourteen-hour drive, Sidney had to wait behind a herd of Highland cattle before making his way back up the hill. One of the cows in front of him pissed copiously just to ensure that her visitor had no romantic illusions about the scenery.

Sidney then stumbled as he stepped out of the car, his legs weakened by the journey and his senses unused to the proximity of ditches so close to the road.

He opened the gate to the cottage and Amanda heard its creak, coming out to ask him not to let the sheep into the garden before she told him anything else. She looked tired and thinner than he had remembered, and was dressed very simply in jeans, boots and the kind of jumper he had given to the jumble sale.

"I'm sorry," she said after giving him a welcoming but half-hearted kiss. Her voice sounded distant, as if Sidney still hadn't quite arrived.

"I've brought whisky," he said.

"I've already got some. I hoped you'd come. I even prayed."

"You were that desperate?"

"You're the only friend I can rely on."

"You look very well," Sidney lied.

"I know I don't. But I'm here. And I feel better."

"It must be the sea air."

"I've had to shop for outdoor clothing but it's hopeless these days; you either have to dress like a teenager or a granny. There's nothing in between. Not that I need expensive clothes any more. I think I'd rather live simply and like this."

Sidney took his suitcase from the car and Amanda showed him into the cottage. There were three bedrooms, a small kitchen, bathroom and a living room with an open hearth. A peat fire was burning, even though it was August. "I get so cold," said Amanda. "But it's cosy being alone."

"I hope I'm not disturbing you."

"Do you have news of Henry?"

"I don't think he will be prosecuted."

"Then I'm glad."

"He's worried. He thinks you're not coming back."

"I'm not," said Amanda. "Is that so very wrong?"

"You plan to live here?"

"No, Sidney, I'll return to London but not to Henry. I need time to think about my life. I want to live differently; to be alone. Have you been instructed to bring me home?"

"I have come to see you. That is all. My visit has no other purpose."

"I hope you can stay for a while. Does Hildegard mind?"

"Thank you for asking."

"I do love her, you know. I hope you realise how lucky you are in having her?"

"I am very fortunate."

"Even if it's hard sometimes to know what she really thinks. I suppose we all have that in a marriage. Only I wouldn't want her to disapprove. You would tell me if she did, wouldn't you?"

"I wouldn't be here if she was unhappy about it."

"I must write and thank her; although that seems an odd thing to do, I suppose. I don't really know how to behave any more. How long can you stay?"

"I'm not sure. I think a couple of days."

"You might as well, now you've travelled all this way. Would you like something to drink? There's food too. I haven't very much, though. I've got a little routine going. Cornflakes in the morning; soup, bread and cheese at lunchtime; an omelette at night. One of the farmers brings me milk and eggs. They're very kind here. Charitable. I've been thinking a lot about that."

"Living a simpler life."

"I don't know if I can abandon everything; but I think I have to live differently, Sidney. Perhaps charity only means something if you give away so much that your life is altered."

"You need to preserve a sense of yourself, Amanda. Perhaps your wealth is what makes you who you are."

"But what if I want to be someone else? Don't we all have enough? Everyone I know is so greedy and so frightened, so unwilling to make sacrifices. But that's what your faith is about, isn't it? Making sacrifices."

"I do think we often need to be judged less by what we say and more by what we do. Deeds, not words. The truest test of character is how we behave towards people who can do nothing for us."

"I don't think I can go back to London unless I have changed in some way. And Henry, well, there's too much to forgive. Do you know that he was spending so much on his first wife that he was starting to hide it from me? That's what I can't abide. The drip, drip, drip of his lies. Are you sure he didn't kill her?"

"I am. And Geordie thinks so too."

"Why did she hate him so much? Was it because of the child? Henry said he had told you about that. I hope he did. If he's lied about that as well . . ."

"No. He told me. I wondered if you had suspected something like it?"

"I think I always knew. It was why Henry was so anti-adoption. He didn't want to be reminded of it all. Not that he was the one who suffered. It was his wife who went through it all. He's been such a liar."

"I think he was trying to protect you."

"I am not a child, Sidney."

"I know that."

"But I can't see a way out. Sometimes so many things mount up in front of you that you don't know where you are. It's like being here on the island when the clouds come over and you can no longer see the view. It happens so fast."

"But there are also times when the sun shines through."

"You once said they were 'God's promises'."

"An old clergy friend told me that. Children like to hear it."

"One has to keep one's promises, I suppose."

"That is the idea."

"'For better, for worse . . .'"

"Unless everything becomes untenable, the situation changes so radically . . ."

"Which, in my case, it has, I think."

"No one would ever say that it's been easy for you."

"We've made promises to each other as well, Sidney, haven't we?"

"I'm not sure they were *promises* exactly."

"Always to be friends."

"I know, Amanda . . ."

"At least we should be able to keep that."

They went out for a walk on the headland before it was dark. The coastal path took them out towards the Cuillins. The air already had the feel of autumn. The berries in the rowan trees were turning from tangerine to scarlet; the swallows and house martins were searching for late-summer flies; the wind came on across the heather and thistle. It began to rain. Soon it would be night and then, in a few days' time, they would travel south back to their homes and, for Amanda, a future that was as uncertain as it had ever been. What will she make of her life now, Sidney wondered, and what place will I have in it?

The Return

It was a Tuesday in early September 1968, and Mrs Maguire had summoned Sidney to Grantchester. Rather than meeting at her house, she had requested a rendezvous at the Orchard Tea Rooms. This was odd, as she always disapproved of spending money on something that she could do perfectly well herself, and she hated waste. She also looked smarter than usual and, having been complimented on her appearance, she explained that she was wearing the woollen navy Windsmoor jacket her sister had left her. She had to look her best because something dramatic had happened.

"It's my Ronnie," she said. "He's come home."

This was news indeed. Mrs Maguire's husband had disappeared during the war. Everyone presumed that he had been "missing, presumed dead" but his "widow" was so hazy on the details that Sidney always had the slight suspicion that Ronnie Maguire was still alive. Perhaps he had found a girl in Singapore or South Africa (he had fought with the Cambridgeshire Regiment in the Far East) or he had returned to a mistress and second family back in England? A detailed conversation about the matter had never been encouraged.

"It's been twenty-five years. More than the time we were together. I don't know what to think. I thought he was dead. He just arrived on my doorstep with a suitcase."

"Have you asked him where he's been?"

"He's a bit cagey about all that. Tells me he can't remember everything but hopes it will all come out in time. He says it's taken him all these years to find a way home. I'm not sure I believe him."

"And he's staying with you?"

"I've put him in my sister's room. Even though it's been two years since she died, I've only just got used to being alone. It's very confusing to have a man about the house mucking it all up again."

"Is there anything you'd like me to do?"

Mrs Maguire was almost afraid to ask. "Could you pay us a visit? I'm not sure Ronnie's quite himself."

"Do you mean that you're not sure it's really him?"

"He's filled out. I suppose we all have. And he's redder and fuller around the face than he used to be. Breathless too. He was always such a fit man."

"I suppose it's age. None of us are getting any younger, Mrs M."

"I know that. But he used to be so handsome. I think he must have let himself go. But there's more . . ."

"Something alarming?"

"I'm not sure. He didn't recognise the brooch he gave me when we were courting. You know the one? I've told you about it."

It was eleven cultured pearls on a sprig of silver leaves. Mrs Maguire wore it on her best blouses.

"He also talked about a dance we went to in Great Yarmouth. I've never been there in my life. Do you think he might be confusing me with someone else?"

"That's possible. Memory can be fickle. But he is definitely your husband?" Sidney repeated.

"I'd like to think so," Mrs Maguire replied. "I do know my Ronnie. He's just not the man I'm used to. I don't know whether I'm angry or glad. I'm not sure how I'm supposed to behave."

"I suppose it might be a question of how much you're prepared to forgive," said Sidney. "When would you like me to come?"

Over a second pint in the Eagle that Thursday evening, Sidney asked Geordie how much he knew about the original disappearance. If Ronnie Maguire had been "missing, presumed dead" then the War Office would have written formally and his widow would be receiving a pension. However, if he were leading a double life somewhere, wouldn't the police get involved? Bigamy, as far as Sidney knew, was still illegal.

"But living in sin is not," said Geordie.

"And that's what he's been doing?"

"Sounds like it."

"He's also claiming to have lost a part of his memory."

"The convenient bit of his brain that means he doesn't have to face the music. Once a chancer, always a chancer."

"On the other hand, perhaps he had to forget things. I think he was a prisoner of war in Japan. People never like to talk about that."

"Well, he wasn't the only one, Sidney. Do you know what he does for a living?"

"I think he worked as an accountant. Mrs M once told me he was good with numbers. She never liked to go into details."

"Perhaps she knew all along that he wasn't dead? That might have been easier to tell people rather than the fact that he'd done a runner. Saves face."

"I wondered if you could look into the records for me; see if he has any convictions?"

"The criminal thing he's done is to leave his wife. Mrs Maguire's been unhappy for years, hasn't she?"

"She's a good woman, Geordie. She certainly looked after Leonard and me very well."

"Only saw one of you married."

"Well, Leonard's not the marrying kind."

"Sometimes I don't think Leonard's anything at all."

"He doesn't think about that kind of thing."

"Perhaps he makes up for those who think about it all the time."

"Speak for yourself, Geordie."

"I don't mean me. I'm beyond all that carry-on. And so, presumably, is Ronnie Maguire. What do you think he's after? Has his missus got any money? That's the usual line."

"Whatever it is, it's unsettled his wife. She's spent so long remembering him that I think she's built him up into a different person altogether."

Geordie finished his pint. "People change over twenty-five years. I know I have."

Sidney still had a half left. "Do you think Cathy would marry you if she met you now?" he asked.

"I doubt it. I'd marry her, though. Shall I get a top-up?"

"I'd better not. I should be getting back."

"What about you and Hildegard then?"

"I'd marry her today."

"You don't ever wonder what it would have been like if you hadn't met?"

Sidney pushed over his glass. "All right. Put another half in that." As Geordie stood up, he added: "Amanda would never have married me, if that's what you're getting at."

"I wasn't. You mentioned her name."

"You know that it was never on the cards. You were there at the time."

"Do you think she recognises that she made an almighty mistake?"

"Henry seemed a decent enough fellow before we realised how evasive he had been about his past. But we've all got history."

"I don't mean that. I mean not marrying you when she had the chance."

"Perhaps I wouldn't have married *her*."

"Give over, man. Everyone knew you were made for each other."

"But it hasn't turned out like that. And I'm very happy with what I've got, thank you very much."

Geordie went to the bar, paid for the round and returned with the conversation still in his mind. "Hildegard's a good woman, Sidney. No one else would have put up with you. I can't imagine any old wife letting her husband swan off to Scotland. She must either have complete faith in you or given up on you altogether."

"I hope it's the former. But I wasn't 'swanning', I'll have you know. I was persuading a friend to return to her husband."

"And did you succeed?"

"I fear not. Amanda wants a clean break and a new life. She has petitioned for divorce."

"At least that's easier to do these days. I suppose even if she *had* married you the same thing might have happened."

"Charming."

"That is only my opinion, mind."

"Fortunately that situation never arose. In any case, the present circumstances are entirely different; although one has to admit that Amanda's husband had a secret past just like Ronnie Maguire. We've talked about this before, Geordie. If you're determined not to tell people things, then you have no control over the moment of revelation when it comes. Or the consequences."

"Things seldom stay private for ever. I'll give you that."

"Perhaps that's why Ronnie's come back? To spit it all out."

"I've always been interested in the urge to confess, especially towards the end of a life." Geordie pulled one of Benson & Hedges's finest from its packet and lit up. "It must happen with you too . . ."

"People feel the need to make amends; to tidy things up before they go."

"But do you think, Sidney, that sometimes they do it because they feel that they haven't been given enough attention? They're almost annoyed no one has worked out what's been going on and they just want to show what they've done?"

"The confession as a type of vanity, you mean?"

"In criminal cases, yes. People like an audience, the interest taken in them. They are getting the limelight that they previously lacked. They're also intrigued by police procedure. If we get involved then it all becomes a show in which they are the star."

"Even if they are the villain. Like Milton's devil getting all the best lines or the baddie in a panto?"

"I suppose it *is* different with you."

"When people tell me things?" Sidney looked at his pint of beer as if it might provide the answer, took a hearty swig that drained the glass, and gave his reply. "I try to give people the benefit of the doubt and hope they are just wanting to put things right. It's dealing with your own shame. But that too can be a kind of selfishness."

"And do you think that's what Ronnie Maguire is doing?"

"I'll just have to ask him."

"You've got yourself involved?"

"It's Mrs Maguire, Geordie. When I think of all that she has done for me, I can hardly stand aside. I don't want to see her hurt. She's a proud woman; and although she has a confident look to the world, she's as scared as the rest of us underneath it all."

"You don't have to do it."

"She asked me. It's absolutely my duty, Geordie. If I don't help her, if I don't sit with her and alongside her when she has asked for my assistance, then what kind of Christian am I?"

Mrs Maguire thought it best if Sidney first met Ronnie over tea. She would bake both scones and one of her walnut specials; a cake that he had had to wait nearly two years to sample when she was working for him in the vicarage at Grantchester. Perhaps, Sidney wondered, the woman for whom Ronnie had left his wife was a terrible cook and now that her physical charms were waning he had resorted to Wife Number One for culinary comfort?

The tidiness of the thatched house, the aroma of baking, the Michaelmas daisies in the cottage garden at the front and the welcoming atmosphere would have made any Cambridge estate agent gasp. Sidney complimented his former employee on all that she had done and was greeted with the matter-of-fact reply: "I am not prejudiced, but I think cleanliness should come naturally."

Ronnie was waiting in the sitting room. Although fuller in the figure and prone to breathlessness, he had once been a handsome man and still possessed a firm handshake and a twinkle of mischief about the eyes. His thick grey hair and well-maintained beard made him look a little like a Van Dyck painting. He was not tall but carried himself with an air of assurance that was good for another two or three inches. He had also made an effort with his appearance: a navy-blue blazer with a crimson pocket handkerchief, grey flannel trousers and a Cromer Golf Club tie. Sidney noticed that his cufflinks matched his blazer buttons.

Mrs Maguire busied herself in the kitchen; setting out the scones and insisting that the tea take five minutes to brew properly. It gave the men time to introduce themselves. Sidney ventured that he was glad to meet a man he had heard so much about.

"I'm staying in her sister Gladys's old room while she works out what to do with me," Ronnie began.

"I think she will be quite cautious. She's always been careful of her reputation."

"Sylvia's frightened of people thinking badly of her. I remember how she always used to worry if she'd done something wrong."

"She likes to know what the rules are so she can follow them," said Sidney. "And she expects everyone else to do the same."

"She hated it at school if the teacher told her off for anything. We were in the same class when we started. It was 1906. Can you believe that? Things were so different when we were young."

"We used to buy sweets at Percy Noble's hut," said Mrs Maguire, coming in with the tea tray. "It was a tiny shop that sold newspapers, magazines, sweets, cigarettes and minerals, and, Saturday afternoons, cups of tea. Across the road was Smith's, the local carpenter's that doubled up as the undertaker; they still had the village stocks in a shed at the back."

"There was this one hot summer," Ronnie continued, "and a rick of clover and lucerne was set up in the field. It had been damp when they stacked it, but then it gradually heated up inside and burst into flame. It smelled like sweet coffee. I always used to feel sad at the end of summer because I had to go back to school, but as I got older I liked the misty autumn mornings, the flat-racing season, the smell of woodsmoke and beer by the fire. Do you remember, Sylvia, when we first went to the races? We played truant from school."

Mrs Maguire poured out the tea and handed round the scones. She did not need to ask either man whether he took milk or sugar. "It must have been a Saturday," she answered. "I never missed a day except when I had mumps."

"It was a Thursday, in fact, just before the Great War. We were twelve or thirteen. I remember it was after the suffragette threw herself under the king's horse, a couple of years before they switched the Derby to Newmarket. It must have been October. At any rate it was cold; I remember that. You had a new red scarf, Sylvia. We got the bus with my elder brother, looked at horses in the Birdcage and watched by the Ditch Mile in the Nursery. You remember?"

"Can't say I do."

"My brother teased you because one of the horses was called Greedy Girl. You liked White Star. Frank put money on Radway. He was dead two years later. I think it must have been the last time he went to the races."

"You must have gone with someone else, Ronnie."

"It was with you, Sylvia, I promise."

"I think you must have been with Nancy Spooner."

"I didn't. I promise. It was you."

Mrs Maguire checked that no one needed more tea. "Nancy Spooner. I had trouble seeing that one off, Sidney, I can tell you. I remember the dance when she made a play for you, Ronnie."

"Which one was that?"

"The one where she kicked me on the back of the leg in the middle of the Gay Gordons and you didn't believe me."

"I don't remember that."

"I had to have words with her after. You didn't even notice."

"I didn't need to if you took care of it, Sylvie."

"Sylvia. Don't you Sylvie me, Ronnie Maguire. You're supposed to be on your best behaviour."

"I seem to remember you didn't mind when I wasn't."

"Not in front of the vicar . . ."

"He's not a vicar any more. He's an archdeacon; a very venerable man. That's his title, you know. The *Venerable* Sidney Chambers, Archdeacon of Ely."

"It really doesn't matter . . ." Sidney interrupted.

"All the more reason for you to mind your Ps and Qs, Ronnie Maguire."

Despite the confusion over their respective memories, Sidney was reassured that the couple were sufficiently reunited to tease and argue, even if there was much to sort out.

"You mentioned the flat-racing season, Mr Maguire," he said. "Do you know, in all my time as a priest in East Anglia, I've never been to the racecourse at Newmarket?"

"Then you must go."

"I always seem too busy; and I've never quite known who to ask."

"Why don't you ask me? I'm there all the time."

"What are you doing, Sidney?" Mrs Maguire complained. "Are you planning on taking my husband away from me as soon as he's got home?"

"You could always come with us," said Ronnie.

"I've never been a gambler."

"Never too late to start, Sylvia."

"I've taken a big enough gamble letting you back into my house, Ronnie Maguire. Don't expect me to do any more."

As soon as he had gathered up speed on his bicycle and was racing away from Grantchester, in top gear and glad to be returning home at last, Sidney was dismayed to be flagged down by Barbara Wilkinson as she approached her own house with a large bag of shopping. "I see you've no time to visit me these days," she said.

Sidney dismounted. "I am sorry, Mrs Wilkinson, but I am no longer of this parish."

"Out of sight, out of mind, eh? I see you only turn up when there's trouble."

"That's not true."

"Nothing so mundane as visiting a scarlet woman whose son is in prison."

Danny Wilkinson was just beginning the second year of his life sentence; an appeal on the grounds of temporary insanity had been rejected. "You can imagine that my family would take a dim view of that."

"You don't have to tell them."

"You are a very dangerous woman."

"As soon as the show's over, you're off quicker than Ronnie Maguire. I'm surprised you're back so fast. He's left it twenty-five years."

"The situation is altogether different. They are married to each other. We are acquaintances."

"I will tell you something for nothing. That is not the man I remember as Ronnie Maguire."

"People change over time."

"Not as much as that. He's smaller, he's redder and he's much rounder."

"Perhaps he's shrunk with age?"

"If it is him, he's done something very peculiar; although I wouldn't put it past him. He's as crooked as a bag of fish-hooks, that one."

Sidney didn't want to prolong the conversation or point out that this was quite a statement from the mother of a murderer with a wayward sense of the law, and it made him wonder whether those who were quick to judgement (Mrs Maguire *inter alia*) only did so in order to prevent an attack on themselves. They were like unfancied boxers aiming for a first-round knockout because they didn't have any defence.

"It can't be the money," Barbara Wilkinson continued, "as Sylvia Maguire's as poor as a church mouse. Maybe he's after her house?"

"Or perhaps," said Sidney, helplessly, "he wants to make good the mistakes of his past."

On Monday 16th September Sidney's father phoned to discuss an important sporting matter. The Warwickshire cricketer Tom Cartwright had failed a fitness test and pulled out of the England tour with a shoulder injury. The selectors had called up Basil D'Oliveira as a replacement.

"At last they've seen sense. As you know, they should have picked him in the first place."

"But won't the South Africans cancel their invitation?"

"It's possible. But they did say, I think, that they would welcome any team that has been selected purely on the grounds of cricketing ability . . ."

"I like the 'purely'."

"They didn't put it exactly like that. But this should not become a political problem. It's a cricketing matter. Although it's a curious irony, isn't it, that a coloured man should have to leave one nation and play for another in order to return to his birthplace?"

Sidney thought about the question of shifting identity, put down the receiver and was just about to return to the paperwork on his desk when he heard Anna call. She wanted tucking in and a bedtime story.

They read Beatrix Potter's *The Tale of Jemima Puddle-Duck* in which a collie-dog and two puppies

194

prevented the heroine from being eaten by a fox in disguise. When they had finished, Anna looked serious and told her father what had happened during the day.

"Mummy lost Byron."

"What?"

"He ran away. I was scared, Daddy. We were calling and calling and he wouldn't come back."

"Where did you go?"

"By the river. It was all misty and dark. Then it got cold. I didn't like it. Mummy was scared too but she pretended she wasn't. We both did. I wish you had been there. Byron knows what to do when you're there."

Hildegard appeared in the doorway to explain what had happened. "You weren't home, Sidney, so I had to walk him. I was distracted, I admit. I only had twenty minutes before my teaching. As you know, *mein Lieber,* Byron doesn't respond to me as he does to you . . ."

"Obedience has never been his strong point, I'm afraid."

"He wouldn't come at all, Daddy."

Hildegard turned to her daughter. "*Aber letztendlich ist er zu uns zurückgekommen, nicht wahr, meine Kleine?*"

She then explained to Sidney that an unworried Byron had ambled back as if nothing had happened some half an hour later. "It was not good, Sidney. I didn't know what to say or how to discipline him. You said you would be home and I was late for the next lesson."

Anna looked at her father. "You won't run away like Byron did, will you, Daddy?"

"Of course not, darling; now tuck yourself in."

"I didn't like it when you were in Scotland."

"I know."

"You won't go there again, will you?"

"I don't think so."

"*Promise* me you won't."

"I promise I won't go without you. Now snuggle down."

"Honestly," said Hildegard when husband and wife were alone at last. "For Byron to go off like that without any warning. I could have killed him."

"I'm glad you didn't."

"You are fortunate. If you'd been there I might have attacked you instead."

"Then I'm relieved to have been absent. Perhaps that's what Ronnie Maguire was doing; avoiding his wife so often that it became a habit and then he never went back."

"Don't start getting ideas."

"Don't worry, Hildegard. I know I wouldn't last five minutes without you."

His wife thought briefly before her response. "Five minutes you would manage; five weeks is possible. Five years, never."

The trip to Newmarket took place on Thursday 17th October. Sidney picked out an old three-piece suit that had been spared by the moths and a brown rabbit-felt trilby that he thought would be just the ticket for a day at the races. Ronnie was dressed up to the nines in a Donegal tweed sports jacket with a mustard-yellow jumper, a Tattersall shirt and dark-green tie that matched his corduroy trousers.

The two men visited the paddock before the first race to have a look at the horses for impressive muscle tone, shiny coats and bright eyes. The going was good. Ronnie told Sidney they had to choose horses that were bred to stay, often keeping that extra reserve in the locker, ready to spark on the day.

Both men bet on Fortune's Hope at 9–2 in the Chesterton Maiden Stakes, with Ronnie professing inside knowledge. "Humphrey Cottrill, who bred and still owns him, thinks the world of this colt."

"How do you decide who to back?" Sidney enquired.

"I look at the owners, the jockeys and then the horses themselves. Peter O'Sullevan and Jim Joel know their stuff and if Charlie Elliott or Lester Piggott's riding then I'll check the form. I do the basics on the two-year plates and gilts and try not to be greedy. You've got to cover yourself in case things don't work out . . ."

"And does that apply to life in general?" Sidney asked before detecting a flash of frustration in Ronnie's response and regretted that he had raised the subject so early in the day.

"Let's not go into that now. Sometimes a man is led astray. I don't suppose you'd know about that."

"Officially not . . ."

"But unofficially?"

"No one has led an exemplary life, Ronnie. Not even a priest."

"I'm not too keen to explain myself, as you can probably imagine. When you sum it all up it doesn't look too good. But wait, the bell's gone and the horses are off to the start. Let's watch."

They stood at the edge of the stand near the bookmakers so they would be quick to collect their winnings and bet again but, despite being the favourite, Fortune's Hope wasn't even placed, outran by West Partisan, Real Estate and Hickleton.

"I see you don't have God on your side," Ronnie observed.

"Neither Fortune nor Hope, it seems."

"Let's have a drink and another look at the horses. We've got a good twenty minutes until the next."

Sidney was still trying to get the hang of the betting but was intrigued that, as in cricket, so much of it was taken up with the question of *form*. He thought of his father, and how much he would enjoy Newmarket. It would certainly have cheered him up a bit after all his anger and frustration with the cricketing authorities. England's tour to South Africa had now been cancelled and the aftershock was still being felt as recriminations flew. A day at the races would have taken his mind off it all.

A bookmaker was offering tempting odds on an older horse with a good reputation, saying that he had too much class to be done, but Ronnie wasn't having any of it, backing a younger, more promising alternative, telling Sidney, "Those that burn twice as bright burn half as long." Racing, like life, was about taking calculated risks, he said. "It's like the old cliché, Sidney.

If you only do what you've always done you can only get what you've always got."

"And is that what makes you a risk-taker?" Sidney asked.

"I always thought I could lead a better life," Ronnie replied. "But I suppose I was wrong."

"We can't ever predict how things will turn out. The important thing is to try and behave decently."

"Well, I certainly failed at that."

"I know you may not want to talk about it."

"We all have to face the music some day. I'm just sorry I didn't at the time."

"You got someone else to do it for you?"

"Her sister. I asked her to tell Sylvia I wasn't dead, but I wasn't coming back either. I was a coward."

"Perhaps you were frightened of being caught in two minds."

"Let's watch the race, Sidney. All in good time."

Ronnie put a pound on Profit Sharing at 10–1 in the two thirty, while Sidney went for Harry Lauder at 100–8 in honour of his Scottish grandfather, but they had no more luck than they had had before and Sidney was worried about the extent of his losses. How much was he prepared to gamble in a single afternoon? If he lost more than a pound Hildegard would be furious.

The same thing happened in the three o'clock. Sidney put half a crown on Motet at 100–8 in a little musical tribute to his wife, despite Ronnie telling him that betting on a horse just because you liked its name could only lead to disaster. He was tempted to retort that experience didn't seem to be doing much good either as his friend's decision to go for Samivel at 100–6 had been equally unfortunate.

"What's happening?" he asked. "All these horses were well fancied and yet we've lost every time."

"Don't worry, Sidney, our luck will change. You're enjoying yourself, aren't you?"

"Is it always like this? Whatever happened to beginner's luck?"

"Let's go with the nap. Riboccare is 7–2 in the Jockey Club Cup. He's a neat little colt and he'll run two stone better with Lester Piggott on him. Put ten shillings on. I'll pay you back if you lose."

"Don't be silly."

"Trust me, Sidney. I'll put it on for you."

"There's no need for that."

"It's all right. My treat. You'll get almost two pounds back. Let me do it now in case they shorten the odds. I won't be a jiffy."

Ronnie was as good as his word, and the horse ran in by a comfortable half-length, digging in hard towards the finish, bursting past Fortissimo, the previous year's winner, a furlong out.

"It's not just the winning that matters," Ronnie explained. "It's that you suspend your life. When you're at the races there's only one thing to think about. The rest of the world disappears and you lose yourself in the sound of the hooves on the track, the flashes of colour, the speed and the movement. You put everything into the horse you've chosen."

Sidney let him talk. He knew that the secret of having a proper conversation with a man was to have it while pretending to do something else. Like watching cricket with his father, flat-racing was a distraction that allowed serious discussion to feel almost incidental.

"Alice keeps horses," Ronnie said out of nowhere. "I think that's why we got on so well. There was so much we didn't have to explain to each other. We were both brought up on farms."

"How did you meet her?"

"I spent the first year of the war with the Cambridgeshire Regiment on defence duties on the Norfolk coast. We were at Stiffkey on the edge of the salt marshes. Everything that first winter froze solid. It was impossible to get warm. That's when I met her. It was through her brother John. He was in the same battalion. She was only twenty. She had the longest, curliest red hair you ever saw. Green eyes like she belonged to the land, a soft voice and a way of looking that wouldn't let you go. She worked on a stud farm and exercised the horses every day. Sometimes I caught a glimpse as we were doing our own manoeuvres and I couldn't concentrate on anything at all. To see her ride was something I can't describe. John noticed and he teased me rotten. We were on defensive duties, trying to camouflage some double-decker buses.

"'I don't know why you're doing all this,' he said, 'you've got no defence at all.' As soon as I had some leave Alice took me to one of the last of the races at Fakenham. It was just before they had to stop because of the war. She knew her horses, I'll tell you that. I remember we made nearly three guineas. Well, you can imagine what happened."

"You didn't say you were already married?"

"I don't think she knows to this day."

"How on earth did you keep it a secret? You must be a lot older than her. Didn't she ask?"

"I don't know, Sidney. I must have given her some of the old flannel. I didn't intend to do so but the war changed everything. It was a bit of company while there wasn't much going on. I thought the Cambridgeshire Regiment was more like the Home Guard. First we were in Norfolk, then Scotland and then Cheshire. But after Japan came in it all went black. We were sent out to Singapore and then up-country to reinforce the 15th Indian Brigade at Batu Pahat. It was a rum time. We lost so many men. In the end we had to surrender and we became Japanese prisoners of war. The one person who helped me survive was Alice's brother, John. I don't know how we got through it all but somehow we did, and when we got back to England I knew I wasn't ready to go home. I didn't even know what home was any more. I couldn't imagine it. I just stayed with John in Holt, near Stiffkey, where it all began. Then I saw Alice again and couldn't leave her. She had a child by then, my child, a little boy. He was called Frank after my brother. Then we had two more very quickly and I could hardly go back to Sylvia after that. I didn't want a confrontation. It was best to say I was missing, presumed dead."

"And you were happy?"

"For a long time."

"Does Alice know you're in Grantchester now?"

"I don't think she cares too much about my whereabouts at the moment."

"You left under a cloud?"

"I made a mess of things, Sidney. Money, really. It wasn't another woman or anything like that. I suppose I couldn't settle. But let's not spoil the day. There's another race and our luck's turned. We have to take advantage of fortune when it comes. I can't tell you everything at once. It's been too long a life."

Emboldened by his victory in the previous race, and having just witnessed horse and rider in perfect rhythm, Sidney backed Lester Piggott with an each-way bet on Grey Portal at 100–30. The horse came third with Ronnie triumphing once more with Zarco, at 13–8, winning by six lengths and a short head.

"I don't want to tell Sylvia too much about all this," said Ronnie. "I wouldn't want her to think any the worse of me. You know how judgemental she can be."

"She has much to criticise."

"I am aware of that. But she wouldn't like it. I think she'd rather not know. She likes to be in control of things."

"She's always wanted the first and last word."

"And I'm minded to let her have them."

Ronnie placed a pound on the favourite, Spring Glory, in the Highflyer Stakes at 7–4 ('He beat Jacobus by five lengths at York. This is a dead cert, I'm telling you') whereas a sentimental Sidney, mindful of the time of year, put half a crown on Advent at 100–6.

Neither horse was placed and both men ended up down on the day. Despite the revealing and informative nature of the conversation, Sidney could not help but feel that his first day betting at the races was probably going to be his last.

The next week was spent on routine tasks in Ely: the preparations for Christmas, visiting the sick and learning a modern musical accompaniment to the liturgy that was pitched at attracting young pilgrims.

The news from Grantchester was sparse. Dr Robinson had been called in to check on Ronnie Maguire's wheezing chest, Barbara Wilkinson had written one of her desperate letters (in turquoise ink) to ask if Sidney had done anything about "the imposter" and Malcolm Mitchell telephoned to say that he had been offered the incumbency of St Bride's Church, Fleet Street. This was the journalists' church and Malcolm was beside himself with happiness. It could not have been more perfect, he said. He would now be able to live properly with Helena, their weekly commuting could cease and they could begin to think about starting a family. He was sure that this had been the result of Sidney "putting in a word" and wanted to thank him for the kindest thing anyone had ever done for him.

The gratitude was cheering and Sidney was in a particularly good mood as his wife prepared the first casserole of the autumn. He picked up a spoon, tasted the sauce, and added a little paprika. Hildegard asked him what on earth he was doing.

"I am savouring the stew of destiny with the spice of fate."

"Leave it alone, Sidney. Nothing is safe when you are near. Not even an innocent *Eintopf*."

"Suspect everything! Leave nothing to chance!" Sidney joked, wrapping his right arm round her waist.

"But trust your wife," she replied, giving him a little kiss on the lips. "That's the point of marriage. It should be the one part of your life where there is no doubt. You must know that by now."

Sidney stepped back to open a bottle of wine. "But what if my beloved alters her personality before my very eyes?"

"Don't be ridiculous."

"People are changed by marriage."

Hildegard began to make the dumplings. "I think we're supposed to improve each other. That's what it says in the *Church Times*."

"I didn't know you read it."

"I have a look and try to understand what you are thinking."

"I'm not sure you'll find it helpful. But that doesn't matter. We may well become different people through marriage but the question is — how much of our original selves remain? Do you still feel German, for example, or have you lived here long enough for that no longer to be an issue?"

"My nationality will never leave me. It is who I am. That's why I want to take Anna next summer; to show her that she can feel at home there too."

"Do you think you would feel more yourself if you went back?"

"And we lived there? I don't know, Sidney. I miss the language, the people and the food. I miss the white *Spargel* in the spring; the raisin bread and the Christmas markets. I miss the natural world, the forests and the feeling of being at home. But I'm also happy here with you. It is possible to belong to more than one country."

Sidney laid the table as Byron nosed around him, hoping for random scraps of food.

"My father keeps banging on about the D'Oliveira case; especially now the South African tour's been cancelled. I wonder how much we are the products of our nation and whether we can escape the unpalatable past to become different people? Can one ever become something other than oneself? I know that this is the heart of the Christian message, that we shall all be changed, but isn't there a part of us that remains immutable? I mean, take Ronnie. Even though he's clearly married someone else, is he still Mrs Maguire's husband? There's been no divorce."

"And they were married in the sight of God?"

"They were. But he has broken his vows."

"He's the same man."

"But is he? That's what I have to find out."

"And what of Mrs Maguire?" Hildegard asked as she rolled her dough into balls for the dumplings. "What does she want? Why did she ask you to meet them both? You think it was to have a good look at him; but what if she also wanted you to look at her, to check that she wasn't giving away too much too soon? Do you not think you might have been concentrating too much on the man rather than the woman?"

"I think I can look at things through her eyes."

"But what about seeing her through your own?" Hildegard was about to rest her hand on Sidney's shoulder but stopped when she realised it would leave a floury mark on his cassock. "Perhaps I should go and see her instead of you? This may need a woman's point of view."

"That's not a bad idea . . ."

"I haven't been back to Grantchester for over a year. I could look in on Malcolm and congratulate him on his new job."

"He'd like that."

"I might even take Anna and Byron."

"Provided you don't lose him again."

"He is familiar with the Meadows. I think we'll be all right. And, who knows, Mrs Maguire might even tell me a little more than she has told you? Woman to woman."

"If you could, I'd be grateful."

"I will listen to her very carefully." Hildegard smiled. "But I promise not to be a better detective than you."

"It's not a competition, my darling."

"Sidney, *mein Lieber*, I never said that it was."

The following Thursday, Sidney was emerging from Jesus Lane after a tedious meeting at Westcott House about the training of ordinands in "the modern world" when he saw Ronnie Maguire going into the bookie's. He appeared to have lost weight and his walk was more hesitant than it had been only a few weeks previously. Sidney even wondered if he might have had a fall. There was certainly less confidence about him.

After an awkward greeting, Ronnie confessed that he wanted to put a large number of bets on at the same time: Sir Ivor in the Champions Stakes, The Elk in the Observer Gold Cup and Be Friendly in the Vernons Sprint at Haydock Park. He even suggested that Sidney do the same, as the prices were good and they could get longer odds by betting in advance.

There was another reason for his visit, he admitted. He hadn't been well and he was finding it hard to leave the house. He got so breathless. Perhaps Sidney would like a drink after he had placed his bets. Ronnie wasn't sure when he'd be out and about again.

It would have been churlish to refuse, given how slowly the man was moving, holding his right side and limping slightly, and so they soon made their way to the Baron of Beef. Sidney noticed that Ronnie was no longer wearing his gold watch. He wondered if he might have pawned it. He still had not penetrated the mystery of why the man had left Stiffkey after so many years. All he knew was that it had been about money.

"You would think I'd have known better," Ronnie said at last. "I feel such a fool. But that's where greed gets you."

"You don't have to tell me about it."

"I don't mind. You could take it as a warning, although I don't think you'd ever be so foolish. I've seen how cautiously you bet."

208

"Perhaps I take enough risks on other things, Ronnie. Besides, I don't have very much money."

"You don't need much to get in a mess. All you need is a bit of fortune to begin with. You mistake it for talent and then you're doomed."

"Sylvia told me that you had always been good with numbers."

"That's one way of putting it."

"You're an accountant, aren't you?"

"I was. I did the books on the farm. Then I started to help a few other people with their tax and finally, just over ten years ago, I got myself an office in Holt. Nice staff. We did well. I started recommending investments for clients and ways of saving tax. It was all perfectly legit, avoidance not evasion. Then I thought we could do with a stockbroker and I met this bloke at the races. He was a friend of Alice's brother: Terry Grant. Some people called him Cary because he had the good looks and the charm and Terry sounds a bit like Cary if you're not listening properly . . ."

"He had the patter."

"Certainly did. We started off quite cautiously. Inflation was around 3.4 per cent, the rate for savers was 3 or 4 per cent and in the first few years our clients were averaging a 7–8 per cent annual return. That was good enough, but others were making a bit more and I asked if we could push it on a bit."

"You asked? Or he suggested that you did so?"

"He was the kind of man who could make you think it was all your idea. He started talking about South African mining stocks; not just gold and diamonds but better value and faster profits in underpriced minerals: titanium in Kenya, copper in Uganda, platinum in South Africa and Rhodesia."

"I thought there were sanctions against Rhodesia?"

"There are. Terry said that made the chance of profits greater. There were fewer deals and plenty of people who still wanted the products and who were prepared to pay more. I don't know how true that was. I never got the chance to find out. The idea was that they were all minerals with a future: titanium in the aerospace industry, copper wiring in electronics, platinum in shipping. Like Harold Wilson, he went on about the white heat of technology and the consumer revolution, the metals used in cars, fridges, music systems, all the growth industries for which there was public demand. We all want cars, we all want to travel, we all want the best of modern life, and here was a chance to invest in the raw materials. It couldn't fail."

"Except that it did."

"Human error. Terry never invested at all. He took money from new investors, gave us back our half-yearly profits, which were always better than we had been expecting, 12–15 per cent, and persuaded us to put more and more back in. He even gave Alice a pair of diamond earrings to keep us sweet. Finally, the returns were so good I remortgaged the house. I thought we could pay it all off, go to the Caribbean, live the life of Riley. Then Terry disappeared off the face of the earth. God knows where he went. At first I thought he might have had an accident or that he was dead. I even worried about him. Then I realised. What a bastard. He just vanished. No one knew where he had gone, not even Alice's brother, who was supposedly his best friend. He lost money too. The worst thing was . . ."

"You hadn't told Alice you'd remortgaged the house."

"How did you guess?"

"It's why you're here."

"That's about it. She went crackers when she found out. We were about to lose everything. She had to talk to the bank, sell the horses, get other friends to help. I was kicked out sharpish. I had a suitcase and a wad of cash and that was that."

"What about your friends?"

"I didn't want the shame. I just had to get out. And then I thought of Sylvia and what I'd done and I wondered what had happened to her. Perhaps I could do one thing in my life to make things right. It's a stupid idea, I know, but I haven't been thinking straight. You won't tell her all this, will you?"

"It's not for me to say, Ronnie. It's for you."

"I don't know what I'm doing any more. But I'd like to earn some money back for her. Leave her a bit to be going on with."

"Do you mean that you're planning to move on? You've only just got here."

"I'm not sure she can keep me. Besides, none of us carry on for ever."

"You're not old."

Ronnie began to cough and reached for his packet of cigarettes as if it might contain the cure. "I'm nearly seventy. I'm not in the best of health. I can't take anything for granted, Sidney. You know that. I'm sorry you're involved in all this. You'll tell me the right thing to do, won't you?"

At the same time, Hildegard was seeing Mrs Maguire. They had not found it easy to adjust to each other in the past, but a mutual respect had taken hold over the years and both women knew that this was not a relationship that benefited from confrontation. Hildegard recognised that she was going to have to proceed carefully if Sylvia Maguire was to confide anything personal.

Both Anna and Byron had been left at home with a babysitter (the original idea of taking them had been mere bravado) and Hildegard, like her husband, began by complimenting her host on her appearance, her cottage, her tea and her cake. "I was expecting more sign of a man."

"I've got my husband trained. We've also had a bit of a clear-out. Sold some of my sister's clutter."

"I see."

"Gives us room to move. I only hope we don't have to set up a bedroom down here. Ronnie's finding the stairs a bit difficult."

"Is he unwell?"

"He gets breathless. We've had the doctor round. They had a bit of a chat but I'm not party to what they tell each other."

"I'm sure you could ask questions afterwards."

"I think I'd rather not know if it's anything serious. I don't like the future ruining the present."

212

"And I imagine you have a lot of the past to catch up on."

"Oh yes," Mrs Maguire continued. "We talk about what it was like all the time. I've got a few photographs and we keep going through them: the school, the shop, the farm. Would you like to see? There's one of me on a pony and Ronnie pretending to be a scarecrow."

She fetched out an old album. "We can't remember who everyone is, that's the only thing. Ronnie tries to help out and sometimes I think he makes up stories just to please me. I'm sure I never pushed Nancy Spooner out of a boat, but he says I did and it was the funniest thing he ever saw. My memory isn't what it was. Normally it's the recent things. I used to think I was quite good at my childhood, but sometimes memories are like those propeller seeds that get caught in the wind. That's one of the first things I remember. We called them whirlybirds. I was running along a line of elm trees trying to catch them with my friends. Whoever got the most was the winner. The sun was so bright. I had a little green dress, I think. I must have been about five, the same age as your daughter, Mrs Chambers. I don't know if Ronnie was there or not. I get so confused about time. Sometimes I don't know if it's morning or afternoon."

Hildegard hesitated to bring up something she had already noticed, but the conversation gave her the opportunity. "You used to have a very fine carriage clock on the mantelpiece. Has that disappeared in the clear-out?"

213

"Ronnie said he'd get it valued. He mentioned something about insurance. He took a bit of jewellery too. There's not much. I'm not a rich woman, as you know. I've always had to live carefully. I've only got a few valuables: my mother's silver candlesticks and a set of cruets. I think there's a cup and saucer from Queen Victoria's Diamond Jubilee somewhere. You know that I was born on the day she died?"

"I did." It was the one fact Mrs Maguire shared almost every time they met. "Did your husband take all that to be valued as well?"

"I think so. He had on his mysterious face, the one that doesn't like to be interrupted. He said it would be useful to know."

"And did he say when he might bring the items back?"

"A couple of weeks, I think. He wasn't very clear and I didn't like to ask. I don't want to make him cross."

"It was good of you to let him back."

"Didn't have much choice if I wanted company, did I? And vows are vows. Not that they matter much to Miss Kendall, I hear — or rather, Mrs Richmond."

"That has been unfortunate. Divorce is never easy."

"Did Sidney really go all the way to Scotland to fetch her back? That's what people are saying. She's led him a merry dance. It's a pity her husband couldn't do it himself."

Hildegard was silent for a moment, deciding that it would not be wise to talk too much about the ways in which a reluctant spouse could be persuaded to return home.

Mrs Maguire continued. "I'm glad he found you. The alternative doesn't bear thinking about. Miss Kendall was always too posh for him."

"And I'm not?" Hildegard asked spontaneously, unable to check herself.

"I don't mean that. You're a first-class woman in every way." (Hildegard knew Mrs Maguire had not always thought this but kept her discretion.) "I sometimes wonder how you put up with him."

"I think we all have to find ways of coping with our husbands; and most of the time we have to disguise the fact we're doing it."

"That's where Miss Kendall went wrong. She didn't have the patience."

"And is that the secret of marriage, do you think, Mrs Maguire?"

"You have to keep hoping it will all come right even if you have to wait until the very end. Ronnie always loved me. Why would he come back if that wasn't true?"

"Did you always know he was alive?"

"I suppose I did, but I didn't like to admit it, especially not in public. It was easier to blame his absence on the war. He was in the Far East. A lot of men never came back. My sister told me she thought he was up north somewhere but I didn't believe her. If he was in England then why wouldn't he want to see me again? Then she said she thought Ronnie was in South Africa. Gladys never got her story straight and I didn't know where she was getting her information. She said it was his sister. I was sure Ronnie never had a sister.

Perhaps it was the other woman, but I never liked to talk about that."

"You knew there was one?"

"It was obvious, I suppose. But I didn't want to imagine such a thing because I knew if I thought about it too much it would be all I would remember. I had to hold on to what we'd had ourselves. Then I could hope for the future."

"And are you glad he's come back?"

"He's taken his time about it, I must say. It's not an easy thing to forgive. I've been on my own so long."

"I suppose it depends on how many sacrifices you are prepared to make."

Mrs Maguire had a thousand-yard stare in her eyes. "The reason I married him was because he gave me a feeling of being safe, even when I was a child. I didn't like being on my own. I was always afraid something bad would happen. Then Ronnie came along. That was a good thing. I knew where I was when I was with him. Then he went away and I was a child all over again, trying to catch propeller seeds in the wind, not knowing how I would ever get home. And that's where you need to be, Mrs Chambers. That's enough of my prattling. Anna will be needing to be bathed and put to bed."

Ten days later Geordie popped up to see Sidney in Ely. He felt like a bit of a chat, he said, and wanted to get away from his normal routine and talk about something different over a couple of pints in the Prince Albert.

216

"Ronnie Maguire?" Sidney asked.

"Could be, but I never quite know what I'm going to get with you. It could be cricket, jazz, marital secrets, trips to Scotland, who knows?"

"I'm sure you can enjoy just as much conversational variety at home."

"You're wrong, Sidney, and I like this pub. It's small enough to be snug, they do a good beer and they leave you alone. What more could a man want?"

"I wish you lived here," said Sidney. "I don't have anyone else to have a drink with."

"I'm sure that's nonsense. There must be the odd clergyman with a need to get away from it all."

"Alas, the only other priest prone to distraction has his eyes firmly set on the ladies."

"And you don't?"

"Steady, Geordie."

"Any news on the returning hero?"

"He's a rogue, of course. Hildegard's seen Mrs Maguire and suspects he's been pawning her valuables . . ."

"With her agreement?"

"It seems so, but that's always a grey area. Hildegard also thinks he's a bit of a drinker. She noticed a whisky bottle in the bookcase."

"That's very observant. At least you and I haven't got to that stage; unless your wife's had a bit of practice already, spotting these things at home."

"It's a slippery slope, I'm told."

"Indeed. Fancy another?"

Once they were on to their second pints the men discussed gambling, the pawn shop and the possibility of alcoholism.

"I like to think I'm all right when I know people who are worse," said Geordie.

"You must see a lot in the force."

"It's not just the police. There were a couple of Scots blokes. Actors. They used to come in at opening time for a sharpener to get over their hangovers. Three double white spirits: that's a double rum, a double gin and a double vodka, poured into a pint glass and topped up with Guinness. That set them up. Then they were ready for the day."

"It's amazing they survived."

"They didn't. They were both dead before they were sixty."

"I've spent some time with Ronnie," said Sidney, returning to their principal subject. "He carries a hip flask and likes to keep himself topped up, but I don't think he's that bad. I've never seen him late in the day, mind you."

"I hope Mrs Maguire doesn't have to put him to bed."

"He's been going there of his own accord quite recently. Not as fit as he once was. He has difficulty breathing. There are mood swings too, I fear. He can say some very dark things."

"And are they directed towards other people in any way?"

"No. Only to himself."

"I wouldn't want any violence towards his wife. Then we would have to step in."

"I think he's quite capable of beating himself up. I think that explains the drink and the gambling; life hasn't turned out as he had once hoped."

"These things often become self-fulfilling prophecies."

"He's hoping to make some big money on the horses, he said, 'before it's too late'. I don't know whether that means before he runs out of money or before he dies. I know he placed some tremendously large bets on the racing at Haydock yesterday. He had some sure-fire tips and was hoping to make as much as two or three hundred pounds."

"Haydock, you say. Yesterday?"

"That's right."

"Well, he won't have made any money there."

"How do you know?"

"Fog. The racing was abandoned. He'll be no better off than he was at the start of the day."

"At least that means he won't have lost the money. But it might make him do something desperate."

"What's he playing at?" Geordie asked. "It just doesn't seem right. Do you think he's planning on disappearing all over again?"

In early December Hildegard saw Mrs Maguire once more and reported on their conversation at bedtime. "She told me she wasn't sure why Ronnie had come home, but then she said to me, 'Why ask too many questions? Does anything matter if we're happy? It'll soon be Christmas.'"

"Perhaps it doesn't matter. People are sometimes content with delusion. It could be the fear of hurting each other. I wonder if we'd do that."

"I'm not sure, Sidney. Would you like me always to tell you everything I think and know?"

"I don't always know what you are thinking."

"It would be terrible if you did."

Sidney climbed into bed. "I think there is a right and a wrong time to say things. I have always been honest, but there has to be some privacy in thinking. We cannot always control our thoughts and sometimes they rise up, embarrass and frighten us. We have to judge when and what to say. We can't just blurt out all our feelings. That would be terrible."

Hildegard turned on to her side to face her husband. "It would, even from you."

Sidney stroked her cheek and continued: "Not everything needs to be said out loud. There is such a thing as silent understanding and I'd like us to think we both know each other better than anyone else."

"That doesn't mean we take each other for granted."

"Certainly not."

"Because I know you'd tell me things if you had to."

"Of course."

Hildegard cuddled in to her husband. "I wonder how much the Maguires have said to each other. It must be so difficult; what to say and what to leave out; how to be honest and how not to cause hurt. They are both so proud and so vulnerable."

"And I'm not sure how much time they've got left. At least it's not too late."

"I don't know, Sidney. We need to look after Mrs M. I don't think this can end well."

Any attempt at resuming normality the following morning was undone by the fact that both husband and wife had forgotten Amanda was coming to lunch. They had to pretend that they had always known and rustled up a quick shepherd's pie they had been planning to have that evening.

"Don't worry *at all* about me," said Amanda. "I know perfectly well how busy you both must be. Would you not prefer it if I took you out?"

"No, I have it all prepared," said Hildegard. "Unless you'd like to see Sidney on your own?"

"There's no need for that. I've spoken to him quite enough recently. And we have to catch up, Hildegard. You know I love you *equally*."

It was clear that despite a certain brittleness, and a fear of being caught off her guard, Amanda did not want to make too much of the recent trip to Scotland. Nor did she particularly want to discuss her failing marriage. She just wanted to spend time with people she loved.

"That's the point of our friendship. It doesn't matter which one of you I am with. I can talk, knowing that you will tell each other anything I say. That's right, isn't it, Sidney?"

"He did tell me about Scotland; and about your decision," Hildegard replied.

"Never mind about me. I need some distraction now that I am back in circulation. What's been happening *to* you?"

The Chambers were initially reluctant to go into detail about the Ronnie Maguire case, given Amanda's recent history. However, they then realised that their guest's experience would provide a unique approach to the situation. She was also in such a combative mood that her opinion would be given quickly and directly. It therefore wasn't long before they furnished Amanda with a full account of what Sidney described as "complicated shenanigans".

"We didn't want to tell you too much about it," Hildegard explained. "Other people's lives . . ."

Amanda's response was as forthright as they had hoped. "Oh, you've no need to show any sensitivity with me. Things are what they are. Have you asked about Mrs Maguire's will?"

"Not yet."

"Whyever not? She might have changed it; particularly after her sister died. Who knows, Sidney, she might even have left her house to you."

"I very much doubt it. Besides I think Ronnie Maguire's due to die first. He's not in the best of health."

"Then why do you think he's come back?"

"Atonement."

"It's a bit late for that, isn't it?"

"As a minister I must remind you of the Christian teaching that it is never too late."

"I hope that doesn't apply to Henry."

"I'm afraid it does."

"Well, you're not going to have any luck convincing me on that one. His opportunity for forgiveness lapsed a long time ago."

"Your mind is made up?"

"I've seen a lawyer and please don't either of you try to persuade me all over again. How can I keep living with him and how can I ever know that there aren't more secrets? One can never get a straight answer from him about anything. I've decided to go ahead with the divorce and that's an end to it. It sounds like Mrs Maguire should do the same."

"I don't think she can."

"Nonsense. This is Mrs Maguire we are talking about. She can do anything she puts her mind to. Do you want me to go and tell her myself?"

"That won't be necessary, Amanda."

"Then you might as well hear my other news."

"Romantic?" Hildegard asked.

"Not at all. I've given up all hope of that. In any case, it's far too soon. The situation is this. I've got a new job in the Department of Prints and Drawings at the British Museum. I am going to be their deputy curator."

"That's marvellous," said Sidney.

"I know I told you that I was having thoughts about a completely different life but this was too good an opportunity to give up. The collection is little short of astonishing. There are over fifty thousand drawings and two million prints from the thirteenth century to the present day. It's a complete treasure trove: Dürer, Raphael, Rembrandt and Goya."

"It will be a new life for you," said Hildegard.

"I'm starting with some research on Michelangelo. They have a fascinating selection of his work from different stages of his career. I can give you both a private tour. Yesterday I looked at a preparatory drawing for Adam on the Sistine Chapel ceiling. It is such a wonderful opportunity to examine an artist's first thoughts. I can study all those sketches and the beginnings of ideas and understand the formation of style; how things eventually become what they are. It's such an overlooked area. We spend all our time looking at the finished article, never at the early stages. So I'm going to throw myself into my work. I think it'll be much safer than chucking myself at a man."

A few days later Mrs Maguire telephoned to say that Ronnie's condition had deteriorated. The doctor and the vicar had both come but neither was as comforting or consoling as Sidney. She wanted to hear his voice and have him beside her. It was the only thing that would feel right.

Sidney could hardly say no and it was one of those rare times in his life when he knew, *exactly*, that he was behaving as he should, as both priest and friend; not that this was about him at all. He shouldn't be vain, he corrected himself, his presence should be entirely at the service of others.

"It's been a bit difficult, I have to say," Mrs Maguire began. "I've done my fair share of nursing but that was a long time ago and I'm frightened of making a mistake. I'm so anxious about most things these days. It's like going for a walk and being sure you're going to fall over but you don't know when. You can't trust a single step you take."

She showed Sidney into the living room, where a bed had been assembled. Ronnie was asleep.

"He's asked me to put some money on the horses, said it will help tide me over, but you know I'm not very good at that kind of thing. My father used to call gambling the devil's work."

"I am sure that a bet at this stage in both your lives won't do too much damage."

"I don't like to think of my old dad looking down on me."

"Perhaps he'll turn a blind eye."

"You've always been a wild one . . ."

"I trust that the Lord is merciful, Mrs Maguire. It's my only hope."

"'In very present danger'."

"You know your prayers . . ."

"I know my Bible too. It keeps me right."

"You're an example to us all, Mrs M."

"You should call me Sylvia."

"I think that's Ronnie's prerogative. Has he been sleeping long?"

"He always naps after an early lunch. We eat at midday, you know. I think it gives him an excuse to have a drink. Then he sleeps. He'll wake in time for the racing, don't you worry."

"I'll wait for him."

Sidney looked at the supine figure lying in front of him in his navy-blue-and-burgundy-striped pyjamas, breathing erratically. He prayed as Ronnie slept:

"Hear us, Almighty and most merciful God and Saviour; extend thy accustomed goodness to this thy servant, Ronald, who is grieved with sickness. Sanctify we beseech thee, this thy fatherly correction to him; that the sense of his weakness may add strength to his faith, and seriousness to his repentance. That if it shall be thy pleasure to restore him to his former health, he may lead the residue of his life in thy fear, and to thy glory; or else give him grace so to take thy visitation, that after this painful life has ended he may dwell with thee in life everlasting, through Jesus Christ our Lord. Amen."

Mrs Maguire placed her hand on his and Ronnie woke up, uncertain where he was. He smiled on recognising Sidney.

"Now I know it's serious," he said and began to sit up.

"Don't stir yourself on my account."

"It's good of you to come," Ronnie gasped, before lapsing into a fit of coughing. "I don't suppose I've got much longer."

"We live in hope."

"I think I ran out of that a long time ago."

Mrs Maguire turned the television volume back up so they could catch the racing. She said she would leave the men while she tidied up. Ronnie fancied a flutter on Beau Champ in the Palace Handicap Steeplechase at Sandown Park at 5–2 and then Privy Seal at 8–1 in the three forty-five. He still thought it was cowardly just to back the favourites and there wasn't enough money in it, but he didn't want to take any more risks. He wondered if Sidney could place the bet for him.

"I'd like to win so I can manage a bit more than paying for my own funeral. That's not a very good way to go, is it?"

"You'd leave a clean balance sheet."

"That's one way of looking at it. But I want Sylvia to know that at least I tried to look after her. I'd like to leave her with a decent amount of money. This is the only way I know how to earn it. She disapproves of the gambling but what can you do? It's all I know. You will explain everything to her, Sidney, won't you?"

Soon after placing the bets and leaving the bookmaker Sidney called in on Dr Michael Robinson at his surgery in Trumpington. He hoped that their long friendship might excuse a little indiscretion.

"What are Ronnie's chances?" he asked. "I know he's not well."

"I'm afraid it's not looking good," his friend replied. "Mr Maguire is in the final stages of emphysema. I don't think I am breaching any confidence in telling you this as it will be perfectly obvious to anyone with even a smattering of medical knowledge. The man should be in a hospital, but his wife wants to care for him at home and I think we can allow that. It's probably because he wants to keep smoking and drinking and that's not going to make much difference to the final outcome. The damage is done, his heart is weak, and so eventually he'll either have a heart attack or be unable to keep breathing. I've organised some nursing visits and I'll call in when I can, but at this stage the duty of care is as much your job as it is mine."

"Do you think he's fully aware of how little time he has left?"

"I know he is. And his wife knows too."

"Mrs M?"

"Is there another?"

"I'm afraid there might be."

"Then someone should tell her. Mr Maguire has made it very clear that he doesn't want a lingering death."

"Will you help him when the time comes?" Sidney asked.

"I will do as much as I can to make him comfortable. But I will not be able to 'help' in the way I think you mean. There's only so much I can do within the laws of the land. But you know, Sidney, I must get on with my labours; people who require medical rather than moral assistance."

"I thought you provided both?"

"I wouldn't want to do you out of a job, Sidney, would I?"

What lay unspoken between the two men was the memory of a series of deaths in the February of 1954 when Dr Robinson had been suspected of helping patients on their way into the unknown with larger than average doses of morphine. It was only after a frank exchange on the potential difference between God's will and the nature of a merciful death that the two had become friends, united by a common desire to alleviate suffering and comfort the afflicted.

"You know," Dr Robinson continued, as he picked up his Gladstone bag and held open the door for Sidney's departure, "I have often puzzled over the phrase 'a lingering death'. Other people might refer to that simply as 'life'."

Before he settled back down at home, Sidney took Byron out for a walk on the edge of the fens. The stooped, bare trees looked like a parade of old soldiers from the First World War. There was a fine rain but it was nothing that would get either of them wet. Sidney could almost hear Mrs Maguire's words telling him it was "only a bit of bange". She had so many of the ancient East Anglian words for the weather. He had once heard her describe the misty drizzle over a riverbank as "dinge on the draw-ground" and an evening fog as a "roke over the holm". He wondered how soon all those old expressions would be lost.

It was dark before four. When he got back to Cathedral Close he poured himself a whisky and took down a volume of John Donne. He wanted to reread "A Nocturnal Upon St Lucy's Day" and think about death, the afterlife and the hope of love renewed after resurrection:

> Study me then, you who shall lovers be
> At the next world, that is, at the next spring:
> > For I am every dead thing,
> > In whom love wrought new alchemy.

When he had finished, and after he had thought for a while, he knew that he could not afford to be melancholy any more. He should go back out into the kitchen, see his wife and daughter, be glad of their company, and enjoy the simpler truths life had to offer.

Ronnie died early on the morning of Sunday 15th December, and Sidney visited his widow that very day. Mrs Maguire told him of her husband's sharp decline after the doctor had seen him and how he had kept throwing off the blankets in the final stages.

"Either his feet were frozen or his shoulders were too cold. He didn't want me to tuck him in; he wanted to be free. I was sad that I couldn't help him enough."

"You did all that you could."

"I wanted him to go happily. He won the treble at Chepstow: The Sentry, Oberon and King Candy. That's nine pounds and five shillings on a one-pound stake. He was proud that I'd swallowed my principles and put the money on for him, even if it did mean leaving him for longer than I wanted to. It was good to get out of the house, though. It gave me a bit of time to think. He handed me a fiver but I only risked a pound. Didn't tell him. Still, it paid out and I told him that he had a winner at the last. He was still fighting it, you know. He didn't like to be told. Even by death. He went the distance, every furlong, and I was with him when he crossed the line. He even thanked me. Said he was glad he'd made his decision. Seen me at the beginning and the end of his life. You can't say more than that, can you?"

Sidney remembered his father's words in the D'Oliveira case. Cricketers must surely be judged on merit alone. Perhaps Ronnie, despite his terrible history and his obvious flaws, had proved his form after all.

The next day was Anna's fifth birthday and also the end of her first term at school in which she had played one of the sheep in the nativity play (hardly the starring role, but there was no favouritism for clergy daughters).

She was given her first Sindy doll, a Booma Boomerang, a *Jack and Jill* annual, some Lego, and animals for the farm. Hildegard's mother had sent her a series of wooden buildings to make a little German town, and her sister a traditional *Hampelmann*, or jumping jack, in preparation for what they hoped would be a homecoming visit the following year. A trip to *Chitty Chitty Bang Bang* was also promised.

Amanda and Leonard arrived as dutiful godparents. Leonard seemed to have an extra spring in his step, whereas Amanda was still watchful, as if fate had one more trick up its sleeve or she was frightened that people might accuse her of something other than divorce. She had brought some paints and reminded Anna that one day they would go back to Florence together, when her goddaughter was older, and she would show her the most beautiful drawings in the world.

Sidney was saddened by the idea that there would never be a time when all his friends were happy, and the contrast with the children's exuberance as they played their games of Pass the Parcel, Musical Chairs and Blind Man's Buff only increased his sense of melancholy. He would have to pull himself together for Christmas and find his hope again.

Perhaps, he thought, he could look to Mrs Maguire as an example? She had taught him how to understand all was to forgive all; and that by thinking beyond her immediate self, loving hopefully and sometimes beyond all reason, she had found a better way to live than filling her life with suspicion, fear and self-doubt. If that involved an element of misconception then was that really so bad? Who amongst us had not preferred the comfort of illusion or deceived themselves in order to deal with the difficulties of life — sometimes hoping for the impossible — knowing that even if their aspirations were implausibly far-fetched, it was better to take that risky highway rather than remain on the low road of caution and despair?

He lit the five candles on his daughter's cake and cheered as she blew them out in turn.

"That's so I get five wishes instead of only one, Daddy."

A German Summer

As the Apollo 11 astronauts prepared to land on the moon, the Chambers family was engaged in a rather more prosaic adventure: a two-week visit to Rügen Island in East Germany. Hildegard had spent her childhood bicycling under its chalk cliffs and playing on its long stretches of silver sands and wanted her daughter to experience something similar, a holiday more memorable than the family's usual two-week bucket-and-spade trip to Cornwall. Anna would see her grandmother, learn a bit more of the German language, and even experience a taste of communism.

Sidney had initially been reluctant to come since, on a previous visit, just before the Berlin Wall went up, he had been arrested on a trumped-up charge of spying. Hildegard had needed to pull many strings in order to get him out. It was just as well that her father, Hans Leber, had been a martyred communist hero in the early 1930s. As soon as the Stasi realised who she was they had taken a more lenient view, but Sidney was determined to avoid trouble if he ever went back to East Germany and made it clear that he would have preferred an uneventful seaside holiday in England. He was, however, persuaded by his wife's need to see her mother and for Anna to appreciate the delights of a country she had never visited. In other words, he was outvoted.

They were staying at the Villa Friede, on the Strandpromenade in Binz, an imposing three-storeyed Bäderstil building with a white façade adorned with balconies, verandas and a decorated frieze containing symbols of peace and friendship. Hildegard remembered all the architectural details from her childhood and delighted in pointing them out to her daughter. A neat garden with white roses and sea buckthorn faced the sea and the wide stretch of sands. It was, Sidney imagined, the kind of place Thomas Mann would have stayed when contemplating the philosophy of time, illness and death.

The villa was owned by local government official Günter Jansen, his wife Maria, and their son Jürgen. Günter was an old admirer of Hildegard from her schooldays. He was a small, wiry man with a neat moustache and sharp shoulders; a former athlete who still believed in keeping his body in shape and his wits about him. He was a middle-ranking official responsible for housing and construction in the Free German Trade Union Federation, an organisation that technically owned his establishment, since most hotels had been taken into state control in the early 1950s. But no one who visited the Villa Friede could be in any doubt that Günter and Maria Jansen still ran the show, and that this almost certainly involved a series of under-the-counter financial arrangements that required secrecy, energy and persistent watchfulness.

Maria was a fine-featured, dark-haired woman with almost translucently pale skin, a high forehead and small but luminous amber-brown eyes that carried a melancholy allure. In the West it would have been assumed that she had perfected the stylish "no make-up look" but in the East this was achieved simply by wearing no make-up. She dressed mainly in black and spoke little, clearly finding it pointless to keep up with her husband's relentless front-of-house optimism. Instead she preferred to work behind the scenes, overseeing the hotel staff, the kitchens and the bedrooms, while keeping an eye on a son who had grown so large she could no longer believe that she had ever given birth to him.

Jürgen was a quietly inventive eleven-year-old boy who was always making something out of wood or wiring, whether it was a crystal radio, a remote-controlled car, or a miniature helicopter. People at school called him a *Mondgucker*, a moon-gazing idiot, but he was far cleverer than he let on, a loner who clung to his parents, continually wanting their approval and their love, only to find that they did not have enough time to provide the amount he craved. His favourite activity was to ride in the sidecar of his father's prized MZ motorbike along the sea front, urging him to go faster and faster, leaning into corners, and shrieking with delight if they ever had a near miss with a passing car.

Hildegard watched with quiet amusement as every morning and evening father and son exchanged the Young Communist League salute:

"*Für Frieden und Sozialismus: Seid bereit,*" Günter declared. "For peace and socialism: be prepared."

And Jürgen replied with his right hand held high, fingers together, palm out, with his thumb aiming towards the top of the head and his little finger pointing towards the sky: "*Immer bereit.* Always prepared."

Sidney had wanted to ask his wife about her nation's twentieth-century tendency towards ideological extremism — the full-circle swing on the watch from communism at eight o'clock over to fascism at four and then back to communism at eight again — but he hadn't dared. Instead he listened carefully whenever Hildegard told fragments of its story through the memory of her father, while her mother presented family history as one of revolutionary struggle. Sibilla Leber was already ensconced in the hotel when they arrived and insisted that they all pay tribute to her husband's memory by attending a special Friendship Festival that weekend. This was a celebration of socialist solidarity involving music, gymnastics, sport and military display. It would be a perfect opportunity, she said, to witness East German idealism in practice.

After everyone had polished off a hearty breakfast of ham, hard-boiled eggs, *Brötchen* and home-made *Sanddorn* jam, the families got the children down to the beach. It was a mild summer's day with a light breeze and the idea was to make the most of the good weather before the wind picked up. They settled into a couple of *Strandkörbe*: open-faced, sheltered and hooded wicker beach seats that could seat a family of four. Lena Jansen, the family matriarch, soon arrived to check that all was well and to reminisce with Hildegard's mother, repeating their old sadness that it was such a pity their children couldn't have married each other.

It soon became clear that Günter, despite being wed, still carried a torch for Hildegard. While Sidney started to build a vast sandcastle with Anna, his host sidled up to her in a *Strandkorb*, leant in closely and spoke in rapid German: "I remember, Hildy, when you first came here. Your father was still alive. You thought you were lost in the woods and I brought you home. It was getting dark. Everyone was worried. You could see the moon. We held hands."

And Hildegard replied: "That was forty years ago. We were so little. So much has happened that I hardly remember my childhood. I often wonder what it would have been like if I'd never left."

"I wish you hadn't."

Sidney's German was not fluent, but he understood all too well what Günter meant. Maria was irritated too. She got out of her chair and vented her frustration on her son and on the equally annoying dachshund that yapped around them.

"Go and swim in the sea and take Franzi with you," she shouted. "Play in the waves. Leave us in peace."

She put down a beach rug and laid out a little picnic with herring, dried toasts, apples and cheese, and handed out glasses of a drink made from sea buckthorn that was supposed to increase energy. Not that Jürgen needed any more. The boy ate all the time. It was as if he was trying to consume his own hunger.

As he ate, Günter made relentless pronouncements on contemporary politics, the evils of Western capitalist greed and the injustice of the global economic system. This was a man who was used to an audience. Despite his oleaginous approaches to Hildegard, Sidney almost admired their host's authoritative way with those around him. Perhaps he could learn a thing or two from someone who managed to disguise his more outrageous assertions with bold gestures and confident laughter, implying that anyone who disagreed with him was an idiot.

It was well known, he assured the Chambers family, that American interests were imperialist and corrupt and that their expansionist plans always punished the decent working class. He then demolished a salted hard-boiled egg and left, saying that he had both party and business matters to attend to. There was a building that he had promised to inspect on behalf of the trade union federation. It had once belonged to Thomas Pietsch, one of the family's oldest friends, who had died in the spring.

Lena Jansen told Hildegard's mother all about it. The dead man had given up hope, she said, but then he had never been the same since he had lost his business after the war and been imprisoned on a charge of political corruption. It had been a shame, but Thomas Pietsch had never known how to play the system; unlike her son Günter, who knew everyone, had always been popular (and should have married Hildegard).

She suggested that they pay his widow a visit. "We have to stay true to our comrades despite what happens to them. It is easier for you, Sibilla. Your husband was a hero."

"But he died. What is the point of a dead hero?"

"It is better than a living coward."

"Thomas Pietsch wasn't a coward. He was naive and greedy. That is all."

"At least his son has learned. He is a clever boy; just like my Günter. And Jürgen is clever too. He could have been your grandson."

"That was not to be," Sibilla Leber replied, "but I never imagined my daughter would marry a priest. It must have been the shock after her first husband died. That's the only reason."

"He seems decent enough for an Englishman."

Sidney realised that he was being talked about. He was now forced into a position in which he could not help but overhear the conversation but had to pretend that he was preoccupied with something else. This was a difficult act to pull off, particularly as he needed to listen intently in order to follow the German and understand what the two women were saying. Hildegard saw what he was doing and smiled. She was going to let him stew.

Sibilla Leber dropped her voice and continued talking about her son-in-law without mentioning him by name. The wicker seats were cocoons that muffled sound and prevented anyone else listening in properly.

Sidney wondered if they had been deliberately invented to avoid surveillance. Whether he sat on a picnic rug or joined people who were already talking, he could not feel he belonged in this strange lunar landscape, populated with myriad space-like modules amidst the craters in the sand. "The clergyman is perfectly respectable, I suppose," Sibilla Leber went on, "but he's too curious. He pokes his nose in where he should keep well away." She kept repeating the German word for nosy: *neugierig, neugierig, neugierig*. "You can see him thinking about other people all the time and judging them. I don't like it."

"You don't have to see him so much, Sibilla."

"Hildegard tells me all about him. She won't complain because of what happened with her first husband — you know he died in circumstances she has never explained to me — but I'm certain this one neglects her. Family comes last for him and not first. That man always has his nose in other people's business."

Sidney could not decide whether or not he was meant to hear all this, much less understand it. It was so annoying that he was not able to interrupt and put his case. What business was his marriage of theirs? He began to dig so furiously around the moat of Anna's castle that he showered her with sand, making her cross.

The two women talked about their visit to Thomas Pietsch's widow. Her son Otto had apparently done well in the construction industry. He had worked hard and kept his nose clean, unlike his father and unlike

240

Sidney, who was still referred to as *neugierig, neugierig, neugierig*. These old biddies really had a nerve.

Maria said in passing that she didn't trust Otto Pietsch. His father had died too young. He was only sixty-four. Perhaps his son had helped him along the way?

Her mother-in-law was appalled. "That's a terrible thing to say."

"Perhaps I'm speaking the truth?"

"There's no need to say these things out loud."

"What does it matter?" Maria said quietly.

Lena Jansen leant close to Sibilla and whispered for all to hear. "Our hostess is unhappy. Her husband doesn't love her, but how can he when he still has feelings for Hildegard? She should have her hair permed; wear some lipstick like your daughter."

Sidney had had enough. He picked up his bucket and spade and took his daughter off to make a better sandcastle nearer the water's edge. Despite being "family", they were some of the rudest people he had ever met.

In bed that night he did not like to criticise them directly. He was well aware that to complain about his mother-in-law so early on in their holiday would be an act of folly, and to raise the subject of Hildegard's friends and relations so soon after their arrival could only cause trouble.

However, he didn't want to let the matter rest and decided to try a roundabout route by talking to Hildegard about Maria Jansen's unhappiness.

"I have never known her to be content," his wife observed.

"She seems to have given up on life."

"She finds her son difficult; her husband too. I don't think she likes the politics. It makes them vulnerable."

"Do you think it's also because she knows Günter would rather have married you?"

"If you behave, you have nothing to fear."

"Did you ever think what that might have been like?"

Hildegard sighed. "It was what our parents wanted."

"And Günter too."

"Maybe. But I had no intention of doing what everyone expected. I wanted to choose for myself; and I did so. Twice." She pointed her finger. "Don't make me have to decide one more time, Sidney."

"I am always fearful of that possibility."

"Don't be absurd."

"I am serious. You might think differently about our marriage now you're back in Germany."

"This is a very different country now."

"I can't help but feel this is where you belong."

"No, Sidney. We have made a new home in England. Although I cannot forget who I once was, nor the lessons of my childhood."

"Perhaps none of us can. Nor should we . . ."

Hildegard continued. "The idea of belonging changes as you grow older, don't you think? It's hard when we don't own our own home and you work in the Church. I think sometimes that you would prefer to be a constant pilgrim."

"I feel most at home when I am with you and Anna. It doesn't matter where we are."

"But you need your distractions."

"That's not always true."

"More often than not. You may be concerned about my feelings now that we have returned but I am also worried about *you*, Sidney. Will there be enough entertainment? So far there has been no crime and no lonely perfumed women. What are you going to find to amuse yourself? Perhaps, now that we are in a foreign land, you will be thrown back on your resources, without the protection of your past, your country, your church and your friends. Maybe I will see the real Sidney at last?"

Anna Chambers was excited by the imminent possibility of men walking on the moon. She had brought her little telescope from home in the hope that she might be able to see them land. Her mother hadn't had the heart to tell her how improbable this was, but she did promise to wake her up in the middle of the night so that she could see the event on television — provided the East Germans showed it.

This did not seem likely. There were only two state channels and there was so little chance of picking up reception from West Germany that Rügen was known for being part of *Tal der Ahnungslosen*, the Valley of the Clueless. Instead, the children watched the mishaps of Clown Ferdinand and his caravan.

"Jürgen loves it when people fall over," said Günter, laughing loudly, believing that if he found something amusing then other people must too. "He thinks it's the funniest thing in the world. He'll try and trip you all up, just you watch. He likes his fun."

"*Es ist so lustig*," said Jürgen.

"This is boring," Anna told her mother. "It's not funny. I want to see the men on the moon."

Sidney wondered when they were going to go out and sample the delights of a local brewery. Günter finally obliged by taking him to his favourite *Bierhalle*, a large two-storeyed building that doubled as a cinema and community meeting hall, with bright yellow walls decorated with stucco reliefs of gymnasts, dancers and musicians.

Outside, an oompah band played "*Wein, Weib und Gesang*" and all around them people were toasting each other: "*Prost, prost, Kamerad! Prost, prost, Kamerad! Prost, prost, prost, prost, prost, prost, Kamerad! Wir wollen einen heben: prost, prost prost!*" As they spoke they moved their glass to their head, chest and stomach — *Zur Mitte, zur Titte, zum Sack, zack, zack* — before downing the beer in one.

Günter bought the first round of drinks and they spoke in a mixture of English and German, helping each other out whenever necessary. He said that he was surprised Sidney had agreed to come on such a holiday. "I thought the British preferred France."

"It's the first time we have been here as a family. Hildegard is keen that Anna should keep in touch with her German heritage."

"Some exiles would prefer to forget that."

244

"I think my wife is of the belief that you can't ignore history."

Günter began to extemporise on a theory of social improvement, in which everyone strived for a future that evolved from the workers up rather than the aristocracy down. "You have to work with people who are all planning for a better tomorrow." He continued: "And this is not always clear. It is not just the politicians but the town planners, the people in construction, the police. We have to be consistent. Ideology is more important than money."

"Although money does matter, I suppose."

Günter clapped him on the back. "A typical capitalist response. You must buy the next round of drinks!"

As the conversation wore on, Günter revealed his plan to take over the Pensionshaus Garni.

"Wasn't that once Thomas Pietsch's hotel?" Sidney asked.

"Not any more."

"Does his son know?"

"He will find out. He's over there."

Otto Pietsch was a large bleary-eyed man with sloping shoulders who had reached that stage in life when it was too late to reverse the process of letting himself go. He was with his friend Karl Fischer and a female drinking companion in a skimpy cotton dress that was a size too small for her. They were already half-cut, shouting out traditional banter to their friends: "*Es trinkt der Mensch, es säuft das Pferd, doch heute ist es umgekehrt!* Men drink and horses guzzle, but tonight we're wearing muzzles."

After half an hour, another of Günter's friends, Rolf Müller, pulled up in a two-toned Wartburg police car. Sidney was worried they might have done something wrong, that they had all been too loud or too drunk, but he was quickly informed that they had not been loud *enough*, and that Rolf, an officer in the criminal investigation department of the Volkspolizei, was determined to enjoy his night off. Günter owed him money, he said, and he could start by paying off his debt *in beer.*

"Tut den Durst nur immer löschen," he began to sing,
"doch mit Wasser das laß sein.
Wasser das gehört den Fröschen
doch den Menschen Bier und Wein."

Günter translated:

If quenching thirst is your sole aim
Then water will do you just fine.
But water belongs to frogs
While humans have beer and wine.

Sidney was uneasy. He could not quite believe the camaraderie that was on display. He felt that everyone was going through the motions of having a good time in order to avoid any true show of feeling; that those around him were willing everything to be all right even though they knew it probably was not.

He had seen this before, in England and in war-time: the hope that if you *pretended* that your morale was good then it might *become* good. There was something desperate about the night. Perhaps, he thought, it was because people worried that if they had stayed at home others might talk about them, report on their activities and arouse suspicion. They felt that they had no choice other than to be part of the show. Their forced conviviality was an attempt to demonstrate that they all belonged, that they were all in this great social project together, no matter what, hiding their terror of being exposed and alone for those rare moments of privacy in which no one could catch them out.

As he bought a round of drinks, Karl Fischer mumbled something about fate and death. Sidney couldn't quite make out the sense; he was unable to establish if the man was even talking to him and the volume of noise made comprehension difficult, but he knew the words "*Tod*" and "*Schicksal*". He had heard them often enough. A few moments later, Günter leant forward and pronounced with an almost drunken melancholy: "*Freundschaft ist weit tragischer als Liebe. Sie dauert länger.* Friendship is far more tragic than love. It lasts longer."

Sidney wasn't sure these men were really friends: Günter Jansen, Karl Fischer, Otto Pietsch and Rolf Müller may have slapped each other on the back, given out drinking toasts and made their arrangements to see each other at the festival that weekend, but their comradely behaviour felt practised rather than meant, something they hoped might be true while knowing all along that it was no such thing.

Back at the Villa Friede, the children were incapable of such pretence. Any parental hope that they would play happily together soon proved over-optimistic. There was a valiant attempt at a family game of rounders on the beach, but the sad fact was that Jürgen was uneasy in other children's company and preferred to construct things on his own with a soldering iron.

Günter gave his son the usual communist greeting on his return home: *"Seid bereit."*

"Immer bereit."

Jürgen told his father that Karl Fischer had paid a visit earlier.

"He didn't mention that when I saw him."

"He came with a new transistor for the radio I am making. Then he talked to Mother. They told me to leave them alone. I asked Uncle Karl to help with my tape recorder but Mother wouldn't let me so I watched them without them noticing. Mother likes Uncle Karl . . ."

"We all like Uncle Karl, Jürgen. He is a very good electrician."

"Mother smiles when he comes and is sad when he leaves. I wrote it in my book. It's like the one you have."

"Let me see it," said Günter. He turned to his wife. "I didn't know Karl was here, Maria. Why didn't you tell me?"

"Because I didn't know he was coming either."

"You were alone with him?"

248

"Not for long. I am never alone. There is always somebody watching or wanting something." Her husband looked as if he might hit her, but before he could do anything Maria added, "And I never smile. You know that."

"Perhaps you should be flattered by the attentions of men at your age."

"I'd rather be on my own."

She had just managed to settle the children down to bread, onions and *Bratwurst* and was not in the mood for a fight. As far as she was concerned, there were still nine days to go of this overpopulated intrusion. She just had to live through them.

"Jürgen has been trying to record all our conversations on his cassette recorder," Hildegard announced in an attempt both to explain the situation and deflect from its seriousness. "It'll be you next, Sidney. Anna's bedtime story. He'll probably want to record that too. Just you wait."

"Am I reading to her?"

"You promised, remember? Every day of the holiday."

Anna was at an open window, looking through her telescope at the night sky. Sidney watched as she began an imaginary conversation.

"Hello, Mr Moon, how are you today?"

She answered herself in as low and booming a voice as she could muster. "I am very well. But what are you doing walking all over me?"

"I wanted to see if you were made of cheese."

"I AM made of cheese."

"Can I eat you up?"

"That would take a *very long time*."

"If I start eating you will I turn into cheese?"

Anna noticed her father was in the room but didn't seem to mind. Glad of an audience, she carried on with the moon's low voice. "Do you have a cat, little girl?"

"No, I have a dog."

"Does he like cheese?"

"I think he does."

"Does he want to eat me too?"

"He's not here at the moment. He's in England."

"And where are you?"

"I'm in Germany."

"Do you like Germany?"

"I don't think I do. I think I'd rather be with you, Mr Moon."

Sidney said it was time for bed. Anna asked for *his* story and her father then made up a fairy tale about how the moon shone and moved through the heavens, how it was accompanied by individual spirits to keep it clean and how those spirits pulled travellers up into the night sky in their sleep, letting them dream the most beautiful dreams.

It seemed astonishing to be part of a time when you could look up at the moon and know, as you did so, that two American men were walking on its surface.

"Are the astronauts there now, Daddy? Can we see them?"

"It's too far away."

"Can they see us?"

"I don't think so."

250

"And will they see God?"

"Perhaps, my darling. If they wait long enough."

"How long will that be?"

"As long as a good night's sleep. Close your eyes now."

"I don't want to." Anna looked towards the doorway. "What's he doing?"

Jürgen had been listening. He was holding out a microphone. He had not been able to understand the English (he learned Russian at school) and asked them what the story was about. When Sidney told him, he replied simply:

"I've been to the moon," he said. "When I lived before." Then he turned and walked away.

Anna said that she was afraid of the boy. She didn't like it in Germany. "You don't either, Daddy, do you?"

"I'm not sure. I think I am waiting to find out more."

"I'm worried all the time here, Daddy."

"It's because you are not at home, my darling."

"Mummy says this is her home."

"She doesn't mean that."

"What does she mean then?"

"She is thinking what it was like for her when she was your age. It's hard for you to understand."

"No it isn't!"

"It doesn't matter."

"It does, Daddy. I'm frightened. It's that boy. I don't like him."

"Jürgen means no harm."

"But he's scary, Daddy."

Sidney gave his daughter a cuddle. "Don't you worry. I will look after you." His daughter smelled of wool and warmth and milk. He remembered her as a baby. How much longer would she have such trust, such innocence?

Anna held on tightly to him. "I don't like his dog either. Do you think a wolf will come out of the forest and eat him?"

"I'm afraid not."

"But if a wolf did come and eat him you would be happy?"

"I wouldn't like to see that," said Sidney. "But I wouldn't mind if that dog Franzi ran into the forest and never came back."

"But you won't go into the forest, will you?"

"I'll only go if you come with *me*; and you must only go if I am with *you*. Is that fair?"

"And when you tell me a story tomorrow night can it just be you and me?"

"Of course it can," said Sidney, tucking his daughter in and realising, as he said this, that tomorrow they would all be at the Friendship Festival.

It took place at the northern end of the small town of Prora, the site of one of the most ambitious examples of Nazi architecture ever built; a three-mile-long series of hotel buildings erected between a long beach and a large pine forest. It had been designed to give twenty thousand workers a holiday every year but the war had put a stop to its construction and the project had never been completed. Two central blocks were currently used by the police and the East German army, but the bulk of the site had been left unfinished amidst the sand dunes, a Nazi white elephant that now served as a powerful demonstration of the folly of political grandstanding and social engineering.

Sidney and Hildegard walked through the areas that had not been sealed off by the authorities while Maria took the children to the beach to eat ice creams and build sandcastles.

"Why don't they convert all this and use it for holidays today?" Sidney asked.

"It would be too expensive," Hildegard answered. "It might even require a large amount of investment — or even private ownership — and that's far too capitalist a concept for this country. You could talk to Günter about it. As an upstanding member of the Socialist Unity Party, he has the philosophy of collectivisation written on his heart."

She explained that in 1953 there had been a concerted attack on private property during *Aktion Rose*, a government initiative to nationalise hotels and holiday homes.

"One February night a total of four hundred police set off in buses from Rostock to arrest the biggest landlords. It was a deliberate attempt to scare off anybody with money or individual ambition."

"So how did Günter survive? He still has a hotel," Sidney asked.

"Technically he doesn't own it."

"It looks like he does. How does he manage that?"

"Collusion," Hildegard answered. "You know the saying, '*Wasser predigen und Wein trinken*': someone who preaches water but drinks wine? That is Günter for you. And he was lucky. There were snowstorms at the time of the raids. They slowed down the police's progress and cut off the roads. Günter and his father were able to hide evidence and make their defence. Others were not so fortunate. But it is not a good idea to speak too much about this. You can observe everything that's going on, but keep your thoughts to yourself."

"I'll bear that in mind," said Sidney.

"This building may be a relic of the past, but people in the East only replaced one form of dictatorship with another. Many of the judges under National Socialism remained in their posts. Only the laws changed. Günter may laugh and joke and tell you all sorts of things but he's a dangerous man."

"Really?"

Hildegard looked round to check who was near them and warned that it was possible they were being followed. "That man over to the right behind us."

"Where?"

"Don't look now."

"What do you mean?"

"It's the shoes that give him away. He was watching us back in Binz. Now he's tying his shoelaces. That has to be a message to another operative."

"Perhaps his laces have simply come undone."

"I don't think so. There's a man ahead who has just raised his hat. He's probably going to take over. Günter could have arranged all this. He's probably bugged the whole hotel."

"Including our room?" Sidney asked.

"And even his own. Why do you think Maria has the radio on all the time? Günter is an informer. He's probably spying on his own wife. That's why she answers him so provocatively. She is perfectly aware that other people can hear her, and she wants them to know just what she thinks about it all. Nowhere is safe to talk. Trust no one. Not even me."

"That's ridiculous."

"Everything in this country is absurd, Sidney."

"So that's why Günter has done so well for himself."

"As a good communist, he helped his father when private property was taken into public ownership. Even now, he must have the police in his pocket. But you must act as if you know nothing, and you cannot be too curious. In England, a question may be a form of politeness or a statement of interest. Here it is a form of attack. You need to be very careful what you say, Sidney. Don't push it any more than you have already. I've got you out of prison in this country once before; don't make me do it again."

The Friendship Festival began with a parade of Young Pioneers paying tribute to their founder Ernst Thälmann and raising banners depicting a hammer and compass surrounded by a ring of rye. Jürgen sang a song about a little trumpet player who had communism in his blood and kept everyone's spirits up with his socialist belief and his ready smile.

There was a gymnastic display, some track and field events, a family obstacle race, a tug of war and what appeared to be a showdown between a group of tractors designed to demonstrate the superiority of East German engineering. More bizarre, however, was a mass mock baptism during which groups of boys and girls were taken into the sea by a man dressed as the figure of Neptune. He was painted green, wore a fake beard and held a trident.

"I don't think you'd find this in the Church of England," said Hildegard.

"Some priests do use the sea. But they draw the line at fake beards."

"The Bishop of Ely can be a bit of a show-off."

"I think he stops short of painting himself green."

Jürgen recited a poem, "Neptune's Prayer", before he was dunked in the sea and christened *Schleimige Seegurke*, "Slimy Sea Cucumber", which everyone found amusing. His mother and father applauded loudly when their son was presented with a certificate to celebrate a healthy initiation into the mysteries of folk tradition. Günter then left for celebratory drinks in the home of his great friend in the Volkspolizei.

Rolf Müller lived in a block on the resort grounds that had been originally designed as staff accommodation but now housed the police, officers of the National People's Army and several local civil servants. In the early evening he took "the usual gang" of Günter, Otto Pietsch and Karl Fischer back to his house for a carefully orchestrated celebration with schnapps and a crystal vodka known as "the blue strangler". Despite a half-hearted invitation to include Sidney and Hildegard, it was pretty clear that this was not a night for outsiders, and the visitors were relieved to escape another evening of enforced jollity.

Günter was clearly in festive mood and told them not to wait up. He was planning to make a night of it and wouldn't be back before dawn.

"Will you be careful on the way home?" his wife asked.

"Don't be so anxious."

"You are lucky to have someone to care."

"I always take the road along the railway line," Günter told Sidney. "It is completely straight. All you have to do is rev it up and keep on until morning. The motorbike does all the work. It knows where to go. There is no need for anyone to worry about me. The bike will get me home."

The next morning they were woken with the news that Günter was dead. He had either driven off the road or been hit by a car that had not stopped. It was an accident, Rolf Müller informed the family. Every year there was some kind of fatality. It was tragic that this time the victim had been Günter. He may have been a big man but he had a very thin skull. He had not been wearing a crash helmet.

There were no witnesses, and the first motorist who had stopped confirmed that Günter was already dead when she found him in a ditch. Even though she was a nurse, there was nothing she could do. She thought he had turned over and gone into a tree. Rolf Müller was very sorry. Günter had been one of his closest friends.

Maria Jansen turned on him. "Why could you not look after my husband or save him from his drunkenness?"

Rolf replied, in as kindly a manner as he could, that Günter was not a man who could be told what to do.

"Where was he found?" Hildegard asked.

"Just outside Binz. There is a blackspot. So many times this happens."

"He said the road was straight."

"There is a turn across the railway line; first right and then left on to the main road into town. We think he misjudged it in the darkness, lost control on the bend and went into a skid."

"What time do you think it was?" Sidney asked.

Rolf Müller was surprised by the question. "I sent them home at three in the morning. Günter wanted to stay longer but we had all had enough."

"And it was still dark?"

"Yes."

Sidney persisted. "He told me that he would come home when it was light."

"He changed his mind."

"Was he very drunk?"

"He was good at hiding it. Because he is, he was, so convivial, people could never tell."

"There was no rain last night, the roads were dry," Sidney continued. "And he knew that road so well. It's very unfortunate."

"It certainly is," Müller snapped in German.

258

Sibilla Leber turned to her son-in-law. "You are being too nosy." Again, she used the word *neugierig*.

Hildegard put her hand on her husband's arm and apologised on his behalf. "Sidney is upset when people die, needlessly, in pain and alone."

"As a priest he must be used to it."

"Every death is different," said Sidney. "And each one matters."

Hildegard told Anna to play quietly in their room. She was going to have to support Maria when she broke the news to Jürgen but, at that moment, she was more concerned about her husband. "It could have been you, Sidney. You could have been riding with him. I cannot bear to think how he died."

"Pray for him."

"I am anxious about you. I am sorry that I have not been kind."

"Nonsense. You have behaved perfectly to all of us. This is your home."

"Coming back makes me nervous. I can admit that now."

"And now we have more important things to think about."

"One accident and everything is changed."

"I think someone must have hit him," said Sidney. "Even when drunk Günter knew the road too well to just veer off like that."

"If that was the case then why didn't the driver stop?" Hildegard asked.

"He should have done. He must have felt the impact on his car."

"You are assuming it was a man? A woman found him. A nurse."

"Whoever it was, I suppose they will not have wanted to stop and spend any time with the authorities. If they had been drunk as well, then they would be charged. It's just odd that it happened on such a straight road."

Hildegard began to weep.

Husband and wife were silent for a while, holding each other and taking the news in when they heard Jürgen cry out. He was shouting that it couldn't be true, his father was a brilliant driver; he had promised his son that he was going to live for ever. He screamed at Maria: "Someone has taken Father. I will find out who it was and I will kill him. I will kill. I will kill. I will kill." The boy banged his head against the door until it bled.

Anna started talking to the moon again.

"Mr Moon, what makes you so bright?"

"I have a light inside me."

"Do you ever go out?"

"No, I don't."

She began to whirl herself round and round in circles. "I go round and round and round and round and round for ever and ever and ever and ever until everyone goes dizzy and falls down dead."

And she fell to the floor.

Sidney and Hildegard attended Sunday morning service at the local Protestant church with Maria and Lena Jansen. Sibilla Leber had already been to the early service and stayed behind to look after Jürgen and Anna. The church was an austere late-nineteenth-century red-brick building resting on a hillock of woodland on the road to Putbus. The choir sang Bach's Cantata for the Tenth Sunday after Trinity: "Behold and see if there be any sorrow like my sorrow". Lena and Hildegard wept. Günter's widow stared blankly ahead. She was so pale, so still.

Sidney prayed for the dead man's soul, hoping his prayers would reach God in a country so hostile to belief. He wondered what price the priest had had to pay for accepting the notion that an alternative socialist heaven was being built on earth. What compromises did he have to make? Would it mean a double life? Was that the same kind of existence that Günter had led, pretending to be one thing while being another? As he contemplated the communion service he remembered Hildegard's observation about their host's hypocrisy: *he preaches water but drinks wine.*

Günter must have had enemies. But this was not the way to think, Sidney chastened himself; not now, in church, in a foreign land where no one wanted him to raise the questions he was burning to ask.

The music continued to tell the story of the destruction of the temple in Jerusalem. It was a tale of sorrow, sin and zealotry, exploring the tension between God's anger and Christ's mercy, and built up to a deluge of destruction and despair. The text, taken from the Book of Lamentations, spoke of punishment, judgement and storms of vengeance before a final sorrowful chorale asked that sinners should not be allowed to get away with their wrongdoing. It was a grim message for a Sunday morning, with a quietly prayerful ending, and the family returned home in an even more sombre mood than when they had left.

On reaching the sea front they found that Jürgen's grief had manifested itself in the strangest of ways. He was sitting on the roof of the Villa Friede, refusing either to speak or come down.

Sibilla Leber was in despair. She had been so busy looking after the children she hadn't even started on the lunch. "There is nothing we can do or say. I don't even know how he got up there. I can't see any ladder."

Anna explained what had happened. "He keeps talking about a sparrow in a nest. I think he wants to be a bird."

"I will speak to him," said Maria. "Go inside, everyone. I think we need to be alone."

It took her almost an hour. After she had persuaded her son to descend, Jürgen went to his bedroom, slammed the door and refused to come out. His mother left him some food on a plate. The family only saw him the next morning when he sat out at the front of the house with a tape recorder, listening to the same section of tape again and again, leaning forward with an earphone in his right ear. Play. Stop. Rewind.

Sidney asked the boy what he had recorded and what he was listening to.

Jürgen did not answer but concentrated on his tape. Perhaps he was listening to his father's voice. Play. Stop. Rewind.

262

Maria told Hildegard that she was almost relieved her husband was dead. Now she didn't have to worry what might happen to them all. The worst had happened now. People might even leave them alone.

"Don't say such things," Hildegard counselled, tacitly pointing out that the kitchen was likely to be bugged.

"I can't help it. I speak my thoughts. I can be less afraid."

"You have always dreaded such a time?"

"I expected it would happen one day."

Hildegard tried to comfort her. Maria had known love and it would come back to her. She would remember the best of her marriage, the happy times.

"I am not sure I have ever known happiness. Günter took pity on me. That is all."

"I think it must have been more than that."

"His father insisted on our marriage. You had already married, Hildegard. My parents said it was a good idea. They thought I was the only suitable woman left for him."

"And you didn't love him?"

"I knew he still loved you; but I accepted him. I would be looked after. Everyone told me that. Even him."

"You have good friends," Hildegard reminded. "Otto Pietsch, Karl Fischer . . ."

"Oh, friends. Yes, of course. They are supposed to bring comfort. Perhaps they will. Karl is always kind to me, it is true. He came this afternoon. That is one thing that will be easier, I suppose. His visits. Günter was always jealous, so suspicious. And there was no cause for him to be so. Karl and I are friends; that is all. He is someone I hope I can trust and in this country that is not always so easy."

That evening, while walking on the beach where no one could overhear or record their conversation, Hildegard and Sidney discussed the accident once more. "I was wondering . . ." Sidney began tentatively.

"Go on . . ."

"My father once had a motorbike with a sidecar, a second-hand Norton with a Swallow two-seater. I think he paid a hundred and seventy-five pounds for it. He let me have a go and it was heavy to handle, I can tell you . . ."

"I know what you are saying . . ."

"Quite hard to turn that lot over."

"Günter could have fallen asleep . . ."

"Unlikely on a bend and with the breeze in his face."

"We don't know he had that. In fact we don't know anything."

"I just don't think we're getting the full story, Hildegard."

"In this country that is normal."

They both knew that the dead man's participation in the revolutionary socialist movement had garnered him enough medals to prove that he must have been a member of the Stasi. But surely he was not important enough for this to be some state-sanctioned murder? He was only *der Hecht im Karpfenteich:* a big fish in a small and fairly irrelevant pond.

264

They would have discussed Günter's death further but they saw Karl Fischer approach. He was wearing dungarees and was carrying his electrician's toolbox, telling them that he was on his way to help out a friend. He was reluctant to be dragged into a meeting but once he had been spotted there was no escape. Hildegard offered her condolences, saying she knew that Günter and he had been friends for a long time.

"We were at school together. We both did well."

"Your fathers must have been very proud of you as you grew up," said Sidney.

"We were proof of their beliefs; examples of good parenting, ensuring the health and happiness of the working class."

"Was it hard to live up to their expectations?" Sidney asked.

Karl Fischer put down his toolbox. He could see that this was going to last longer than he had hoped but he didn't want to appear rude. "Hans Leber was the great orator. Werner Jansen, Günter's father, was more of a politician, like his son. He could play the game. The politicians liked him. When the party leaders came to Rügen they asked for Jansen's advice."

"About what?"

Karl hesitated for a moment, uncertain where the conversation was leading and when he could move on. "They wanted to know how to make the island open and accessible to everyone; how to give the workers better holidays. Less private ownership. More state control. The Jansens saw to that. It wasn't so hard."

"Some people found it more difficult," Hildegard observed. "I heard Otto was upset about the way in which everyone failed to support his father when he ran into all that trouble. I'm sure he must have talked to you about it, even at the festival."

"They lost their property. You know that. But Otto's father was greedy. He didn't reveal how much he had when they asked him for details. And so he was punished. Günter and his family couldn't defend him without endangering their own security. Neither could we, I am afraid."

"Did your father ever see Thomas Pietsch in prison?" Sidney asked.

"Visits were not encouraged. Only his family went. But we all attended the funeral in the spring. It was a sad time. Now there's another. We must look after each other in our grief."

"And you help Maria Jansen?"

"I try to be a good neighbour. That is all." He stopped, hoping that his answer would be sufficient, but Sidney said nothing, forcing Karl to continue. "I don't think Maria has ever been happy."

"Why do you say that?" Hildegard asked.

"You know the answer. Why do you make me say it? She knew her husband loved you."

"That was so long ago."

"It doesn't matter. She never had any confidence. I once told her that she would look lovely if, instead of having her hair swept back so tightly, she had a fringe. It would be pretty. She told me that she was too angry to be pretty. Günter was a bully like his father. I hope

Jürgen will not be the same when he finds a woman to love."

"Has Maria ever sought your help?"

"What do you mean?"

What Sidney really wanted to say was this: "Did Maria Jansen ask you to murder her husband?" But he could hardly do that now; even out on an open beach with no one close enough to overhear the conversation. Instead Hildegard explained that everyone was so upset about what had happened that they had started to come up with all sorts of theories. They were all highly improbable, she said. It was just that no one could quite accept that Günter Jansen, a larger-than-life jovial figure, had simply driven off the road.

"You suspect something else? Something deliberate?" Karl Fischer picked up his toolbox. "I believe that Günter was drunk. It was an accident. These things happen. Fate takes its course. If you think it is something else then you should talk to Otto. His father was the one who suffered at the hands of Günter's family. I have to leave you now."

Hildegard agreed with Sidney that Günter Jansen's recent attempt to acquire a property that had once been the Pietsch family home could be seen as a provocative act.

"We should see the widow, Sidney. I am sure Hanna Pietsch could tell us things."

"Would we need an excuse to go?"

"My mother is already planning a visit. We just have to find a way of joining her. If her son has only recently found out how culpable the Jansen family were in putting his father in prison all those years ago, then he might have been angry enough to do something about it."

"And all the men were together that night. It could have been any one of them, I suppose."

"Karl has a soft spot for Maria, Otto may want revenge for his father's imprisonment, Rolf is owed money. They also know each other well enough to create a conspiracy of silence. But Hanna Pietsch may tell us more. I'll have a word with my mother."

Sibilla Leber was immediately suspicious about the visit; why did Sidney have to come too?

Hildegard described her husband's pastoral gifts and his interest in seeing all walks of life. The fact that Hanna Pietsch lived in social housing was a side of Germany that tourists never normally saw. A visit would, she said, be an exemplary demonstration of the care given by the communist party to the poorest members of society.

The Pietsch home was salutary proof of how far the family had fallen. Having owned a beautiful twelve-bedroomed Bäderstil villa in the 1950s, mother and son now lived in a concrete block of flats next to a fish-processing plant and a patch of industrial wasteland; reduced to two bedrooms with a tiny lounge and bathroom. Communal washing hung from a shared green, but the large discharge pipes from the factory that snaked around the building compromised any chance of clean air. Sidney thought it would have been hard to live with any pride in such a place.

Hanna Pietsch expressed her sorrow for Günter's death, especially after such a happy night.

"It was not so happy at the end," Sibilla Leber observed. "But fate punishes those who think they can defy it."

"I know they all drank too much," said Hanna. "My son could hardly walk when he came through the door. He slept for most of the next day."

"Is he here now?"

"Otto has gone away for a few days. I am not sure where."

"What time did he get home that night?" Hildegard asked.

"It was already light. I think it must have been almost five o'clock. I heard him come in. He made such a noise."

"And he had been with Günter the whole time?"

"Karl too. And Rolf. They are good friends."

"And do you know if they all left Rolf's house together?"

"So many questions," Sibilla Leber muttered.

Hanna was unperturbed. "I imagine they did. Otto often drives them all home. But his car was outside when I went to bed. I checked because I thought he was home already but he was not. Then I was glad he had not taken it. I do not like it if he drinks too much. I think Karl must have been driving them. They never tell me. He has a car too. He can afford a better model. He knows how to work the system."

"And Otto does not?" Sidney asked.

"He did not have such a fortunate start in life. It was hard for him to find work. The authorities thought we were decadent and so we had to look even poorer than we were. It was difficult to do this at first and then, in time, it became easier and easier. We became very poor. Otto still drives his father's car. It is old, like me, and it keeps breaking down, also like me. It makes him so cross."

"Is he often angry?"

"With his father for dying; and with me for living."

Hanna Pietsch explained how they had stayed in the same flat for over fifteen years. It was not how they had once lived, but she could not complain and she did not want to draw attention to herself with the authorities, believing that the limitations on her freedom were mitigated by the fact that the state would always look after her.

Sidney was impressed by her forgiving attitude, considering what had happened in the past, and he said so.

"You know about that?" Hanna asked.

"He knows about everything," Sibilla Leber interrupted, before muttering the word *neugierig* once more.

"I suppose everyone has heard the story," Hanna answered, "even tourists like you."

"My husband is not a tourist," Hildegard pointed out, but it didn't matter. Hanna Pietsch didn't seem to worry who was listening to her.

"Public shame, no matter how long ago, can never become a secret. Our lives are summed up in so few

270

ways: Sibilla is the one whose husband was a communist hero; Günter was the one with the unhappy wife; I am the old widow whose husband was in prison."

"Did your husband blame anyone for his imprisonment?" Hildegard asked.

"It was only to be expected."

"In private, did he think Günter's father was responsible?"

"He didn't like to see his friend profit at our expense. But you know what they say? *Wo Geld kehrt und wendt, hat die Freundschaft bald ein End.* All friendships soon turn cold when money is involved."

Sidney took over once more. "Was your son aware of his father's feelings?"

"Otto did not know the Jansen family was directly responsible. He only found out recently, after my husband died. Someone told him at the funeral."

"And was he angry?"

"I think so. But he didn't behave any differently in public. Only at home. Emotion can be dangerous in this country. People do not like to talk about how they feel. It makes them vulnerable. Then others can take advantage."

Sibilla Leber said that she was surprised Hanna was speaking so freely.

"I am too old to care," the widow replied. "What can they do to me?"

"Do you know where Otto is?" Sidney asked.

"He just said he was leaving for a few days. He wanted to get away. He never tells me where he is going. He doesn't have to, I suppose. He is a grown man. That does not mean I do not keep the food ready for him. But it's hard. Do you have a son, Mr Chambers?"

"No. I have a beautiful daughter. Anna."

"My husband always wanted a boy but I think I would rather have had a little girl. They are better at looking after their parents."

Sidney could see that Sibilla Leber was about to interrupt and contradict this statement but thought better of it.

Hanna Pietsch continued. "Now I am old I do not know what will become of me. It would be easier if I still believed in God but too much has happened for me to do that."

"He is still there," said Sidney, "waiting for you."

"I cannot hear him calling. Perhaps it is too late for his mercy."

Sidney leant forward. "God's love will not let us go. He is with us. His love surrounds us. His call still summons us."

"Then he may have to wait a long time. I'm tired now. I do not like these questions. Please leave me."

As they left the building, Sidney put his arm around Hildegard. She was shivering. He saw how sad this visit home was making her. He wished they had not come.

The following day the Chambers family drove off to the Jasmund woods above Saßnitz to cheer themselves up a bit. Anna had been promised a trip to an enchanted forest where she could imagine all her favourite fairy tales with woodland settings coming to life: *Hansel and Gretel, Little Red Riding Hood, Snow White* and *Rapunzel*. Hildegard said they would discover an almost holy wilderness, the true and ancient Germany amidst the high trees, shallow ponds and sunlit clearings. It would be their own adventure, just the three of them, alone and together in a homeland she had always known and loved.

She hummed the Bach chorale "Now all the woods are sleeping" as she drove up the tree-lined hill on the edge of Saßnitz, passing a church that was almost entirely hidden by forestation. They then found themselves in a vast and eerie landscape, gravid with mystery and possibility. There were no lower branches on the densely planted beech trees; nor was there bracken on the ground to obscure the view. Instead, the forest stretched out before them, immense, unbounded and unknowable. There were paths to prevent them getting lost but it was difficult to tell where any of them led. There was no horizon; only an infinity of possibility. After walking for almost an hour, the family sat in a little hollow, enjoyed a picnic, and then lay down and looked up at the sky.

"Hello, Mr Moon, when are you coming back?" Anna asked and found there was an echo.

"Hello, hello, hello. Mr Moooooooon!"

Overhead they heard starlings, jays, the odd crow, and, in the far distance, the cries and laughter of children sounding as if they came from another life, a previous generation calling back to them across time.

"This is more like home," said Hildegard. "No people, no ideology, no conflict. A land that survives them all. This will still be here when everything else is past. Do you believe in the wisdom of the forest, Sidney?"

"Isn't the idea that people go into the woods to be tested in some way? They almost always get lost but they come out a different person. What was lost is found. You can't get more Christian than that."

"It's a risk, isn't it? You may get lost and you might even die."

"But, as Shakespeare has it, out of this nettle, danger, we pluck this flower, safety."

"If trees could speak . . ."

Anna was inspecting the hollow of a beech that might have served as the entrance to a magical underground kingdom. "Trees can't speak, Mummy. Don't be silly."

Hildegard smiled and called back to her daughter. "I like being silly sometimes, Anna. Don't you?"

"Not all the time. That would be silly."

"So," Sidney concluded, "being silly all the time is silly?"

"Yes, Daddy, but not as silly as you and your stupid questions."

As they drove back, Sidney confessed that he was still troubled by Günter's accident. The official account didn't make sense.

"It will be hard to contradict," Hildegard pointed out. "And it will be unpopular if you make your feelings known. The police are telling a very straightforward story. It was dark and late and it took place at a familiar blackspot."

"Jürgen suspects something," Sidney continued. "I feel sure of it."

"You think Günter was run off the road by someone he knew? By Otto? Is that why he has disappeared?"

"Don't you think that there is something wrong about the way the authorities have closed this without any investigation? They aren't even looking for the driver."

They passed the first sign for Binz. "Isn't this the road where it happened?"

"It is," said Hildegard.

"Then can we stop at the site of the accident? There can't be that many turns out of Prora. It's only four or five kilometres."

"We don't want to be questioned by the police."

"Humour me, my darling. Just for a moment."

"It may not be so funny if we're arrested. They don't need an excuse."

"We can pretend to be lost."

"On a straight road?"

"Or to have broken down. It won't take long."

Hildegard pulled over. "Five minutes only," she said. "Come on, Anna, we're going exploring."

"Is it a treasure hunt?" Anna asked.

"Yes. We need to find ten pine cones and three tyre tracks."

Once they had got out of the car, Sidney made his first observation. "Günter would have had to stop to turn left."

"Unless he didn't."

"But even if there was no traffic, he would have had to slow down when crossing the railway tracks. It's hard to believe he could have been travelling fast enough to skid."

"I've got three pine cones already," said Anna.

Hildegard looked for evidence of where Günter's bike must have ended up. At first they could not find any. Sidney suggested searching further up the road. Eventually, with Anna's help, they found an indentation in the ditch.

"I think that's where a wheel's been, Mummy. And there's a piece of metal. Look, it's a mirror . . ."

"Well done, Anna. Now see if you can find some more cones."

"This may be part of Günter's wing mirror," said Sidney.

"That's odd," Hildegard noted. "It's before the turn."

"Unless he was going the other way?" Sidney asked.

"I think we have to assume he was travelling home."

Hildegard thought out loud. "Which means that either he took the turn before or he was hit by a car coming from the opposite direction. He could have been knocked backwards and dragged along. If that is the case, we need to inspect the bike."

"Also," Sidney observed, walking to a narrow turning point by the railway line, "if he emerged here, instead, he still wouldn't have had enough time to build up sufficient speed to lose control and kill himself. He was hit, I'm sure of it."

"Another piece of metal, Daddy."

"Good girl."

"But if it was deliberate," Hildegard replied, "whoever did it must have known exactly when and where Günter was going to be on the road. They could even have followed him . . ."

"There could also have been a second driver."

"Do you mean Otto and Karl could have been working together?" Hildegard asked.

"And even with Rolf Müller."

"That really would mean trouble," said Hildegard. "We should get back."

Anna had found seven more pine cones and declared herself the winner. She hoped they could have ice creams on the beach when they returned to Binz.

"There is a phrase in German," Hildegard said, as she started the car once more, "*auf dem Holzweg sein*, which means 'to be on the wooden path'. It comes from the idea that when huge trees fall in the forest their trunks open up a new way through the woods. Travellers follow it, get lost and end up nowhere. I think you call it 'barking up the wrong tree'. I hope we're not doing that."

"And is there a phrase for barking up the right tree?"

"There is — *auf dem richtigen Weg sein*. We just have to find it."

On their return to the Villa Friede, they discovered that Rolf Müller had paid a visit. Someone had reported that they had seen Hildegard, Sidney and their child "acting suspiciously" on the main road. He now demanded that Mr and Mrs Chambers left matters well alone if they wanted to avoid arrest. Sidney did not like to ask on what charge, as he knew by now that anything could be made up to suit: spying, probably.

Günter's motorbike was also available for collection from the *Volkspolizisten*. Maria Jansen could pick it up in exchange for a necessary payment, ideally in Deutschmarks, the West German currency.

She sent Sidney and Hildegard. Once they got to the station on Jasmunderstraße, Rolf Müller ticked them off for their curiosity and reminded the "honoured guests" that the investigation had been concluded. Günter had driven off the road. No other vehicle had been involved. As they had suspected, it was a simple case of a drunken driver losing control at an accident blackspot. The bike was not in perfect condition, the tyre pressure was down, the brakes were worn, and there were plenty of scuffs and scratches from previous incidents which indicated that the victim was persistently reckless.

As Hildegard went to complete all the necessary paperwork and pay a fee, Sidney took a closer look at the bike. Most predominant were traces of pale-blue paint on the left of the back mudguard; if Günter had been driven off the road, this was the most likely colour of Trabi responsible: the same as Karl Fischer's car.

He started working away with his fingernail and discovered what he thought were two different types of paintwork; both pale blue and dark green. Someone had gone over the original damage in order to disguise it. It had not been done well. This was either all too hasty or a deliberate attempt to incriminate someone.

Hildegard emerged from the office and announced that the bike would be returned later that day. Both the paperwork and the police inquiry were complete. Just before they left, however, Sidney could not resist asking Rolf Müller one last question. "Did you get your money?"

"What do you mean?"

"I remember in the *Bierhalle;* how you told us all that Günter owed you *money*, but he could start by paying off his debt *in beer*."

"I don't remember that."

"Perhaps it doesn't matter."

"Those kinds of debts are cancelled after a death."

"What will happen to the Pensionshaus Garni?" Sidney asked.

"The one Günter was going to take over? It will stay within state control. No one will profit."

"There's no chance of Otto Pietsch being able to look after it? It used to belong to his father."

"That is impossible. Why do you ask?"

"It doesn't matter."

"I think it does. I have noticed that you are persistent, Mr Chambers."

Hildegard stepped in. "My husband likes to know how everything works. He is curious in that way."

"Politics is best left to the politicians: the Church to the clergy. Each have their own way of doing things, and if things are not explained that is not always so bad."

"I think it is better when everything is out in the open," said Sidney.

"Do you really?" Müller continued. "I thought priests preferred mysteries."

"That's probably why he feels so at home here," Hildegard interrupted, keen to dilute the tension.

"I'm not sure that I do," said Sidney.

"Then it's probably just as well that you won't be here for much longer," Rolf Müller concluded. He began to move away, keen to get back to his work.

"Could I ask one more question?" Sidney pressed. "I think Günter Jansen's body was found on the right-hand side of the road?"

"That is correct; towards Binz."

"I'm sorry, I don't understand. We drive on the left in England and so it is sometimes confusing."

"I am sure you don't need to worry. You will not be doing much more driving here."

"I don't intend to. It would be too dangerous. I just wanted to know, if the victim left the road and fell into the right-hand ditch, why the angle of impact on his bike is from the left? That would imply that someone hit him from the side as he crossed the road; quite violently, perhaps even deliberately."

"He fell to the right. There was no other vehicle involved."

"With the bike dented on the left."

"He must have turned over."

"With a sidecar?"

"He was travelling at speed. We know Günter liked to drive fast. There is no mystery to this. It was late and dark and the man had drunk too much. He was keen to get home. He made a miscalculation. That is all. Please, no more questions. This is your last warning. My colleagues are not so tolerant of interference."

Back at the Villa Friede, Hildegard tentatively asked Maria if she had seen Karl Fischer.

"He came to offer his condolences."

"What about Otto Pietsch? Has he paid you a visit?"

"He was not so fond of my husband."

"Did you ever see them argue?"

"Once; after his father's funeral. Günter said Otto was drunk, making accusations. He went to see him afterwards."

"Was it about the Pensionhaus Garni?"

"I wouldn't know."

"Günter was going to take it over. It had belonged to Otto's father."

"Nothing 'belongs' to anyone for long. Why does it matter now that everyone is dead?"

"Because Otto seems to be missing. His mother doesn't know where he is."

"Perhaps he has gone away."

"Would you know where?"

"Karl might. They are friends."

"And would Karl tell you?"

"Why would he do that?"

"Because you love each other. You have no secrets."

Maria almost smiled. "You think it is all as simple as that?"

In Jürgen's room, Sidney tried once again to ask the boy about the night of the accident. "Is there anything you want to tell me?"

Jürgen said nothing but handed Sidney an earphone. Once he had checked it was in his guest's ear properly, the boy turned the knob of his cassette recorder. Play. Stop. Rewind. He had to go over the actions several times before Sidney could understand that he was listening to part of a conversation between Maria and Karl Fischer. They seemed to be talking about a sparrow or a starling, a *Spatz*, which could not find its nest. He would have to ask Hildegard.

"*Hat der Spatz seinen Baum gefunden?*" This was Maria's voice. "Has the sparrow found its tree?"

And Karl had replied, "*Ja, sein Nest ist am Boden.* Yes, his nest is on the ground."

That evening, Hildegard and Sidney visited Karl Fischer. He lived in a modern detached house, not far from the Villa Friede on the Wylichstraße, with the sea at one end of the street and a lake at the other. Three iron swallows decorated the frontage.

As they had suspected, Maria Jansen was already there.

Karl Fischer expressed his surprise but gave them a tentative welcome and asked them to sit down. Hildegard apologised for the intrusion. She and her husband just wanted to ask about the night of the Friendship Festival. There were a few things neither of them could understand.

282

"Death is always hard," Karl replied.

"But we wanted to ask about the living."

"It's difficult to remember. Everyone had drunk so much."

Sidney decided to take a risk. "I think you were sober enough to drive. You gave everyone a lift."

"It doesn't really matter how we all got home, does it? The fact is that Günter did not."

"And I think you, and perhaps all your friends, know why."

"Of course we do. He drove off the road. The police inquiry has concluded."

Hildegard hesitated. "Rolf Müller has told you. Already?"

"It's obvious."

"I am not sure that it is," said Sidney. "We looked at Günter's motorbike and found traces of paintwork at the rear. We think he may have been hit by a green car."

"Mine is blue."

"But Otto's is green."

"Then talk to Otto."

"He is missing."

Karl sighed. "This really isn't any of your concern, Mr Chambers."

"But it is interesting that you use the word 'concern'. You have all been trying to make us think that if this ever became a case of murder then it would be motivated by revenge. Günter Jansen and his father were responsible for the ruin of Otto's family. Otto Pietsch only discovered this recently, at his father's funeral. He drives a green Trabant. Now he has disappeared. Why? Because his mother must have warned him this might happen. If anyone thought Günter's death was not an accident then the Pietsch family would have been made a scapegoat all over again."

"Otto is probably in Berlin."

"It does not matter, because I think that you were driving his car on the night of the accident."

"Why would I do that?"

"Because you decided to split the responsibility for Günter's death."

"I don't understand why you think any one of us would want to kill a friend."

"Let me try and explain," Sidney began. "Then perhaps you can tell me if it is true or not."

"I don't see why we should listen to you," said Maria.

"Have patience," Hildegard cut in. "It is probably safer to know what people are saying about you than not."

"Rumours never help anyone," said Karl.

"You gave everyone a lift home," Sidney continued. "That you admit."

"I do."

"But you didn't go home yourself."

"I didn't?"

"No, you did not; at least, not immediately. Instead, at Otto's house, you switched cars. You got into his dark-green Trabant because everyone had seen you in your pale-blue car all night. Otto either knew exactly what you were doing or was too drunk to notice you take his keys. You knew that if there were green paint marks found at the scene of the crime, no one would think it was you because your car is blue; and if anyone did see a dark-green car then it would be easy to blame the Pietsch family because Otto had a motive for murder."

"This is not what happened."

"I think it's close enough. You left well before Günter. Rolf Müller knew of the plan and detained him so that you had enough time to take Otto's car and lie in wait. You parked just beyond the bend, out of sight, probably with your lights off."

"If I did that then I would be the one most likely to be hit."

"But you weren't. I think you had some form of communication with Rolf Müller. He gave you a warning when Günter was leaving. You waited for him to approach the bend. As soon as you saw him you accelerated, hit him from the side, pushed him into the ditch and drove on, probably back to Rolf Müller's house. He then reported on 'the accident' and made sure that the evidence fitted the explanation. Otto is missing because his car is missing. He has taken it far away, probably with traces from Günter's motorbike on the front left bumper."

Karl Fischer was unmoved. "You've no evidence for any of this."

"We have your words. They are on Jürgen's tape recorder. He liked to keep it running on record; something he probably learned from his father. He played me a little section. I had to ask Hildegard what it meant. Maria is heard asking: '*Hat der Spatz seinen Baum gefunden?* Has the sparrow found its tree?' And you reply: '*Ja, sein Nest ist am Boden.* Yes, his nest is on the ground.' The Sparrow was Günter's nickname from school. You both knew he was going to die."

"That tape could mean anything."

"I think it is clear."

"Even if it is, who will you tell this fantastical story? Rolf Müller? He will be amused if this is your attempt to make sense of it all. Then, if you persist, he will be annoyed. And that won't help you."

"I hope Rolf Müller will be chastened and pursue a conviction. And if he does, then you may not be so confident in your answers. We think he retouched Günter's bike to add a little blue paint. Insurance, so that he could blame either you or Otto, whoever paid him least to keep quiet."

"You have been so inventive, Mr Chambers," Karl Fischer replied. "You have worked so hard when you should have been on holiday. It's such a shame, and in such a beautiful landscape. You must have missed so much."

"I don't think I've missed anything at all."

Maria Jansen spoke at last. There was no point continuing, she said. It was one man's word against another's. Everyone at the Villa Friede would wonder where they were. "Anyone will think this story is crazy."

"You all worked together," Sidney insisted. "Otto Pietsch's family was ruined by the Jansens and they have waited thirteen years for vengeance. Rolf Müller has bad debt, thought he was being outmanoeuvred by

Günter's corruption and made sure that he would profit from any 'accident' and loss of property. And you two love each other."

"You would know our feelings better than we do ourselves?" Maria asked. "How can you say such things?"

"I am not judging you."

"But you have accused us. And I don't believe you can prove anything at all."

"Günter's death was an accident," Karl Fischer resumed. "If you suggest anything different we will make counteraccusations. We will create so many stories and so much paperwork that no one will ever know what truly happened. We might even find a way to make you look responsible yourself, Mr Chambers. You are a stranger and an amateur. No one will believe anything you say unless you would prefer to stay here for five or six years in order to try and prove your theory. Prosecutors and the police will give up. Nothing can be done. It's too much work over the death of a man nobody liked."

"Günter always thought he was popular."

"He was deluded," said Maria. "He made everyone around him miserable."

"Not his son."

"Jürgen was afraid of him, just as I was. Neither of us ever loved him." She turned to Hildegard. "You know what it is like to be married to the wrong man."

"You don't mean Sidney?"

"No. Your first husband. The one who killed himself."

"He was murdered," said Sidney.

"That was not the story we were told."

"Let's not talk about this," said Hildegard.

Maria would not let her go. "You have found happiness. Why can't I?"

"I think you know the answer to that. You will find happiness only when you confront the truth."

Karl cut in to prevent any admission of guilt. "The Jansen family started the treachery a long time ago. They used us all."

"And so what was," Sidney asked, "in one generation a tight group of friends becomes, in the next, a closed circle of deceit?"

"You could say that. In fact you can say what you like. No one will listen to you."

"I wonder if you will be able to live easily knowing that this crime is on your conscience?"

"I have conscience enough," said Maria at last. "Although I don't feel any better; only that the pain cannot be as bad as it once was."

"People think that death will help matters," said Sidney. "That it brings on an ending. But it seldom does. The things that trouble us are the hardest to forget. If we do something rash, hoping a violent act will overcome a past horror, then we double the agony."

"Perhaps if I'd known you before," said Maria, "you would have told me. You preach the selfless life. And I know Jesus said we had to love our neighbour as ourselves. But so many people hate themselves; how can someone like me love their neighbour, or even their husband, if they cannot love themselves?"

288

"By understanding that the greatest happiness often comes from outside."

"That's easy for you to say."

"No," Sidney answered firmly, "it's not at all easy to say, much less to practise. But that is what faith involves. It's not only a question of belief in God. That may even be the easy bit. It's faith in other people that counts."

"Even when they let you down?"

"Especially when they let you down."

"And if they keep doing so?"

"Sometimes you do have to walk away," said Sidney. "I know that. It's not always a sin to give up on people — but it is to kill them."

The "holiday", such as it was, had come to an end. The Chambers family made their farewells and Sibilla Leber said that she hoped they might visit her in Leipzig for Christmas.

"You know how you always loved it as a child, Hildegard. You were so excited when your Advent Calendar came and I remember how you used to fill your shoes with grass so early for the Feast of St Nicholas. One year you even filled them twice, hoping that he would come back and put sweets in them all over again!"

"I know, Mother, you say this every time I come home; but Trudi did that. Not me."

"I wouldn't be guilty of such a mistake. We could make *Stollen* and gingerbread houses and dress the tree with the family decorations. Anna would learn about our traditions and sing carols as they are supposed to be sung — in German."

"Christmas is difficult for us, Mother, as you know. It is a busy time of year for Sidney."

"He can't be in church all the time. Indeed, from what you tell me, he is not there very much at all. I am surprised . . ."

"You could always come and stay with us," Sidney interrupted gallantly.

"I prefer my own home. But it is kind of you to offer," Sibilla Leber replied. "I know you don't really like coming here."

"That's not true, Mother."

"I am sorry. I don't mean to be rude. Forgive me." Sibilla was suddenly tearful. "I don't always remember that I have two daughters. You are so far away. And I do like seeing my little Anna. She is growing so fast. She reminds me of you, Hildegard. She has the same imagination. I hope you are proud of her."

"We are."

"Don't spoil her. She needs discipline. When will she start the piano?"

"Next year, I hope."

"That's good. One family tradition will continue at least. Please don't make it such a long time before you come back, my beloved. If it's for my funeral I shall be very angry."

The Chambers family took an evening train to Lübeck, crossed the border, and travelled back into West Germany as night fell. Sidney was glad to be on his way home at last but fretted that things had been left unfinished. Justice had not been done. Hildegard tried to console him by saying that he couldn't be expected to win every battle, especially in a foreign land.

"And remember, those students in Cambridge avoided punishment when that necklace was stolen. You turned a blind eye there."

"That was theft rather than murder and they were young."

"Is morality relative?"

"I think punishment should fit the crime. But in this country there are so many laws it's hard to keep track. Everyone is so watchful, so suspicious. Even when people are supposed to be enjoying themselves they aren't able to relax."

Anna slept on her mother's lap and the train sped on towards Hamburg. Hildegard asked why her husband thought himself so responsible for the happiness of others. Some people were never going to be content. It was a delusion. Why expect them to be something that they could never be?"

"Because I am a priest. I have to believe that we can all be redeemed."

"I am not sure Maria will ever be convinced of that, despite her faith. Some people cannot escape themselves."

"Have you ever felt like that?" Sidney asked.

"During my first marriage, yes, towards the end; and sometimes in the past, during the war. But let's not talk about that now."

"Coming to Germany has made me remember all over again how different our lives were before we met. I think it was listening to Bach last Sunday, sung in German in a German church as it would have been two hundred and fifty years ago. I try to keep in mind the fact that you haven't had an easy life — not since you were a child."

"After my father died. That's when so many children grow up; when the first parent goes, no matter how old they are. It happened much earlier to me. I am not alone in that."

"No, but then there was the war."

"And after it, I took some risks," Hildegard admitted. "I left my homeland to form another life. I do not like to complain. I always have music, just as you have faith. That is my consolation. And everything has been better since I met you . . ."

"As it has been for me."

"And as it could be for Maria if they all escape justice."

"Do you understand what it must have been like for her?"

"I don't know, Sidney. I don't think I have ever had such desperation. But that does not mean I do not have moments of loneliness. Sometimes I have to submit to the sadness and let it pass. They are not because of anything you have done. They just come."

"There are times when I don't quite know how to help," Sidney replied, "and I leave you to your piano or your thoughts. But I am sure I should do better. Priests are like doctors. They often neglect those closest to them."

"When you are exiled from your own country and then come back, as I have done, you feel that you are a stranger in both places: too German for England and now too English for Germany, or whatever country my homeland has become. And I am not a proper communist, like my father, in spite of what everyone thinks. I look at the GDR and I see what is happening and I do not feel his successors are doing such a great job. I don't think that this is what he imagined when he fought and died for the cause thirty-five years ago. And so I cannot help but feel separated from all that hope and history. My mother is the same. She won't admit it . . ."

"She has to keep the flame alive."

"It's hard for her, Sidney. You think she does not like you but you should not worry about that. If I had married Günter it would have been the same. She has never liked anyone who is not my father. And he was not a saint, never mind what she says."

"I wish I had met him."

"I wish you had too; and I sometimes wish I had known you earlier. But then we were different people and we may not have loved each other. So perhaps it is just as well. You can be a different kind of hero to our family, Sidney . . ."

"I think heroism is dangerous."

"Don't worry. You are far from being one in the traditional sense."

"What about the untraditional?"

"There is still hope. Look at Anna sleeping. We must be her anchor."

"And we will be," Sidney promised. "Both of us."

They looked out of the train window to see a firework display over Hamburg. It was as if people were sending their own miniature rockets to the moon, bursting with light and transient colour. "Do you think we will ever have a normal life?" Hildegard asked.

"Not a chance," her husband replied. "Do you want one?"

"Not in a million years."

Hildegard smiled, took her husband's hand and studied it. "If only I could tell our future."

Love and Duty

There were many times in Sidney's life when he felt grateful for the opportunities God gave; when he found himself in a situation he could not have been in had he chosen a different profession. Some of them had been difficult and tragic, yet there were other, more consoling and surprising moments of respite. One of them was his unlikely attendance at the Royal Albert Hall to hear Pink Floyd play on 7th February 1970.

Roger Waters, whom Sidney had first met on the Meadows after the theft of Olivia Randall's necklace, had provided him with a pair of tickets. Sidney had been at the start of so many things for him, he said, and he had been the accidental inspiration for one of their finest songs. The bass player and co-lead vocalist of one of Britain's most exciting "prog-rock" bands did not specify the exact track but sent an LP care of the cathedral so that Sidney could experience "how it all blends together".

Hildegard was teaching in Ely until seven that evening and Geordie was investigating an arson attack on a Cambridge antique shop, so Sidney invited Amanda to accompany him. He had not seen her for a while and asked his wife if it would be all right, saying that he wanted news of his friend's job and her life post-divorce. Hildegard said that she would be amused to discover what Amanda thought of such avant-garde music and, even though it might cheer her up, she was pretty sure their friend would complain about the volume.

Sidney was distracted on leaving Ely, missed the train he had intended to catch, and was late. Amanda smoked a cigarette and fretted as she waited, worried about missing the beginning of the concert, only to be told that these events never started on time anyway. A student in a T-shirt and jeans then told her that she looked pretty cool for a woman "her age".

Amanda had not taken kindly to the remark but was, none the less, flattered that the younger generation had paid homage to her elegance. She was wearing a Hannah Troy white silk dress with a black front panel, flared elbow-length sleeves and what appeared to be a clerical collar, half black and half white.

"I can't be good all the time and I need to dress up in the evenings otherwise I get too depressed. Besides, I thought this might amuse you, Sidney. Never grey. Just black and white. That's what you get and, at the moment, because of your tardiness, I'm afraid I'm feeling pretty black. You must never leave me to wait on my own in public again. I haven't got the cheekbones for it."

Sidney looked stricken and then caught her eye. He could see that she didn't really mean what she was saying. "I'm glad you're back to your combative best," he said. "But don't worry. I think we'll be all right. We've got a box so we can slip in and out. And Roger promised he'd send up some drinks."

"You don't get that at the Proms."

"I don't think they let you take anything in to Glyndebourne either. Things are looking up."

The concert began with a frenzy of strobe lighting over a wash of deep red, and a chaos of drums, percussion and bass guitar that Amanda mistook for tuning up. After a couple of numbers the band then settled into "Careful with That Axe Eugene", a number that instantly reminded Sidney of Fraser Pascoe's murder.

"Do they sing at all?" Amanda shouted into Sidney's ear. "Or are they just going to wail?"

"I think the lyrics come later."

"Now I know why it's called 'prog-rock'. They play every chord in turn and hold on to each one for as long as possible."

"I think this is just the build-up. I'm rather enjoying it. Have you ever heard anything like it?"

"We've had twenty minutes of this and nothing has built up to anything at all."

Things livened up with "Sysyphus" and "Atom Heart Mother" but Amanda insisted that the music sounded like the space-age soundtrack for a film she had no intention of seeing. The evening was not exactly a success and Sidney wished Hildegard had been able to come. She would have been more broadminded about the soundscape and amused by the seriousness of performers tripping to their own music before a crowd of secular charismatics.

Amanda cheered up by the time they got to dinner. She had persuaded the maître d' at Mirabelle to let them eat late, and ordered champagne as an early celebration of Sidney's birthday. There were only a few days left before Lent and she told him that if he was going to stop drinking this year, he might as well stock up now.

"I don't think it works quite like that, Amanda."

"I don't know how you do it. Abstinence from anything is such a bore."

"Restraint is the road to redemption," Sidney replied, quaffing his first glass.

Amanda laughed at the gulf between word and deed and they were almost back to their old routine. She was relieved to be able to speak, saying that she had only agreed to come to the concert as it gave them a chance to talk properly afterwards and resume a bit of normality. She still found social events difficult and she had lost some of her confidence in situations where she didn't know people well. But she was enjoying her new job at the British Museum. In fact she had already discovered a "sleeper": a previously misattributed work which she thought to be a presentation drawing of a young male nude by Michelangelo for his friend Tommaso dei Cavalieri. The circumstances were still hush-hush.

"It seems you have 'a saucerful of secrets', to quote from one of the songs of tonight. Is it exciting?"

"Well, I think it's a lot more interesting than that farrago of noise, I must say. If you ask me, Pink Floyd's main secret, if that really is what they call themselves, is how on earth they persuade people to come to their psychedelic howling."

"I liked it. All those lyrics about setting the controls for the heart of the sun and the man making the shape of questions to heaven."

"I couldn't understand a word of it. In any case, you're just saying that to be provocative."

"We have to move with the times."

"I don't know, Sidney. It doesn't seem so long ago that we were jiving to jazz."

"You were doing the dancing, Amanda. I was only watching."

"I distinctly remember you jiving. Quite badly, in fact."

"An aberration of my youth."

"It's depressing to dwell on past mistakes." Amanda put down her menu. "I think I'll have the crab and avocado, or maybe the devilled kidneys. That would require some additional red wine. That's probably just as well, as I'm in need of fortification."

"That sounds ominous."

"I'm afraid it is," she continued, after dispatching their order. "There's something I have to tell you."

"Oh, golly, Amanda."

"I should warn you, it's quite awkward."

"Is it about the divorce?"

"No, that's all done and dusted."

"And it's not Henry?"

"Not at all. He is no longer any part of my life."

"Then perhaps it's a new admirer?" Sidney asked, attempting a comical raise of one eyebrow.

"Don't be silly. Even if I had one I'm hardly likely to tell you at this stage. No, it's trickier than mere romance." Still Amanda hesitated.

"What is it then? Spit it out."

"Leonard."

Sidney's voice jumped an octave. "Leonard?"

"Your former curate."

"I *know who he is*. I didn't realise you had been seeing him."

Amanda signalled to the waiter to refill their glasses and told him off. "It's always so annoying when you store the bottle away from the table. Please don't." She then turned back to Sidney. "We're friends too. Leonard's one of the few men in whose company I've never had to worry if there's any ambiguity of feeling."

"Do you mean you worry about most men?"

"Yes. That's why I've stopped seeing them. I don't like meeting new people. They either want my 'understanding' about their marriage, or they flirt and hope for something more, or they talk about some kind of business initiative or charitable foundation in a roundabout attempt to extort money."

"I would have thought that marrying Henry had put a stop to all that."

"Well, now I've put a stop to him."

"And so you were having lunch with Leonard?"

"Drinks. I took him to Claridge's. He likes places that are a teensy bit camp, as I am sure you can imagine."

"I never really think of Leonard in that way, mainly because I don't think he sees himself as anything other than a celibate priest."

"Which is why our conversation was so troubling, Sidney."

"How was that?"

"He asked me for money."

"Leonard?"

"Quite a lot. Fifty pounds. A loan."

"Did you ask him what it was for?"

"Personal reasons, he said. Perhaps he's got himself into terrible debt? He did say that he was in a pickle."

"And did you agree to lend it to him?"

Amanda hesitated as their starters were delivered to the table. "I did. I said I would give it to him in cash next week. As you know, I like Leonard very much and he seemed quite relieved. Then we talked about Michelangelo and the British Museum."

"Ah, yes. T. S. Eliot. Women come and go talking of Michelangelo."

"Actually we talked about the sonnets. Leonard was very helpful. He knows them, of course.

"Veggio co' bei vostri occhi un dolce lume,
Che co' miei ciechi già veder non posso . . ."

"Italian was never my strong point, Amanda."

"But detection is."

"What do you mean?"

Amanda leant back in her chair and folded her arms. It was a familiar gesture that always meant trouble. "You know perfectly well, Sidney. I'd like you to talk to Leonard as soon as you can. You need to get to the bottom of all this. You're his friend, aren't you? Something, or someone, is making him frightened."

After his return from London, and his abandoning of yet another course of Lenten abstinence on the dubious grounds that "tension" and his "volume of work" required the necessary consolation of alcohol, Sidney picked up the phone to hear that his presence was required in Cambridge. Geordie announced that the arson victim who had prevented his attendance at the Pink Floyd concert needed a pastoral visit.

"I think you know him. He remembers you from that case we had when we first worked together: Lord Teversham, the man who was killed during a production of *Julius Caesar*."

"What's his name?"

"Simon Hackford."

"Good heavens!"

"What's wrong?"

"Yes. I do remember him."

"Hackford is, as you may know, something of a homosexualist."

"Not '-ist', Geordie. He is simply a homosexual."

"They say they're one in twenty these days."

"I'm surprised the figure is so low."

"You have a way with these kind of people, Sidney. I thought you could be of assistance."

"I hope I have 'a way' with everyone, Geordie, whoever they are and in whatever situation they find themselves."

"The thing is, the man doesn't want us to investigate. He says the stress will get to his nerves. I hope it's not an insurance scam like the photographer we had a few years back."

"I don't think Simon Hackford would set fire to his own shop. He loves those antiques too much."

"At least there wasn't much damage. It certainly wasn't a professional job; they used the kind of Molotov cocktail any amateur could knock up in a shed; although the lock was picked, so it did take some knowhow."

"No witnesses?" Sidney asked.

"None so far. You don't get many of them at two in the morning."

"A local man?"

"Possibly, but Hackford's well liked and it's hard to find anything against someone whose main love, apart from the obvious, is eighteenth-century English furniture."

"Perhaps it was meant as a warning. Something to scare him?"

"It could be that. I'm not sure, Sidney. I'd like you to have a word with Hackford. He's Leonard's friend, isn't he?"

"You know that?"

"I was waiting for you to tell me; and I have noted that you deliberately didn't hand over the information, even when I gave you the opportunity. Don't think you can keep things from me, Sidney. Our friendship comes first."

"Priests do have their own code of confidentiality."

"That doesn't seem to have stopped you in the past. Hackford trusts you. Thousands wouldn't."

"I think you'll find thousands do," said Sidney with uncustomary arrogance. He was not going to let Geordie have the last word.

Simon Hackford's antique shop was situated in Trumpington Street, almost opposite the Fitzwilliam Museum, with four clear windows in which were displayed a tasteful collection of china, landscape paintings, portraiture and traditional English furniture. The front door had been destroyed and there were scorch marks across the floor, but the main area of the blaze had been confined to a walnut chest and gilded mirror. As such, the physical damage was relatively minimal; the emotional trauma of such a deliberate attack, Sidney suspected, was likely to be worse.

The proprietor was a well-preserved man in his early fifties, dressed in a three-piece double-breasted Prince of Wales suit, as if the layers of cloth could give him some form of protection against the modern world. His was a look of quiet decoration; discreet but stylish cufflinks, an understated watch, a pale-blue spotted handkerchief, and a navy silk tie worn over the same Turnbull & Asser shirt his father had owned. Tradition,

304

perhaps, and a belief in the aesthetics of connoisseurship, had meant to keep him safe from contemporary barbarism.

Hackford was known for his ability to spot high-quality silver. He had made money after finding a lost set of apostle spoons but had then let his most lucrative patron down by failing to spot a Gainsborough at a country auction. In the early 1950s he had been part of a lavender marriage, the result of both parties trying to please their parents, but since his divorce some five years previously he had been careful to keep a low profile.

He told Sidney that he could not imagine anyone who would have wanted to burn his shop down.

"Leonard's been so on edge," he added.

"That's unlike him."

"About the Bedford thing."

Sidney was confused. This was new information and had nothing to do with the arson. "What Bedford thing?"

"You must know. You're an archdeacon."

"But not in Leonard's diocese."

"He's being considered for a bishopric."

"Leonard? But he's only been at St Albans for three years."

"They like him there."

"A bishop." (*And before me!* Sidney thought before being ashamed of himself.) "Whereabouts?"

"Bedford. It's vacant."

"I've just recommended one of our own clergy for the position. But Leonard would be far better."

"He's not so sure. Will you talk to him, Sidney? Not about this, but about his future. I've been so worried. He's been such a supportive friend and I don't want to add to his anxiety." He waved his arm in the direction of the fire damage. "I am sure this was just a one-off."

"It does seem unfortunate. You haven't had any unusual visits recently? People watching when you lock up?"

"The police have asked about all that. I've told them I'd rather not make a fuss. It's probably not even worth claiming on the insurance. I'll just have to cough up."

"But your shop has been attacked. The police can't stand idly by; otherwise the perpetrators triumph. We have to defend ourselves against those who would do us ill."

"But what if I don't want a confrontation? What if I am happy with my privacy?"

"Is something else troubling you, Simon? Something that you would rather tell me than the police?"

"It doesn't take too much to make me nervous. If you could have a proper chat with Leonard I would be grateful. I don't want him getting all worked up about my worrying."

"He'll be concerned about you, I'm sure."

"Talk to him, Sidney. It's not been easy recently. He'll tell you."

Rather than arranging to meet Leonard directly, Sidney took a more tangential approach, using the opportunity of their joint attendance at a forthcoming conference at Church House to discuss matters informally. He did not want his former curate to think he was barging in, but he was pretty sure they would both have limited patience with the bureaucratic minutiae involved in the formation of a new synodical form of government for the Church of England. The possibility of a mutual escape was almost guaranteed.

It was a bitter afternoon when they emerged into the Westminster gloom. Sidney offered Leonard a toasted teacake and a warming brew at the Army & Navy store. After reviewing the events of the day and exchanging ecclesiastical tittle-tattle, he pressed his friend for a little more information. He had heard rumours . . .

Leonard hesitated, his teacake suspended midair. "Rumours?"

"About a forthcoming appointment."

"I don't think that's likely. I am sure it will all go away." Leonard resumed eating as if the swallowed teacake would also involve the disappearance of the subject-matter.

"A bishopric?"

"I have let them know that it is too soon."

"You don't want it?"

"I don't feel I'm ready, Sidney."

"And is that the only reason?"

"Pretty much."

Leonard's lack of a direct answer convinced Sidney to press further. He asked if everything was all right. Why hadn't he been told, for example, about the arson attack on Simon Hackford's shop?

"I didn't think it was anything to do with you."

"But Keating is the investigating officer. He's your friend too."

"Simon doesn't want a fuss."

"When did you last see him?"

Leonard turned to his tea. "Everything's been a bit difficult recently."

"Is there anything you want to tell me?" Sidney asked. "You haven't run into financial difficulties or anything like that?"

"No, nothing, really. But thank you for your concern."

Sidney felt that he was getting nowhere. He tried a more oblique route to the heart of the matter. "I was with Amanda last week . . ."

"And how is she?"

"We were talking about her potential discovery of a drawing by Michelangelo. I'm sure she must have mentioned it when she last saw you."

"She did." Leonard perked up, relieved to be talking about something else. "We had a long discussion about Renaissance theories of beauty and the quest for the ideal; how we, as mere mortals, may have to start from people we love and the world around us, but the idea is to transcend our merely sensual experience and reach out for the divine."

"A religious approach to art, almost?"

"Exactly. How successful those artists were at following their prevailing beliefs is another matter. I said that it's probably easier to grasp the theory when in the presence of a beautifully proportioned young man or woman but it's a lot harder with people who've got their flesh in all the wrong places. Amanda was quite amused."

"Oh, I think she likes a balance between scholarship and larky conversation."

"I don't think I've ever been that risqué before. But, with her, you feel you can say anything. She gives you confidence, don't you think? I suppose that's why you've always got on so well."

Sidney stuck to his guns. He was not going to be sidetracked into a discussion of his affection for a woman who was not his wife. "Why have you asked her for money, Leonard?"

Leonard put down his teacup and their companionable mood was gone. "She told you?"

"Amanda is my oldest friend."

"She is a friend of mine too. She promised it would go no further."

"You know what she's like."

"I trusted her."

Sidney thought that Leonard might walk out, but they hadn't paid and he was not the type to make a scene. "She is worried about you; and now I am too. Why do you need the money, Leonard?"

"I don't want to tell you. It would put you in a difficult position."

"Is it something illegal?"

"Not according to the laws of the land. Although it is not something that is spoken about very much in the Church."

"Does it concern your private life?"

"Do I need to spell it out?"

Sidney decided that he would have to help his friend get to the point, whether he liked it or not. "Is someone blackmailing you, Leonard?"

"I knew as soon as we started this conversation that you would guess. I wish we hadn't got into all this."

"You know that I am one of your greatest supporters. I will do nothing to harm you. And I am still your priest."

"Have you always known?"

"I have not thought about your life in that way at all. You are just my friend Leonard to me. And your friends love you for your Leonard-ness, whatever that might entail."

"People used to be more private about things."

"That did not always help matters. Secrecy can bring forth its own terrors."

Leonard looked for a distraction — a piece of teacake, another cup from the pot, but there was nothing left. "I think a man's private life is his own business."

"We talked about this when you first became my curate. Our vocation makes it more complicated."

"And sometimes more simple if only God is privy to our thoughts."

"That does not make life any the less true."

Leonard thought for a moment. "Do you think the Church will ever accept people like me?"

"You are here, Leonard, working in the Church."

"But you are different, Sidney. You turn a blind eye."

"You do not force me to look."

"And so a man's feelings should remain hidden, you think?"

Sidney tried to balance friendship with duty. "There is the question of tact: offending others, drawing unnecessary attention. You know the reasons given. The Church doesn't like these things out in the open. Nowadays people are all too keen to declare their emotions; just because you *feel* something deeply doesn't mean that you have to tell everyone about it. There's a lot to be said for discretion."

"Some would call that hypocrisy."

"As I say, not everything has to be transparent. It is perhaps less painful to keep these matters to oneself."

"But what if one is so in love that you want to declare it to the world?"

"Then tell me, Leonard."

"It's Simon. Is that a shock?"

"I know it's Simon. I saw him yesterday."

"Has he told you anything? I mean about . . ."

"He has not. You tell me."

"It's quite a long story. He came for the Feast of St Alban in June, when we decorate the shrine with roses. It's in memory of the legend that roses grew from the ground where his blood was shed. You remember, Sidney?"

"'So among the roses brightly shines St Alban.'"

"Simon brought a little bouquet he had picked from his mother's garden. It was odd because they were a creamy yellow, and I told him that I had never liked the colour and he told me that he had gathered them specially because the crest of the city is yellow and blue

311

and he wanted to bring something appropriate. He was amused because one of the varieties he had chosen was called 'Rambling Rector'. I hadn't ever discovered that he knew about roses but then there was so much about him that I didn't know, and I realised then that I *wanted* to know.

"We had lunch in the White Hart and then we went for a walk round the lake and across to the Roman theatre. He'd never seen it. We talked about drama, and that production of *Julius Caesar* during which his old friend Lord Teversham was killed. He said it all seemed a lifetime ago and that he had felt alone ever since his death. I think we talked a little about the nature of friendship and he came back for tea. I'd made one of Mrs Maguire's walnut specials. She gave me the recipe when I left Grantchester. It was her little farewell. She told me that she'd never given it to anyone else and it would have to remain 'our secret'. Simon and I sat together and I can't really remember what we talked about because my head was filled with the delightful terror of what might happen next. When the time came for him to leave and get his train I knew that I didn't want him to go. It was silly really. He got up and went into the hall and I opened the door and a handshake was insufficient and a hug embarrassing, and then he just kissed me and everything changed."

"You don't have to tell me, Leonard."

"It's quite all right. I understand it now. In the past, I didn't know that I was a homosexual. I didn't think I was anything. It didn't bother me very much. But then there was someone. Simon. And I fell in love. It didn't

312

feel 'unnatural' or 'abnormal' at the time. It felt right. Do you know the poem by Southey that has the words 'Not where I breathe, but where I love, I live'?"

"I do." Sidney had once said those same words to Hildegard, and he thought about her now, as Leonard talked about falling in love and how right it felt.

"When you and I first met, Sidney, I noticed how tactful you were when I didn't know who I was. I think we had a conversation about the Archbishop of Canterbury's position on the matter. Then there was the death of Lord Teversham and Ben Blackwood and the Wolfenden Report. Before then they thought that a love of another man was something that could be cured; that such feelings were temptations that should be resisted. But I don't believe that a Christian should ever renounce the possibility of true love, even if it is earthly, flawed, and doomed by mortality. We have to acknowledge the possibility of becoming better people, of being made more than we ever could be on our own, of having the capacity to love. Surely to deny that would be to commit the greater sin?"

"You don't have to deny it; but in your position you have to be careful. It can damage your chances . . ."

"Of being a bishop, you mean? I'm not worried about that."

"But you are worried about the blackmail, I presume?"

"It has unsettled me, I have to admit. It's come just when I've found happiness. We'd even bought a double bed."

"You shouldn't tell me that, Leonard."

313

"It doesn't matter. I know you will be discreet."

"I will, but these things can get out. Perhaps the arsonist knew . . ."

"I don't know what he knows. That's the terrible thing. I don't even know who is doing all this."

"The threats are not signed at all?"

"He is using what I take to be an assumed name: Christian Grace; although his is neither very Christian, nor very gracious. He has told me to leave the money in a pigeonhole in the abbey next Wednesday."

"He is a member of the congregation then?"

"He doesn't have to be. Anyone can use them. No one checks. I am supposed to leave it under the letter 'G'. And there's no way of knowing when he will pick it up, so there's no point anyone lying in wait."

"A verger could keep an eye."

"I doubt that's possible. I can't confide in them."

"But, Leonard, it must be someone who knows the workings of the abbey?"

"A fellow priest, you mean? Surely not."

"No, but someone who has sufficient familiarity with the building to know that the scheme will work. I say 'he' because I doubt it's a woman."

"Perhaps not. Although you have had experience of threatening letters before; with Henry Richmond's ex-wife, I seem to remember."

"This is very different, Leonard."

"I suppose it's always unlike any other time. Whoever it is, they can certainly quote the Bible to their own ends."

"Will you show me the letters?"

314

"I can recite them for you. They are burned into my mind."

"And you haven't told the police?"

"I have not."

"Geordie is already involved with the arson attack on Simon's shop. The two crimes must be related."

"No one knows both Simon and me. We don't have any friends or acquaintances in common; apart from you, of course."

"People might have seen you together; on one of your walks, perhaps."

"We have done nothing wrong. You can walk alongside someone in your work."

"Has there been anything controversial recently; anything that you might have done to annoy someone?" Sidney asked.

"I can't think. I suppose I want everyone to like me, just as you do. Is that such a sin? I want to be a good priest, kind to my parishioners, faithful in the work of the Lord. I do not know what I have done to make someone hate me."

"It is almost certainly nothing personal. It is the idea that seems to provoke people to irrational anger. You must try not to take it to heart."

"It certainly feels personal. I hate it, Sidney. It is so vindictive, so filled with the lack of any charity or understanding. How can it be Christian? It makes me lose all my faith in humanity. I'll have to stop. I can't go on like this."

Leonard was on the verge of tears. Sidney reached out his arm in comfort. He couldn't bear it. "Don't be reckless, Leonard. We can sort this out, I promise. It's early days. Be patient, that's all I ask."

"But, Sidney, you are aware that a bishop cannot knowingly ordain a homosexual; and much less can a homosexual become a bishop."

"You are already ordained."

"But in my next job, whatever it is, wherever I am installed, I will have to submit to an examination in the articles of faith."

"As you do every day of your life."

"And people will be there, *judging* me, I know it will never end. What if the man goes on tormenting me? What if this never stops?"

Sidney held on to his friend's arm. "Don't cry, Leonard."

"I can't help it. I'm sorry."

The waitress came over and asked if she could bring the bill. The manager had sent her. She clearly didn't want a scene.

"Remember the prayer?" Sidney asked:

"Anoint and cheer our soiled face
With the abundance of Thy grace.
Keep far our foes, give peace at home;
Where Thou art guide, no ill can come."

"I don't know what to do," Leonard replied, letting go of Sidney's arm and reaching into his pocket for a handkerchief. "I will either have to give up being the man I have become or resign as a priest. I cannot be both."

Geordie Keating was unsurprised when his friend visited him with the inevitable theory that the arson in Cambridge had to be connected to the threats Leonard had been receiving.

"Hackford may want silence, but I am afraid he's not going to get it. Blackmail's always nasty and you can't hide arson. The *Evening News* is on to the story and Helena Randall's found out, so I expect we'll be getting a visit from London's finest soon enough."

"Small beer for her, I'd have thought."

"Actually she was quite interested. Perhaps she's got something up her sleeve."

"She's always been fond of Leonard, as has Malcolm."

"Do you think they are aware that he and Simon are more than friends?"

"Now, Geordie, you don't know that for certain."

"But you do."

"I haven't told you anything specific."

"You don't need to. I know you well enough. Still, I thought it was supposed to be easier for people like that now the law has changed and we're expected to tolerate everything they do."

"You are referring to the Sexual Offences Act?"

"The 'charter for queers', we call it. Not that it makes much difference to me. Homosexual acts committed in public conveniences are still illegal, and the act's provisions do not apply to members of the Armed Forces. It does make them vulnerable to blackmail."

"I remember the Christine Keeler case and the Russian spy . . ."

"Stephen Ward definitely swung it both ways. But what I want to know about the act is why doesn't it exclude priests? I know it's legal, but presumably you boys still take a dim view of this kind of thing. It's a sin, isn't it? And please don't tell me 'it's a bit more complicated'."

"Do you want the full theological explanation?"

"Is there a quick version?"

"There's my version."

"You mean you're all allowed to think different things?"

"The Church is governed by Canon and Measure. Canon is the law and Measure is the interpretation of that law. Are you with me?"

"It doesn't sound so very different to my world. But I think I'll need another pint before you go on."

"There have been some very good lectures on the subject by Norman Pittenger at King's. We could have gone together, Geordie. That would have created a bit of a stir. We could have held hands in the back row."

"Are you joking? I wouldn't want people thinking . . ."

"I am teasing. Although some people probably think . . ."

"What!"

"Still teasing, Geordie. You really do have to work on your sense of humour."

"It's not a laughing matter."

"Sin," Sidney resumed after he had bought the second pints, "is generally regarded in Christian thought as a state or condition; it is the separation or alienation from God."

Geordie took a swig of his beer. "Adam and Eve and the tricky business with the serpent."

"The opposite of sin is the 'state of grace' in which the separation or alienation or deprivation has been overcome by God's act in the sacrifice of Jesus Christ."

"And therefore we are redeemed."

"Very good. Pittenger argues that we must distinguish between *sin*, in the singular, and *sins* in the plural."

"Here we go," Geordie replied, lighting up a cigarette. "I knew there'd be some hair-splitting."

"Human sin is when we seek to live in the denial of our dependence upon God and upon others. It is when we live like animals, turning, and here I think Pittenger is rather apt, 'our human existence into something more suited for the barnyard than for the community of men'."

"Rutting and such like . . ."

"Sex, if you would like me to go on, is not, in itself, a sin."

"Depends who it is with."

"Not necessarily."

"Jesus."

"Steady Geordie. The idea is," Sidney continued, determined to get this lesson out of the way, "that sex is God-given. It is promiscuity, exploitation and abuse that is sinful."

"So where does degeneracy come in?"

"Do you mean sex between men?"

"I do."

"The irony is, as I am sure you will know, that most of the sexual practices between men also form part of heterosexual intimacy. What makes the same private actions, performed by consenting individuals, 'disgusting'? You might as well argue that sexual activity between ugly people is not to be countenanced."

"I wouldn't go that far."

"Would you like me to be specific about the actions involved?"

"No thank you, Sidney. We're in a public place and it's quite disconcerting to hear a clergyman talk like this."

"Then let me put you at your ease, Geordie. There are, I think, two things that determine the sinfulness of the act. First there is the *inner spirit* with which it is performed; and second there is the *intentionality*, in which both parties to the act understand the nature of what they are doing. The two persons must be committed one to the other, in such a fashion that neither is using the other. They must give and receive in tenderness, so that there is no element of coercion, undue pressure, or imposed constraint."

"So you are saying that this is the same as in normal relationships?"

"*Heterosexual* relationships, not 'normal'."

"You think homosexuality is normal?"

"I think homosexual acts between persons who intend a permanent union in love are not sinful nor should the Church consider them as such."

320

"Blimey, Sidney."

"I cannot see what is wrong when two men engage in physical acts which will both express their love and deepen it."

"I haven't really thought about it like that."

"Well, perhaps it's time you did. Would you like another pint, Geordie? Or something stronger, perhaps: a little whisky? I'll tell the barmaid that you're feeling a bit delicate, a little faint. It's your feminine side . . ."

"Don't you bloody dare . . ."

"What was I saying about your sense of humour?"

The next morning, unable to concentrate and just before lunch, Sidney put a new LP on the turntable. It was *Ummagumma*, the Pink Floyd album. Roger Waters had sent it to him, and two tracks stood out: "Astronomy Domine", which seemed to be some kind of lilting electronic mystic trance, and "Grantchester Meadows", which included natural sounds he had seen the great bass player record on location.

There was something transcendental about it all. Sidney wondered whether he could buy some coloured light bulbs and turn his study into something more meditative. If he closed his eyes and let the music wash over him, then perhaps . . .

"Daddy?"

Anna shook at his arm, told him the noise was too loud and then announced that she had lost Dizzy, her imaginary friend.

Sidney lifted the needle from the record player and gave his daughter his full attention. This was going to be a difficult conversation. How could one find an imaginary friend? When had Anna last seen him?

"I don't know. I think he's gone away."

"I'm sure he'll come back."

"He didn't tell me he was going."

"Sometimes I don't tell Mummy when I'm going somewhere."

"And she gets cross."

"Are you cross now, Anna?"

"Very. Do you lose your friends, Daddy?"

"I try not to."

"Is God your friend?"

"I hope so."

"Sally at school says I'm making Dizzy up but I'm not. You don't make God up, do you, Daddy?"

"I don't think so."

"But I've never seen God. Like you haven't seen Dizzy."

Sidney was flummoxed by this epistemological immediacy, but if he could not explain the concept of God to his own daughter, what chance did he have with anyone else? He would have to start with the character of Jesus Christ and work up from there.

Anna lost interest almost as soon as he began. "I know all about that," she said. "I'm going to find another friend."

As she turned to leave, Sidney realised that he had failed to notice Amanda standing in the doorway. She had come for lunch. "It's just as well you've got another friend too," she said. "Otherwise you would have been quite alone with your thoughts and, Hildegard has been telling me, that dreadful music."

"It's not too bad once you get used to it."

"I don't think that's really the point, is it?"

"There's a rather amazing track called 'Several Species of Small Furry Animals Gathered Together in a Cave and Grooving with a Pict'. Would you like to hear it?"

"You are making that up. No, thank you."

"How is your Michelangelo investigation coming along?"

"The drawing has been authenticated, so it's all gone rather well."

Amanda explained that the British Museum was to put on a special event to celebrate the discovery of the new drawing. There was going to be some music and a reading of some of the artist's sonnets and she was planning on asking an up-and-coming actor called Ian McKellen to perform.

"I think he's got the necessary flamboyance. I met him at a party and he was wearing a brown corduroy suit and a cravat that was so stylish among all the boring grey flannel. In any case, gay men are so much easier to talk to."

"Mr McKellen is homosexual?"

"He doesn't advertise it, but I think it's pretty obvious. I rather wished Leonard could have been there. I am sure they would have got on like a house on fire. Oh. Perhaps I'd better rephrase that . . ."

"They might well, but Leonard's too troubled to think clearly at the moment."

"You've seen him?"

"I have, Amanda."

"And it is as we feared? His private life?"

"I am afraid so."

"If he'd lived in Renaissance times we wouldn't be having any of this nonsense. To think that civilisation is going backwards."

"Not according to the scientists."

"But morally, Sidney. Whatever happened to tolerance? You should preach about it."

"I do. *You* should come to church."

"I don't feel confident about that. People stare and jump to conclusions."

"No one is judging you, Amanda."

"But I *feel* judged. Just as Leonard does. That's why we get on so well. We both understand what it's like. Are you going to help him?"

"Unfortunately, I think it may take more than money to sort out. Inspector Keating's involved. Helena Randall too . . ."

"And you and me. Goodness, Sidney, Leonard's got the complete set."

"I hope we will prove formidable opponents."

"The blackmailer hasn't a chance; but this gives me an idea. Let me give you the fifty pounds instead. You can see the blackmailer in Leonard's place. That would take the pressure off and you could do a bit of investigation at the same time. I'm so annoyed I didn't think about all this before." She reached down into her handbag. "I've got it in my purse . . ."

"Just a minute, Amanda."

"These are emergency funds, really. I seem to remember doing something like this before when you went off to France."

"I'm not sure . . ."

"Oh come on, Sidney. It will be a true act of friendship; and, for once, you need have no qualms about the validity of your actions. You're the only man who can do it and we'll all be proud of you."

Shortly after Amanda had left, Sidney received a telephone call from Helena with more information. The situation had escalated. The *Daily Mirror* had received letters from "Christian Grace" asking for money for an exclusive on "perverted priests". She had set a reporter on to it, he had done a bit of digging and found the writer's real name: Nicholas Trent. He worked for a furnishing store in Watford.

Sidney remembered the double bed.

"There's not really enough evidence for a story so far, but the man's language is vitriolic. I think we have to be careful. This could get very nasty. I don't like it, Sidney. It might make a great story, but Trent is some kind of moral vigilante. I don't trust his religious certainty. Perhaps I've been listening to you for too long."

"Sometimes I think you haven't listened enough."

"I'll let that pass. I think we should both do something about it. I have some standards and they include loyalty. But we're going to have to act fast to control the story."

"What do you mean by that?"

"We have to frame it in a different way with Leonard as victim."

"Does it have to mention him at all?"

"Not necessarily but Trent will then go to another newspaper. We have to string him along and get what we can. That gives you time to go in."

"Why?"

"I'm doing you a favour, Sidney, a chance to help Leonard before the whole thing blows up — possibly literally, if the arson is anything to go by."

"Oh dear . . ."

"It's the same man, as you and Geordie must have realised. He talks about fire often enough. Here's one: 'the abominable, and murderers, and whoremongers, and sorcerers, and idolaters, and all liars, shall have their part in the lake which burneth with fire and brimstone: which is the second death'. Charming. He lives in Albert Street, St Albans. That should be easy enough to find. I'll give you the address."

Despite all this knowledge, Sidney was cautious. He wanted to do what was best for Leonard and he wasn't quite sure that his friend would want him to go in all guns blazing. He needed to check on his mood and attitude. How easy it was to threaten someone's happiness and derail a life.

He was unsurprised to find that Simon Hackford was with Leonard. The two friends were having a light lunch: omelettes, bread, cheese, water. It was all very Lenten.

Sidney offered to confront the blackmailer.

326

"Do you mean you know who he or she is?" Leonard asked.

"Helena told me."

"What? You mean it's at the newspapers already?"

"She's not going to do anything about it."

Simon Hackford was aghast. "But if she does, we're ruined."

"How is that so? You are the victim of arson, Simon. There is nothing to link Leonard to the case. And you can always deny your relationship."

"What if we don't want to?"

"I don't mean that you shouldn't acknowledge your friendship. You can simply insist on your privacy."

"To the newspapers?"

"I think you can trust Helena."

"But not other journalists."

"And I will deal with the blackmailer."

"Don't you think we can sort this out for ourselves?"

"No, I don't," said Sidney. "Besides, Geordie is involved too."

"You haven't told him about the letters?"

"I haven't spelled it out."

"But you have hinted."

"Please, Leonard. Let me meet the blackmailer for you."

"You've spoken to Amanda about it all?"

"We are *all your friends, Leonard*. Of course we have spoken. We care about you. Now what are your instructions? Will you let me act on your behalf?"

Nicholas Trent's home in Albert Street was a stone's throw from St Albans Abbey and Leonard's house in Sumpter Yard. Sidney scheduled his visit for a weekday afternoon after the shops had closed. His plan was to pretend to be a new member of the abbey clergy, visiting the congregation in order to introduce himself.

Not only was Trent at home, it was his day off. He was a large shambling man, unaccustomed to exercise, and was wearing old clothes: baggy trousers over loosely laced boots, a frayed cream shirt that was not tucked in and a racing-green cardigan that carried the battle scars of breakfast, lunch and, most likely, the dinners of the previous week. He had spent most of the day pottering about and listening to music. It was so hard to imagine him working in a department store, and dressed in a suit and tie, that initially Sidney thought he must have made a mistake, but a further glance around the room convinced him he had not.

The house was filthy. There were newspapers, plastic bags, glue, scissors, unwashed plates and discarded mugs of tea all over the front room, together with empty liquid bottles, sponges, half-burned candles, batteries, pliers and bits of wiring, and a pair of gardening gloves next to a bowl of sugar. LPs were scattered on the floor round an old record player scratching out a bit of Wagner. Aside from the mess, every available seat was occupied by a cat: there must have been eight, nine or even ten of them on the sofa, chairs, in the hall and kitchen or coming in and out of the garden at the back.

328

"Waifs and strays," said Trent, turning off the music. "I try to give them a good home. No thanks to the RSPCA."

"I would have thought they'd be all too happy."

"On the contrary. They keep threatening to take my darlings away. Someone must have reported me."

"You suspect a neighbour?"

"I'm afraid so. People don't know how to leave well alone these days, do they? Can I make you a cup of tea?"

This was a bit rich for a blackmailer, Sidney thought while assessing how much of a health hazard the proffered refreshment might be. "That would be kind."

"Have a seat then. I'll just move Edgar."

"An unusual name . . ."

"I call them after English kings and queens. It helps me remember. I hadn't heard you were coming to the abbey, Mr Archdeacon. It wasn't in the parish magazine."

"I don't start until July. After the sub-dean has moved on."

Trent was at the tap and about to fill the kettle when he stopped. "I wasn't aware he was leaving."

"He's going to be a bishop," said Sidney boldly, wondering whether it was too soon to get on to all this, "although it hasn't been announced yet."

"Leonard Graham?"

"Yes," Sidney replied. "Is there anything wrong?"

"I should think so." Trent resumed his tea-making activities. Sidney remained silent, fending away a cat that was about to leap on to his shoulder. Another made for his lap.

"A bishop? Are you sure?"

"Yes," said Sidney.

"And does the Church of England think that the man has the right qualities for the episcopate?"

"I imagine it does," Sidney replied. "Otherwise it wouldn't have appointed him."

"Unless it wasn't in full possession of the facts. Here's your tea." It came in a cup and saucer that were not as clean as they might have been. "I'm not sure where I've put the sugar."

"It's over there," said Sidney, noticing that it was next to a bottle of nail polish remover. What would Trent want with that? he wondered, before remembering Amanda informing him how flammable the liquid could be. He wished he were with her now rather than forcing out a confrontation in a filthy room. He took a sip of tea. "Is there something you want to tell me, Mr Trent?"

"Leonard Graham is unmarried."

"Perhaps you are too?"

"That is different, I have been unfortunate in love."

"And that may be the case with Mr Graham."

"I fear not."

"You have evidence to the contrary?"

"He has a special friend. They came to the shop."

"Together?"

"Not exactly. Mr Graham hovered in the background while his friend bought a double bed."

"Is that unusual?"

"Men buying beds on their own? It doesn't happen every day, I'll tell you that. And it wasn't for himself. It was for Mr Graham. I had to arrange the delivery to his house in Sumpter Yard."

"I do not see what is wrong with that," said Sidney, playing with a straight bat. "The clergy are not well paid, as you know. Some of us are fortunate to have more wealthy friends."

"And do they buy you beds?"

"They might if I asked them."

"So you see nothing wrong."

"I don't," said Sidney. "What I do think is 'wrong' is this, *Mr Grace*."

"Why are you calling me that?"

"It's not a very appropriate name." He produced a piece of paper. *"Almighty God, unto whom all hearts be open, ALL DESIRES KNOWN AND FROM WHOM NO SECRETS ARE HID . . ."*

"What is that?"

"A blackmailer's letter, addressed to Leonard Graham."

"How did you get it?"

"I presume it is from you."

"I don't know why you would think that. My name is Trent."

Sidney handed over the letter. "Other recent communications contain your real name." He pulled a second missive from his inner jacket pocket. "This is the second note that you sent to the *Daily Mirror*. *'DEVICES AND DESIRES. HIDDEN SECRETS. THE REVELATION OF THE BEAST.'"*

"How did you get all this?"

"Let's just say I know the right people."

"Protecting your own."

"No, Mr Trent. Working against the malign."

"Are you one of them and all?"

"I don't know what you mean."

"A pansy. A queer. A homosexual."

"It doesn't matter whether I am or not."

"That means you are."

"Tell me, Mr Trent, what is it that you find so very threatening about homosexuality?"

"They're perverts."

"All of them?"

"I've seen them hovering round toilets."

"You know that homosexuality is no longer illegal for consenting adults over the age of twenty-one?"

"I don't care how old they are. I am a loyal churchman and a communicant member of the Church of England. Your *friend*," Trent continued with contempt, "is a priest. Doesn't he know that only when he publicly acknowledges that he is a sinner can he receive the grace of God?"

"He does that every time he prays. We all do."

"To think that man gives communion to people."

"He does."

"The grace of God . . ."

"Theologically, you are wrong, Mr Trent. God's grace comes first. His love is prevenient to our response; his forgiveness awakens our repentance."

"You can say what you like. It's disgusting what they do."

"And do you know what that entails?"

"I don't like to think about it. Father forgive them, for they know not what they do."

Sidney took stock. He was not going to let Trent win his argument on religious grounds. "As Christians," he replied, as pointedly as possible, "and you say you are one, Mr Trent, we believe that sexuality is a God-given thing, a wonderful and beautiful thing."

"'Go forth and multiply'? That may be. But how can pansies and lezzers do that, that's what I want to know."

"You are going to cite the Bible, I suppose?"

"The Book of Leviticus, chapter eighteen: 'You shall not lie with a male as one lies with a female; it is an abomination.' Chapter twenty: 'If there is a man who lies with a male as those who lie with a woman, both of them have committed a detestable act; they shall surely be put to death.'"

"Old Testament teaching . . ."

"Then there is Romans, chapter one, verses twenty-six to twenty-seven. You can't deny what it says."

"I think we know far more about human sexuality now than people did in the past. Many of those observations are out of date."

"It's biblical truth, not subject to time but eternal."

"But you don't feel the need to obey other laws found in Leviticus? To follow the regulations against wearing different clothing materials and planting varying types of seed in the same ground?"

"That's irrelevant."

"I'm not sure that it is," Sidney replied, realising that they had reached a stalemate. He was determined to stand his ground.

Unfortunately, so was Nicholas Trent. "I follow the teachings of St Paul, in the Book of Romans which I cited and you did not answer. I don't agree with this permissive society. I know I am in the right, as St Paul was when he censured the Galatians."

"We could talk about this for a long time, Mr Trent, but ultimately I don't think that Leonard Graham and Simon Hackford's friendship has anything to do with us. In many ways it's none of our business. It's not harming anyone else."

"It's an offence against the Lord. They cannot refrain from temptation."

"They may not be as licentious as you imagine."

"You would know, I suppose."

Sidney refused to rise to the challenge. "I think I have yet to meet a homosexual man or woman who does not yearn for a permanent relationship. I don't think homosexuals are very different from their brothers or sisters, and it doesn't help to blackmail them."

"Who said I was doing that?"

"Come, come, Mr Trent. We both know that all these letters are from you."

"If that is the case, what are you going to do about it?"

"Do?" Sidney asked. "Why, pay you off, of course." He reached into his briefcase. "I think the sum mentioned was fifty pounds."

"Now we're getting somewhere. I should have made it a hundred."

"The demand was for fifty and here it is." Sidney placed an envelope on the table. "I hope you feel better for it and use the money wisely."

"I thought I'd give it to charity."

"That's kind of you."

"I don't need the money. It's the principle."

"And what about the morality of blackmail?"

"My cause is just."

"I am not so sure, Mr Trent. And since we disagree with each other's moral position so profoundly I thought perhaps I could take back the money I have just put down."

Sidney's host was appalled. "What do you mean?"

"I would have thought it was obvious. We have your details, I know the police. There is evidence that will put you at the scene of Simon Hackford's antique shop."

"I don't know who you are talking about."

"I find that very difficult to believe. You have Simon Hackford's name from the cheque he wrote for the bed. It was for a large amount and he requested a different delivery address and so you almost certainly asked where he banked. The answer was already there on his cheque book: Cambridge. Any idle enquiry would also reveal that he dealt in antiques. The business carries his name. You don't need to be Einstein to find it."

"I don't see why I would burn his shop."

"Didn't your threat mention 'the abominable, and murderers, and whoremongers, shall have their part in the lake which burneth with fire and brimstone'? There's circumstantial evidence and there are also fingerprints. I note too that you are a keen gardener and that you have, over in that corner, what appears to be a plentiful supply of weedkiller, a substance which, as you almost certainly know, contains sodium chlorate, a highly flammable material."

"Why would I leave that lying around?"

"You appear to leave everything lying around, Mr Trent, including some equally flammable nail polish remover. I don't imagine that you were expecting a visitor."

"You're lucky I let you in."

"An example of your Christian charity, no doubt."

"I lead a good life, Mr Archdeacon. I am a decent man. There's nothing you can do to stop me."

"Fortunately, there is. This could all become awkward for you if and when the police step up their investigation. Even though there was not much damage at the antique shop, these letters don't help your case. Certainly it might be difficult to explain any absence from work to your employer if the authorities come calling."

"I have holiday owed."

"Or your picture in the *Daily Mirror*, the paper you wrote to."

"They have promised anonymity. They'll keep their word."

"I think they'd like to spin the story out for as long as possible. And you know the current thinking, that people who are most hostile to homosexuals harbour homosexual feelings themselves? As I have already established, you are not married."

Sidney almost stopped himself at this point, realising his anger had turned to cruelty, but he was determined to extract as much information as possible so that he only had to come to this house once and never again.

"I am a bachelor."

"Newspapers can make a lot of mischief with the word 'bachelor'. You know the obituaries that state 'he never married'. We all know what that means."

"I may not have met the right girl, yet. There was someone once but she lives in Cardiff. She'll vouch for me."

"None of this needs to happen, Mr Trent. It can all go away."

"Are you threatening me?"

"I am just thinking through what might happen if all this became public. You might destroy Leonard Graham's career but you need to be careful that you don't sabotage your own in the process. Neither the law, nor your employer, will take kindly to your behaviour."

"Do you think so?"

"There is nothing to stop my going both to the police and to the *Daily Mirror* and accusing you of arson."

"How dare you?"

"I don't know, Mr Trent. I must have been extremely provoked."

"You are blackmailing *me*. You are *just as guilty*."

"Have a think about it, Mr Trent. Shall I take the money back or not?"

Sidney certainly felt guilty when he returned to Ely. He had lied and he had been menacing. His threats had bordered on illegality, he knew this, and he wondered how far his behaviour could be excused. Did the potential end justify the means?

He would have liked to talk to Leonard about it but it was too soon. He first needed to relay his news to Geordie, give him the information required and see to his Easter duties.

Not that these were few. As he prepared for the service on Maundy Thursday, the eve of the Last Supper and the washing of the congregation's feet, Sidney thought about the importance of loyalty in the face of betrayal.

Jesus had been loyal to his disciples and faithful to God but did he need Judas to betray him? Had he, in fact, used Judas, as a means to an end, just as Sidney had deceived Nicholas Trent?

He went into the cathedral, knelt down and prayed amidst the gracefully decorated stone of Bishop Alcock's Chapel. He asked for the forgiveness of his sins. Had he done the right things? Had he behaved in a way that befitted the dignity of the priesthood?

He questioned whether he was guilty of treachery in other areas of his life. Were his feelings for Amanda, for example, entirely honest? Was he betraying his love for Hildegard by being so close to his old friend?

He thought of the last time he had seen her and how she had been talking about Michelangelo and his friendship with Tommaso dei Cavalieri; did anyone worry whether it was sexual or not?

"One can be intimate without being physical," she had said. "Like us, Sidney."

"I wouldn't put our friendship on the Renaissance level."

"No," Hildegard had cut in. They hadn't realised that she was in the room. "It's more baroque."

Sidney prayed again and tried to meditate on the complications of love. Surely it should be kept at its simplest. He loved God spiritually, he loved his wife physically and spiritually, and he loved everyone else differently but intensely: Amanda, Leonard, Geordie, Helena and Malcolm, Mrs Maguire, the dean and the fellow clergy. There was no dilution in the intensity of that love, no boundary. He just needed to be better; as a priest, as a friend and as a man.

As he made his way to the vestry, he remembered washing Hildegard's feet before they were married. It was thirteen years ago. Perhaps that was the first time he had realised how much he loved her. If that was how much Leonard felt for Simon, then he had to do all he could to protect that love.

He recalled the words of St Augustine: "Love, and do what you will. If you keep silence, do it out of love. If you cry out, do it out of love. If you refrain from punishing, do it out of love."

Later that night, a wooden hut that was home to St Albans Abbey Scouts, Guides, Cubs and Brownies was burned to the ground. Since the easily destroyed structure was located off Orchard House Lane, the opposite side of Holywell Hill from nearby Albert Street, it did not take long to realise who the culprit might be; not least because Nicholas Trent had lost his patience and warned Helena Randall that such an attack might happen if Leonard Graham (who provided instruction and encouragement for those working towards their Book-reader and Faith badges) remained in his post as a priest.

And so, on Good Friday, just after Sidney had returned exhausted from the three-hour service, Helena telephoned to say that she was going to break her story. She couldn't make any direct accusation as there had not yet been an arrest but she had spoken to Keating and was going to start up her own fire.

"What will all this do for Leonard?"

"I've spoken to him and he's had enough. He does not need to be named initially; but Hackford does. People might draw the odd conclusion, but I am afraid I can't stop that."

"And what did he actually say?"

"He wants it all to end, Sidney. We've got our man. Geordie's on to it. It's all over."

"Not for Leonard."

"He's going to talk to you. He has a plan."

"I hope he knows what he's doing. The Church of England is at its best when everyone behaves charitably and no one makes a fuss. Most things are best left behind closed doors rather than out in the newspapers. I don't like it when we draw attention to ourselves."

"You're one to talk, Sidney."

"This isn't about me."

"No, it's about Leonard; and he's thought it all through. He's made his own decision and I'm sure he'll tell you what it is. I know he's grateful. Just don't expect him to do everything you say."

"But, Helena, it's always so much easier when people obey me."

"For you, perhaps. But not necessarily for them."

On Easter Day, Sidney preached about the supreme love of God; how the central truth of humanity is that we were created to love and be loved; that this was the genuinely integrating factor in human experience. As human beings, he argued, we are flawed and prone to make mistakes, to misinterpret love, misjudge it and fall prey to temptation, distortion and disaster. But what Christianity did, through reconciliation, atonement and redemption, was to release us to love as we are meant to love. After the broken humanity of the Crucifixion, the Resurrection was nothing less than the re-creation of love itself.

Sidney had no qualms about giving it straight. People might think that he was some kind of clerical lightweight, easily bored, prone to distraction, and overexcited by the possibility of a chance to prove his skills as an amateur sleuth, but when he was asked to step into the pulpit and proclaim his faith and acknowledge the divine mystery — one that was far greater than any human mystery he had ever attempted to solve — his purpose was clear. This was his Easter message: that God is love, release is given, freedom is granted and alienation overcome through the sacrifice of Jesus Christ.

The dean congratulated him afterwards. It was, he said, about time Sidney showed the congregation what he was made of, and he was glad to see that it wasn't cotton wool. "There's muscle in you, Sidney, and there's nothing better than a bit of muscular Christianity on Easter Day."

The next morning, Geordie provided Sidney with a lift to St Albans. He had spoken to his colleagues in the Hertfordshire Constabulary and they were due to secure the arrest of Nicholas Trent on two counts of arson and one of "making an unwarranted demand with menaces" under the 1968 Theft Act. Helena had provided written evidence and Simon Hackford had testified on Leonard's behalf.

When confronted in his Albert Street home amidst cats, papers and insurmountable evidence, Trent complained that he had been "betrayed by that damned priest and his gang of friends".

"I have done nothing," said Sidney.

"Like Pontius Pilate."

"It wasn't Sidney that shopped you," Keating told him. "It was Helena Randall."

"The journalist?"

"She got your story. You even confessed the recent arson to spruce it up a bit."

"I didn't admit to the Scout hut."

"You implied that you had done it."

"I don't think I did."

"At the very least you didn't prevent her from drawing conclusions, shall we put it that way? And she taped your conversation; a recording she has given to me."

"This is not how things are meant to be."

"But that's how they are, man. You sent threatening letters. You nearly burned down an antique shop. That was all bad enough; but then a *Scout hut*? What has that got to do with anything?"

"Leonard Graham was going to talk to them about the Easter Monday pilgrimage. People come from all over the diocese. I read it on the abbey noticeboard."

"There could have been children in there."

"It was the night before. I made sure the place was empty. I just wanted to send a message to the sodomite."

"There are other ways of expressing an opinion."

"None that have made a difference. He continues in his pursuit of evil."

Geordie sighed. "He is not 'evil'. He is different."

"He should practise what he preaches."

"I have not heard him preach about anything other than love," Keating continued, assuming instant familiarity with Leonard's doctrinal repertoire. "He loves one man, and one man only, and his private relationship has nothing to do with any of us."

He turned to Sidney. "That's right, isn't it?"

Sidney smiled. His friend was getting the message at last.

The following Tuesday, Amanda held her event at the British Museum. It involved the revelation of the

Michelangelo drawing with some other contextual displays, the singing of the Britten sonnets and a reading by Ian McKellen.

She began with a quick speech about Michelangelo and the Renaissance theory of beauty. As Leonard and Simon Hackford sat closely together in the third row, and with Sidney behind them, she talked about the artist's interest in Neoplatonism and how, despite his stunning rendering of the naked male form revealed in the recently discovered drawing, the *essence* of beauty did not consist of anything pertaining to the human form at all. According to Neoplatonists, such as Marsilio Ficino, it could reside in bodies, and shine forth from them, but in itself beauty was bodiless.

By taking the argument away from physical representation and the human form, Sidney wondered whether Amanda was making a directly personal point, diverting the attention of her audience from any thoughts about Michelangelo's homosexuality and the physical manifestation of his feelings towards a younger man. She talked about a descending hierarchy of beauties; from the absolute beauty of God, through the beauty of the angels, to the delights of the soul and finally ending with the fairness of the human form. The more we ascend, she explained, the more beauty is without form; the closer to earth the more defined in shape beauty becomes. The ultimate aim of art, like that of love, is to reach for the shapeless origin of all shapes, the essence of beauty.

"Doesn't sound much fun," Simon Hackford whispered to his companion.

Not long after, Leonard asked Sidney if they could talk. As well as going over the recent case, it was clear that he had something else to say. He paced up and down the room, as if sitting down would weaken his resolve. "I've decided to leave the Church," he said.

Sidney had not expected such certainty. "Please, Leonard. There's no need to do this."

"I've given it a good deal of thought."

"I'm sure you have. That's what makes you such a good priest."

Leonard stopped at the window, unable to meet Sidney's eye. "Please don't try and talk me out of it. I want to live my life in the open, without hypocrisy. It's what Dostoevsky called 'a freer freedom'."

"You could take some more time to think this through, Leonard."

"You will remember in *The Brothers Karamazov*, Father Zosima spoke of hell as 'the incapacity to love'?"

"I can't recall the passage exactly," Sidney replied.

"I don't want to live a life apart; one of pretence in which Simon and I are only able to see each other in secret, unable to express any affection in public, deceiving both friends and faithful. I cannot hide a love which contains such intimacy that it is almost telepathic; and I only want to share my life with those who will accept us as we are. That is the nature of friendship, isn't it, to walk alongside, as Christ did? Otherwise we are hypocrites."

"Have you lost your faith, Leonard?"

"Not at all. I am still a believer. I just cannot be a priest."

"There are many clergy like yourself."

"Yes — and many of them hide their true feelings, as well you know. Don't ask; don't tell. I'm not sure I want to live like that."

Sidney sat down. Leonard was not asking for his advice. He had made up his mind. Now it was a question of practicalities. "What will you do with your life?"

"So many things; I will help Simon in his business. I think I'll study for the PhD that I always meant to do."

"On Dostoevsky, I imagine?"

"I'll have to get my Russian back up to scratch. And I'll take up a hobby. I think I'd like to learn more about roses, if that doesn't sound too fanciful. Simon's been teaching me; how to graft and so on. I find their beauty so consoling."

Sidney smiled. He may not have been able to keep up with Leonard's Dostoevsky but he knew his Shakespeare:

". . . earthlier happy is the rose distill'd
Than that which, withering on the virgin thorn,
Grows, lives, and dies in single blessedness."

"A Midsummer Night's Dream, I think. You always did know what to say, Sidney."

"You will be such a loss to the Church."

"But not, I hope, to my friends."

"Never that."

"I will still try to lead a good life. I don't intend to go to the dark side. But I can also pray and I can help others; people who are afraid, victims of prejudice.

Perhaps I can do more outside the Church than I ever could as a priest."

"And you will do well, Leonard."

"I hope so."

"I think you know, just as I do, that human loving, however odd it may seem to some, and however differently it might appear from socially accepted norms, is always a pale, imperfect and sometimes distorted reflection of the love of God."

"I will still walk in His light."

"You will. Because whenever we see love or find love — love that seeks faithfulness, acts tenderly, is patient and good and kind and true — then we are glimpsing, and reaching out for nothing less than the eternal love that is at the heart of our faith."

"Thank you, Sidney, for all that you have done."

Sidney rose from his chair. It was time to go home. "I should thank you for all that you have taught me. I am humbled by you, Leonard."

"Don't. You will make me cry again."

"I will try to be a better priest in your absence; and I will try to make the Church a more caring and a more tolerant place."

Leonard reached out and the two men grasped each other by both hands. "St John of the Cross once wrote: 'In the evening of our life, we shall be judged by our loving.'"

"Goodbye, Leonard. But not for long."

Sidney was back in Ely by the middle of the afternoon. It had rained while he had been away but the clouds

347

had cleared and there was enough blue in the sky to patch a sailor's shirt. On the Dean's Meadow, above the host of white and golden daffodils, the trees were coming into leaf. This was the greening of the year, the beginnings of buttercups, clover, docks and nettles. He could see the first buds on the roses in the gardens and wondered if one of them, climbing across a ruined medieval wall, was a "Rambling Rector". It was a pity to be sad on such a beautiful day. It made him feel ungrateful.

These had been strange times for his friends; with Ronnie Maguire's return and death, Amanda's divorce, and Leonard leaving the Church. Sidney needed to get back to his wife and child but, before he did so, he could not help but stop to take in the spring, and worry about all those he loved; their hopes and doubts, their faults and frailties.

He knew that, whatever happened, he had to keep caring for them as truthfully and as loyally as he could. They held him together and they were one fellowship. He would never abandon them and he was nothing without them.

In the evening of our life, he remembered, *we shall be judged by our loving.*

Other titles published by Ulverscroft:

SIDNEY CHAMBERS AND THE FORGIVENESS OF SINS

James Runcie

Six new stories about the full-time priest and part-time detective, set in 1960s Cambridge. On a snowy Thursday morning in Lent 1964, a stranger seeks sanctuary in Grantchester's church, convinced he has murdered his wife . . . Sidney attends a shooting weekend in the country with his wife Hildegard, where they find their hostess has a sinister burn on her neck . . . A firm of removal men "accidentally" drops a Steinway piano on a musician's head outside a Cambridge college . . . Sidney's friend Amanda receives threatening pen letters when at last she appears to be approaching matrimony . . . During a cricket match, a group of schoolboys blow up their school's science block . . . And on a family holiday in Florence, Sidney is accused of the theft of a priceless painting.

SIDNEY CHAMBERS AND THE PROBLEM OF EVIL

James Runcie

It is the 1960s and Canon Sidney Chambers is enjoying his first year of married life with his German bride Hildegard. But life in Grantchester rarely stays quiet for long. Our favourite clerical detective soon attempts to stop a serial killer who has a grievance against the clergy; investigates the disappearance of a famous painting; uncovers the fact that an "accidental" drowning on a film shoot may not have been so accidental after all; and discovers the reasons behind the theft of a baby from a hospital. In the meantime, Sidney wrestles with the problem of evil, attempts to fulfill the demands of Dickens, his faithful Labrador, and contemplates, as always, the nature of love.